THE MARKET GIRLS OF PETTICOAT LANE

PATRICIA MCBRIDE

Boldwood

First published in Great Britain in 2026 by Boldwood Books Ltd.

Copyright © Patricia McBride, 2026

Cover Design by Colin Thomas

Cover Images: Colin Thomas

A CIP catalogue record for this book is available from the British Library.

Paperback ISBN 978-1-83633-312-8

Large Print ISBN 978-1-83633-313-5

Hardback ISBN 978-1-83633-311-1

Trade Paperback ISBN 978-1-80625-800-0

Ebook ISBN 978-1-83633-314-2

Kindle ISBN 978-1-83633-315-9

Audio CD ISBN 978-1-83633-306-7

MP3 CD ISBN 978-1-83633-307-4

Digital audio download ISBN 978-1-83633-309-8

This book is printed on certified sustainable paper. Boldwood Books is dedicated to putting sustainability at the heart of our business. For more information please visit https://www.boldwoodbooks.com/about-us/sustainability/

Boldwood Books Ltd, 23 Bowerdean Street, London, SW6 3TN

www.boldwoodbooks.com

1

1943

The hum of sewing machines filled the air, a rhythm so familiar Amanda could usually ignore it. Twenty women were bent over their machines making uniforms for the troops, work so repetitive they didn't have to think about it. The factory was dimly lit, and the smell of fabric and machine oil hung heavily, mixed with the smell of cheap perfume the women wore. Amanda sat at her small desk, a ledger open in front of her, her smooth forehead furrowed in concentration. For once, she wished she could ignore the background noise of machines and women calling out comments to each other.

'Hey, Amanda! Maisie is working so fast it's a wonder her machine doesn't go up in smoke!' Bethan's voice cut through the drone of the machines. Her dark curls were held back in a scarf and her eyes sparkled with mischief. 'I think she's after a world record.'

Maisie, hunched over her machine, shot Bethan a quick glance, exhaustion showing in the dark rings under her eyes. 'I'm trying to keep up with the quotas, and you should be too!'

Amanda laughed. 'Not looking. And we've got enough to get

on with here. Talking of which, you'll miss your quota if you keep yapping.'

Maisie looked up from her machine, swearing silently. The needle had broken again.

Creeping up behind her, like a cat stalking its prey, silent and invisible, their superior Mrs Duncan made her jump. 'Breaking needles again, Maisie. I swear you break more needles than anyone else. Fix it, quick! You'll get behind.' Her harsh voice echoed around the workshop. She liked nothing better than trying to make people look bad.

Maisie bit back the words she wanted to say. They'd get her fired for sure. She needed the job. She waited until the supervisor had walked on to find someone else to pick on, then began changing the needle.

The bell rang for their midday break, and everyone stopped work and stretched their backs. The three friends continued their conversation as they walked to the canteen. As always, it was a bustling hive of activity, filled with the clatter of cups and the hum of women's voices. The walls were once white, but were now a dull cream, adorned with faded government posters warning that *Careless talk costs lives!* and encouraging ones saying *You can do it!* and *Dig for Victory*. The air smelled of stewed tea and cigarette smoke.

Most chatter was about the latest uniform order from the Ministry of Defence and the inevitable queues for absolutely everything. 'I queued for half an hour at the butcher's and all they had left was a bit of tripe. I'd rather starve!' One small group was discussing a neighbour who was gambling away all the family's money. 'They live on bread and dripping 'cos of 'er. Never learns, does she.' Hearing that made Amanda go cold. Her father was a gambler, always expecting the next bet to make him a fortune. He never learned either. On top of that, he wasn't above betting with the housekeeping money, leaving them short. He even stole Amanda's meagre savings if she hadn't hidden them well enough.

The three friends got themselves some tea from the big metal urn and sat at one of the long wooden tables, unwrapping their sandwiches. They always started their midday conversation comparing them, although they rarely varied – fish paste, Marmite, tomatoes and a bit of cheese if they were lucky. Bethan held up her sandwich. The National Loaf bread was cut so thin it fell sideways as if exhausted and unwilling to be placed next to the sad filling. 'Yuck!' she groaned. 'I swear this bread is more sawdust than flour.'

But their conversation soon turned to other things. 'I'm a bit worried about some figures in the ledger,' Amanda said, still unsure of herself. 'I need to go to the warehouse to count all the bolts of fabric to be sure. I'm probably wrong.'

'Maybe you're just tired, cariad,' Bethan suggested, her tone warm but her eyes serious. 'We've done a lot of overtime recently. We're all worn out.'

Maisie had bought a newspaper on her way to work, but hadn't had time to open it. 'Let's see what's happening in the world, or at least what the government thinks we should know about. Didn't have a chance to listen to the wireless this morning.' She unfolded the newspaper and groaned at the headline: FURTHER RATIONING ANNOUNCED. 'Oh, no, listen to this. "From next week rationing will be expanded, and all citizens will face stricter limits on the purchase of meats, dairy products, and sugar along with items such as cheese and cooking fats." Blah blah blah. We are urged to adapt by conserving supplies.' Maisie looked up. 'What the heck do they think we're doing now, the morons? Conserve supplies indeed.' Her heart sank as she tried to think how to feed the family. Since her mother started drinking, most days she was in no state to shop, let alone cook. A big chunk of the housekeeping was spent in the pub instead of on food for the family. She often felt like she was the mother in the house, looking after her brother and sister when she'd rather be out at a dance or the flicks.

'I know we're all against the black market but who doesn't get something from under the counter sometimes? We have to pay through the nose for it though.' She shook her head. She fiddled with the bottom of her cardigan, mended so many times she could only wear it to work. Her friends knew her mum liked a drink a bit too much but they had no idea how bad things had become.

Amanda sighed. 'I've been doing a few bits and pieces of alterations on the side, even made a dress for someone. The trouble is no one around here has more than two ha'pennies to rub together. I can't charge much.'

Bethan perked up, her enthusiasm shining in her eyes again. 'Really? That's brilliant, Amanda. Why didn't you say before? You could turn it into a proper side business. Get customers from places where people have more money, like.'

Amanda thought about her father gambling away their housekeeping and the way her mother had three cleaning jobs, trying to fill her empty purse. 'What if we think about what you said, Bethan, a little business on the side? Not just me, all of us. We're all good at sewing and we can teach each other if we need to. We could let people know we can do alterations and things, perhaps put some ads in newsagents' windows in other parts of town?'

Bethan's eyes sparkled as she thought of what she would do with the extra money. Her family were poor but they didn't have the struggles the others had. Still, there was never any spare for luxuries or buying themselves treats occasionally.

'You know what,' Bethan said, turning her nose up at her fish paste sandwiches. 'You do some brilliant things with the clothes you get at jumble sales, Amanda. You've got a great eye for what works and what doesn't. Some of your dresses look the absolute bee's knees.'

Outside the window, the rain began to patter softly against the glass, a soothing sound in the occasional lull of conversations.

'She's right,' Maisie said. 'You've got a real talent there, wasted just checking stuff here. We just gotta get our heads together and think what we can do to get more readies.'

Their chatter echoed through the canteen, a brief respite from the reality of wartime life. Amanda felt a flicker of hope. Perhaps they could turn their dreams into something workable, something that could give them a lift from their boring day jobs and everyday struggles. And she'd never told the others, but she was saving to leave home, to get away from her father and get a room of her own somewhere. If they could earn a bit more her dream could come true sooner.

The bell rang, signalling the end of their break. Amanda stood, energised by determination to make something of their ideas. 'Right, girls, back to work. But let's keep talking about this. Let's get the ball rolling.'

2

Six o'clock sharp. Amanda put her father's dinner on the table with automatic precision, a saucepan lid centred on top to keep it warm. Knife and fork lined up. Her mother was tidying the already spotless kitchen. The small house smelled of cooking vegetables and the usual furniture polish made of vinegar and a bit of scarce linseed oil. The wireless played 'We'll Meet Again' softly in the background. It had to be turned off the moment her father walked in or there'd be hell to pay.

The shepherd's pie was padded out with grated carrots and lentils to make it go further. The gravy was thin, but it was the best her mother or anyone else could manage with meagre rations. Amanda had queued for almost an hour to get a bit of mince they'd used, her feet aching after a day at work. Food was always a worry, as was keeping the blackout curtains drawn tight every evening. A single chink of light could bring an air-raid warden pounding on the door threatening fines.

Her father had the biggest share of the shepherd's pie, of course. If his dinner wasn't on the table the minute he walked in the door, he let fly. Sometimes they got the silent treatment. Other times he might wait until his meal was half finished then fling it, plate and all, at the wall and storm out. 'Better grub at the George and Dragon,' he'd hiss.

The clock's tick-tick-tick matched their heartbeats. Four minutes, three, two. Amanda clutched her apron. Her mother flitted around the living room, straightening an antimacassar here, wiping non-existent dust from the mantelpiece there. Her movements birdlike, quiet.

Alert to the sound, they heard his first boot on the stair and froze. Second stair, her mother stopped dusting. Third stair, Amanda's hands were clasped tightly together. By the final stair, the wireless was off and their faces were carefully neutral, merely glancing at each other in silent mutual support. But the familiar sick feeling came in Amanda's stomach. Not quite fear, but as if the lifelong exposure to his behaviour automatically set her body on high alert.

'What's this then?' He was soon peering at the shepherd's pie as if they'd served him a plate of dog turds. His fingers caught Amanda's sleeve, forcing her to stay next to him. She knew never to try to snatch her arm away. But she also knew how to deal with this sort of thing.

'I must go upstairs, I've got the curse,' she muttered. He let go of her arm as if she had the plague. Like most men, he couldn't cope with talk of what he called 'stupid women's problems'.

But she saw her father shovelling the food in his mouth so quickly he never finished one mouthful before the next. 'And you, woman? Is this the best you can do?' This remark, his voice getting louder, was aimed at his wife. She'd worked as a cleaner all day and then done all the housework too. She looked ten years older than she was.

'I... I... I thought it was one of your favourites.'

'Well, it ain't no more!'

A knock on the door made them all still, cutting the tension like a knife through butter. 'Cooeee,' called Mrs Foxon from next door, opening the door a crack. 'Oh, you're having your tea. Sorry. I'm having trouble with the blackout curtains again. Can you come and help me, Amanda? You're so good at this sort of thing.'

Amanda's father always behaved when there were other people around. He wanted everyone to believe he was a wonderful man, a family man, a man of the people to be trusted and looked up to. 'I'm sure my girl would love to help you,' he said with an ingratiating smile. 'Good girl, she is.' The tension on her mother's face relaxed just a little.

A few minutes later, safe in the refuge of Mrs Foxon's kitchen, Amanda began to relax. She loved being with this kind older woman. The wireless was playing some music but it was a happy background, not a countdown to fear.

'Have a cuppa, dear,' Mrs Foxon said with a wicked grin. 'It's all ready and waiting. My curtains are okay, by the way.' She winked. 'Tea in proper china cups and a little shortbread biscuit each. Sorry I ain't got no more. Run out of flour.' The warmth of the tea soon spread through Amanda's hands, and she wished, as she had many times, that Mrs Foxon was her mother. Not that she didn't love her mother. She did. But she knew her mother would never leave her father despite his behaviour. She'd given up trying to persuade her.

'How's work going, dearie?' Mrs Foxon asked. The walls were as thin as wallpaper, and it was best to start conversations in a neutral way. But soon she turned on the wireless so they could speak without being overheard. 'I always try to come when I hear him getting his dander up.' She squeezed Amanda's arm reassuringly. 'I bin thinking. I need a couple of things altered, and so does my friend Florrie. We can't pay much but it would help you to save a bit.' Her voice got even lower. 'Help you get away from him.' She indicated next door with a nod of her head. 'Hang on a mo.' She went to her bedroom and returned with two dresses. They were old-fashioned, but still in good condition. Amanda would enjoy working on them, although she wondered how she would ever find time.

'Can I give you sixpence in advance? We can square up when it's done. You'll need to come round for a fitting soon anyway, won't you?' She continued speaking as she reached into her purse for the sixpenny bit. 'You know, you could make a little business with repairs and things. Have you ever thought about it?'

Amanda laughed. 'More times than I can count. Maybe doing these bits and pieces for you and your friends will be the beginning. I hope so.'

Back home, Amanda was relieved that her father had gone to the pub. Her mum was washing up, the wireless was back on and she was humming along to a tune. If only it was always like that.

Going to her bedroom, Amanda went to her little wardrobe and pulled out an old biscuit tin from Christmases past. As the sixpence went in, she couldn't resist counting her savings again, even though she knew exactly how much she had. Three pounds five shillings and sixpence. Not enough, but it was a good start. She mouthed the amount, almost like sending up a prayer.

Through the thin walls she could hear her mother's shuffling footsteps. But here, in the relative quiet of her room, she could still smell Mrs Foxon's lavender scent, taste that biscuit, feel the weight of the sixpence in her hand. Tomorrow there would be more of her father's behaviour to endure, more meals to serve on time, more moments to navigate his moods. But not for much longer.

Meanwhile, she wrapped the battered tin up in an old nightdress and hid it at the back of the wardrobe again. But tonight, she had sixpence more than yesterday, and the memory of those coins promised a better future.

3

Amanda watched as Maisie ran to the clocking-in machine, batting away the ever-present cloud of cotton fluff that hung in the air like industrial snow. They could taste it on their tongues and it often made them sneeze. The weak morning sun struggled to send long shadows over the room. Even a minute late meant fifteen minutes' pay docked. She didn't like talking about it, but Amanda knew Maisie's mum had lost her job again. She guessed she'd been drunk at work once too often.

She was already at her inspection desk at the side of the workshop, her light brown cotton work coat buttoned to her neck to fight off the cold. Only the dark rings under her eyes showed her lack of sleep. She'd tossed and turned, counting her savings in her head and planning what she would take with her when she finally left home.

Much as she loved her mum, she didn't want to end up like her, old before her time, doing dead-end jobs with a husband who was a waste of space. She thought more than once that she probably would never get married. She'd seen marriages go wrong so often amongst the girls in the factory, never mind the whole of the East End. Once they had kids they were stuck.

Bethan still wore her make-up from the party she'd been to at the US Air Force base the night before. She made it to the check-in machine with one minute to spare. She'd only had three hours' sleep. The GIs knew how to throw a party.

'You'll never guess what happened at the American dance last night,' she began, but there was no time to find out. Before any of them could do more than nod a greeting to each other, the day shift siren wailed. The familiar factory orchestra began – chairs scraped into place on the wooden floor, the soft thud of piles of fabric on the workbenches, the hum of machines starting up. Above it all *Music While You Work* blared from a wireless.

Eight hours of back-breaking work on their Singer sewing machines lay ahead. Then most of the women would have to queue for food before heading home to feed themselves and their families.

Maisie's fingers soon found their rhythm. She barely had to think about what she was doing unless the Ministry changed the order somehow. Then she had to learn a new rhythm. Her thoughts drifted to the chaos she'd left behind at home. Being the eldest child with a sister and a brother was hard. She felt like their mother most of the time. The nearest they'd got often. Ron was ten but sometimes he seemed like he was eighteen, stroppy and sulky, refusing to help around the house or get on with his schoolwork. He knew their mother was often too drunk or hungover to be of much use, but he never helped. Oh no, he thought anything in the house was women's work. Like father, like son, Maisie thought.

'You're about to run out of thread!' Mrs Duncan's harsh voice made her jump. The supervisor seemed to have eyes in the back of her head. 'You gotta keep your mind on the job or we won't meet the Ministry's quota.' She stalked between the rows of sewers, never giving a word of praise but finding plenty to complain about.

'I don't believe she ever got married,' one of the machinists said one day. 'I bet she's one of them surplus women. You know, the ones who couldn't find a man after the Great War. Not enough to go round. Who'd want her anyway?'

That didn't take away the supervisor's authority though. 'Yes, Sergeant Major, no, Sergeant Major,' Maisie said, but not out loud. Head down, she concentrated on her work and was relieved when the bell went for mid-morning break.

Amanda glanced over at her and gave her a sympathetic smile. Her inspection desk gave her a good view of the workshop floor. Through the haze, she watched the daily dance, women bent over their sewing machines, the steady rhythm of their work sending up fresh clouds of textile waste, making them cough. But something else hung in the air – something wrong. Numbers just didn't add up. Fabric in and uniforms out should balance, but they didn't. There were hushed conversations between Mrs Duncan and the warehouse staff too, especially one of them, the warehouse supervisor Mr Turnbull. They often looked furtive but she'd never managed to overhear them.

The three friends stood together in the break. 'We need a meeting,' Amanda whispered to her friends. 'If we really want to decide a way to make a bit extra, we need a plan. When shall we meet?'

Clutching her mug of tea, Bethan groaned. 'Give over. Proper tired, I am, don't make it too soon.'

'You'll need days to get that make-up off, you silly tart!' Maisie said, nudging her so hard she almost spilled her tea.

Bethan moved her tea away from her to protect it. 'Give over.

You don't complain when the Yanks give me little presents and I shares them with you, do you?'

'Girls! Girls!' Amanda said with a grin. 'If we want to earn a bit more we need to get some orders. Anyone got any ideas?'

The break room wireless crackled with a warning that they had five minutes to get back to their machines. Bethan wiped cotton fluff from her lipstick while demonstrating the latest American dance steps. Through rationing and air raids, drunk mothers and unpleasant fathers, they supported each other.

Could they help each other earn more money too?

4

'Mam, have you seen my hair slide? The blue one?' Bethan called down the stairs, her voice just heard over the sound of the Andrews Sisters on the wireless singing 'Boogie Woogie Bugle Boy'.

Mrs Williams was busy mixing another batch of Welsh cakes. With her lot they disappeared as fast as she could make them. 'Check your sister's room!' The kitchen was the warmest room in the house and fragrant with margarine and spice. She sighed as she thought the ingredients for this family favourite were getting harder and harder to find, rationing or no rationing. Flour, dried fruit, butter (she had to use margarine or lard), sugar, egg powder and milk. A bit of jam on top if they had any.

Amanda and Maisie arrived in a flurry of factory dust and excitement, carrying bags with their dance clothes. Amanda's outfit was made out of an old dress belonging to Mrs Foxon, her neighbour. 'You have it, dearie, I can't get it round me belly any more. Them days are long gone, oh, but the memories...'

Amanda held it against her. 'Looks better on you than it ever did on me,' Mrs Foxon had said, admiring the slate-grey cotton dress with tiny white flower sprigs. The skirt was long. It would have only cleared the ground by a couple of inches on her. The collar was white and detachable for washing. Mrs Foxon sniffed it. 'It smells of moth balls after all these years in the back of the wardrobe but give it a good wash and it'll be tickety-boo. You'll look smashing in that,' she went on. 'Do up that belt round that little waist of yours and you'll have the lads queueing up.'

While the two friends took the dresses out to let the creases disappear, Mrs Williams offered them the Welsh cakes. 'Sorry, I can only spare one each. Can't get half the ingredients for love nor money. A pain, it is.'

Bethan came into the room still complaining about her hair slide. 'I'm tamping, I am. I bet my rotten sister's got it somewhere.'

'Still not found it, cariad?' her mother said. 'Have a look in your sister's jewellery box.'

'I didn't steal it!' Mary Ann shouted down the stairs. 'And in any case, you borrowed my last pair of stockings yesterday and laddered them!'

'I did not! Well, you borrowed my best hand mirror and broke it! Mam, tell her off.' She sounded like a sulky five-year-old.

Amanda and Maisie watched this argument, fascinated. At her home, Amanda would have had a clip round the ear from her dad. At Maisie's, there would be a bun fight. But Mrs Williams was unfazed. 'These girls!' she said with an indulgent smile. 'Best of friends they are, really.' She called Mary Ann down from her bedroom. 'Right, you and your sister clear up the kitchen, and no fighting. I expect it to be spotless. I'm going to put my feet up for a minute and listen to the news.'

The sound of Big Ben's chimes announced the news was about to start. 'Here is the news,' the broadcaster read. 'From Moscow comes the official announcement that the remnants of the German Sixth Army at Stalingrad have surrendered. Prime

Minister Churchill has sent a telegram of congratulations to Premier Stalin, hailing this as a turning point in the war.'

Of more immediate interest to Mrs Williams was the latest news about rationing. It was never good. Four ounces of butter a week! How was she supposed to make that go round? She sighed. As the war went on, food got more and more boring, even though the government issued leaflets on how to make something delicious out of nothing.

She picked up the latest leaflet and groaned. 'Thrifty carrot and potato pudding' it was called. All vegetables apart from a bit of powdered egg and some meat dripping. She sighed. She'd give it a try but she doubted it would go down well. How long would this damn war go on, she wondered. People said the tide was turning, but life certainly wasn't getting any easier. Better not to think about it too much. She still had all her family and that was something many women couldn't say. And she had a good husband, something else a lot of local women couldn't say either.

The girls had gone upstairs, and she could hear giggling. The war was fun for some girls, especially if they lived near a military base or a port. Plenty of choice of men, always more fish in the sea if one didn't suit. One of the girls she worked with made two or three dates each night, half an hour apart. That way if one didn't turn up, she met the next one. She giggled every time she talked about it.

Half an hour later, the kitchen was transformed into a beauty parlour. Hairpins and make-up spread across the old well-scrubbed table and the wireless played 'Tiger Rag' while Maisie practised her jitterbug steps.

'You'll never guess what I heard,' Mary Ann said, all squabbles with her sister forgotten for the time being. 'They say there's going to be Yanks at the dance tonight.'

'Americans? Real ones?'

'No, fake ones,' Maisie said, rolling her eyes. 'Of course real ones. They're stationed near here, as if you didn't know.'

Mrs Williams chipped in. 'Remember what your dad says about Americans – all charm and chocolate bars...'

'...but no staying power.' Her daughters spoke in unison, well used to this lecture.

'Right, girls, line up by 'ere and let me look at you. There's posh you are. Got the lines on the back of your legs drawn straight, skirts not tucked in your knickers, a spare tanner in case you have an emergency? Gas masks? Pity your dad isn't back from work to see you all. Pretty as pictures you are.'

Bethan opened the door. 'Oh, no, it's started raining,' she wailed. 'My hair!'

'There's vain you are,' her mum said, handing her an old, battered umbrella. 'Don't do anything I wouldn't do!'

5

The Golden Globe dance hall was humming with the vibrant energy of wartime revelry. A big band on the stage played 'Ain't She Sweet', the brass instruments shining under the colourful lights that hung from the ceiling like stars in the night sky. The air was filled with the scent of sweat, perfume, cigarettes and a heady atmosphere of excitement. The wooden floorboards creaked under the weight of dancing feet, and laughter could hardly be heard over the sound of the music and the feet on the floor.

The three friends and Bethan's sister Mary Ann stepped inside, and took in the sight, smiling, ready for a good evening away from the stresses and strains of everyday life.

'Look at her!' Amanda shouted over the music, pointing to a girl who was giggling as her partner spun her round and threw her over his shoulder. 'I'd never be able to dance like that without being sick.'

Bethan smiled, adjusting her own dress, a deep blue that suited her skin. She tucked her curls behind her ear on one side as she'd seen a film star do in a magazine. 'Don't fret, cariad,' she said. 'We'll soon have lads queueing to dance with us.'

As the music changed to a slower tune, 'In the Mood', the crowd gradually changed, couples drawing closer. In some cases very close indeed and they spotted more than one hand on his partner's bottom. Amongst the crowd of soldiers and civilians, a tall GI caught Bethan's eyes. He stood out because of his confident look, his bright white teeth and a sexy smile that lit his handsome tanned face.

His eyes caught hers and his smile grew wider. He winked and walked towards her. 'Care to dance, pretty lady?' he asked. Without waiting for a response he tugged her hand, pulling her onto the dance floor. It was a slow number and he held her a little closer than she expected when she'd just met him, so she edged back slightly.

'What's your name, sweetheart?'

She liked his accent and although she'd heard a lot of different American accents she couldn't identify them. 'My name's Bethan. What's yours?'

He gave her another dazzling smile. 'Buddy. That's what my friends call me and I hope we'll soon be friends. Where do you come from, pretty lady? You don't sound like the girls around here.'

She was captivated by his charm and smiled back. 'I'm Welsh, I comes from Wales.' She noticed he had pulled her a little closer again and decided not to do anything about it this time.

'Wales? Like the big fish?' He laughed. 'You don't look like a little fish, although you do smell amazing.'

She had had this conversation too often to be amused. 'No, Wales is a country, a separate country but attached to England. We have our own language as well as speaking English.'

'Well, I'll be damned. Who knew?' The music slowed to a halt. 'Can I buy you a drink? I'd sure like to get to know you better.'

Bethan chose a shandy. She wanted to keep her mind working properly when meeting a gorgeous man like this one. They leaned against a wall a little way from the bar so they could hear each other.

'Where are you from, then?' Bethan asked.

'Me? I'm from good old California. Land of sea and sun and good times. I've got a lovely place there with a swimming pool you'd just love to try sometime. I'd certainly like to see you in a swimming costume. I bet you'd look just terrific.' He spent some time telling her about his life in California, how he and his friends would spend lazy days at the beach, swimming and playing games. His energy and laugher were contagious, and Bethan felt a sense of freedom in his presence, as if the worries of the world faded away.

She took a sip of her shandy. 'I'd love to come there. I've aways wanted to go to America.'

'You should come visit. We could have a bonfire on the beach, roast marshmallows, the whole nine yards.' He saw her drink was getting low. 'Let me get you another drink. Something stronger this time.'

'I don't usually...'

'Aw, come on, honey, we should have a drink to celebrate meeting. I know I'm real pleased we bumped into each other.'

While he was gone, she was imagining being there in California. Blue sky, blue sea, soft smooth sand and her sitting there in a new swimming costume sipping what... a cocktail? She'd never had one but she'd read about them in books and they sounded so sophisticated.

Maisie found her before Buddy came back, sweating from her

dances. 'This is such fun! I wish we could do this more often. What do you think of the GI you've been dancing with? He's certainly a hunk.'

Just thinking about him made Bethan's heart beat faster. 'He's so gorgeous. And he's got a house with a swimming pool in California. He said I should go there to visit him.'

Maisie grinned. 'You'd just have to learn to dodge the U-boats first! Well, I met a nice bloke. Local, Frank his name is, he was good to talk to. Works as an engineer on the railways. He's just gone to the gents'.'

But Bethan wasn't really listening, her mind too busy imagining a new life by the beach. Luckily, Buddy came back and brought her back to the moment. He smiled when he saw Maisie and offered her a drink. 'Two lovely ladies in one evening,' he said.

Frank appeared before Buddy could buy the drinks. The difference between the two men couldn't have been sharper. Buddy in his immaculate GI uniform, straight white teeth, a picture of health. Frank, tall but too thin, slightly crooked teeth and pale skin like most people after years of war and poor nutrition.

'Hi there!' Buddy said, pumping Frank's hand. 'I don't get to meet many men who are Brits...'

Frank raised an eyebrow. 'I imagine you spend your time looking for the ladies.'

Maisie was surprised at his response which was quite sharp. But when she thought about it, she couldn't help but agree. There was something about Buddy that wasn't right. He was handsome, well dressed, polite, charming even, but she remembered something her mother once said. 'Never trust a charming man.' At the time she didn't understand what she meant but suddenly she began to.

'Want another dance or a drink?' Frank asked, and he and Maisie left Bethan and Buddy and went back to the dance floor.

'What did you think of him?' Frank asked.

Maisie laughed. 'I wouldn't trust him any further than I could spit him. I only hope Bethan doesn't fall for him. She's such a romantic she'll be planning their wedding by now, and naming their children.'

When the dance ended they went to the bar to get more drinks. 'What can I get you?' Frank asked.

'Just a shandy, please.' Because of her mother's drinking she never drank anything stronger, worried she might get used to it.

While she waited for Frank, she spotted Amanda dancing on the other side of the dance hall. She looked happier than Maisie had seen her for ages, not talking to her dance partner, but her steps matching his perfectly. She caught her eye and gave a little wave of acknowledgement.

Frank returned with the drinks, handing her hers. 'Sorry, I dropped a little bit, it's so crowded in here someone nudged my arm. I'm afraid I'll have to go soon. My gran is ill and I promised I'd call in to see she's settled for the night. Sometimes she forgets what time it is.' He looked into her eyes. 'I've enjoyed meeting you, Maisie, would you come out with me again? Perhaps to the pictures if there's anything on you want to see. I do shift work but I expect we could sort something out.'

She didn't have to think about it twice. 'I'd like that. Hang on a minute and I'll scribble down my address. We don't have a phone.'

He laughed. 'Nor do I, I hardly know anyone who does. But from what you told me we live quite near each other so I can knock on your door or pop a note through if that's okay.'

Buddy had been chatting to Bethan, asking her about Wales. He was a better listener than other boys she'd been out with. She just hoped he'd ask her out again, so she was relieved when a few minutes later he asked for her address. 'I gotta go now, on duty, but I'd sure like to meet you again. Can I write to you and suggest a film one day?'

He didn't need to ask twice.

6

'Okay, who wiped their greasy fingers on the settee?' Maisie was trying to wipe dripping off the settee arm. She looked around at her younger brother and sister who avoided her eye. 'Mr Nobody again, I suppose,' she growled, rubbing harder with a damp cloth and a few drops of ammonia that made her eyes water. She had the wireless on in the background, where *Sing Something Simple* was on. Boring as usual, she thought as she worked.

But she was brought out of her mood when there was an unexpected knocking at the door. Rose, her young sister, immediately ran to the door before Maisie had a chance to even wipe her hands.

'Who are you then?' she heard Rose ask. 'You our Maisie's boyfriend?'

Maisie's heart jumped when she recognised the visitor's voice. Frank! Here? She wasn't expecting a visit from him, and she knew she looked a mess. Her hair was tied up in a turban with an old scarf, she had a tatty apron on over her skirt and wore slippers that were well past their best. She thought briefly of pretending not to be home but Rose would never let her get away with that. Ripping the scarf off her head and running her fingers through her hair, she went to the door.

'Frank! What a lovely surprise. I didn't know you were coming.'

'I hope you don't mind. I had to do a bit of shopping for my ma around here, so I decided to chance my luck that you'd be in. If you've got time we could go to the Cosy Café for a cuppa. My treat.'

Maisie wanted nothing more but felt so scruffy. 'Come on in, Frank. I was just doing some housework, as you can see.' She led him into the living room, making sure he didn't sit where there was the damp patch. As they walked, she whipped off the apron and kicked off the slippers.

Rose went and stood next to Frank. 'You're Maisie's boyfriend, ain't you! You are, ain't you!'

Maisie could have thumped her. 'Rose, go and play outside.'

Rose poked her tongue out at her sister. 'But it's cold out there and Mummy'll be home soon.'

Now her brother Ron sidled up to Frank. 'D'you bring her a pressie? Boyfriends are supposed to bring pressies. Got any chocolate? I like chocolate.'

Frank laughed. 'I'm not a Yank, so no chocolate, and I've only met Maisie once. But I did bring a little something for her.'

Ron's eyes lit up with hope. 'Something to eat?'

Rose snatched the small brown paper-wrapped parcel from Frank's hand faster than a bullet from a machine gun. She sniffed it and her face fell. 'Nah, not chocolate.' She sniffed again. 'I reckon it's soap.' Without asking, she handed it to Maisie. 'Here, make you smell better. Did you think she smelled bad?' Rose asked Frank with a twinkle in her eye.

'She smells lovely now, you cheeky madam,' Frank said with a chuckle.

'Don't listen to them, Frank,' Maisie said. 'They don't know what they're talking about.'

Ron and Rose ignored her. 'Are you rich?' Ron asked, rubbing his fingers together in the universal sign for money. 'Are you going to marry Maisie and live in a big house with servants and everything?'

'And chocolate! Lots of chocolate!' Rose chipped in. 'Can we come and see you?'

Frank laughed. 'Oh, I'm rolling in it. I've got two whole shillings in my pocket right now. Do you think that'd be enough for a big house and servants?'

'Nah.' Ron knew everything. 'That'd cost four shillings at least. Or another shilling if you want a garden an' all.'

Maisie was standing with her hands on her hips. 'Haven't you horrible pair got anything better to do than bother Frank? It's me he's come to see.'

'Just making sure he behaves,' Ron said as if he was looking after her rather than hoping for something for himself.

'Tell you what,' Frank said, reaching into his pocket. 'I've got a couple of thrupenny bits here. Want one each?' He winked at Maisie and continued. 'But we'd have to put off buying that big house a bit if I give a whole sixpence away.'

But Rose and Ron had jumped up and held out their hands. 'I'll buy some pear drops!' Rose squealed.

'Liquorice and a sherbet dab for me,' Ron replied. 'And you ain't 'aving none.' He might be older than Rose, but he wasn't above pulling a face at her.

'Go on then,' Maisie said. 'And make sure you put your coats and gloves on, it's cold out there. Don't stay out long.'

While the horrors had been speaking she had put on her

shoes, finished a bit of tidying and pulled her hair into something she could live with.

'How'd I do with the kids?' Frank asked when they'd gone. 'Think they liked me?'

Maisie laughed. 'They'd like anyone who gave them money for sweets!'

The front door opened with a bang. Expecting it was Rose or Ron back, Maisie was ready to sort them out. But it was worse. It was her mother and she'd been drinking again. She slammed the door behind her and staggered into the living room, stopping when she saw Frank.

She struggled to stand more upright. 'Oh, a male visitor!' Her attempt at a posh voice she sometimes used for visitors was enough to make Maisie cringe. 'How delightful. Are you a friend of Maisie's? I'm Mrs Hawkins.' She held out her hand for him to shake.

Undaunted by the smell of alcohol that hit him, Frank smiled pleasantly and shook her hand. 'Yes, I'm Frank. I was in the area and came to see if she had time to come with me to the Cosy Café for a cuppa.'

Maisie cringed listening to her mother trying to impress Frank. Her mother was swaying as she spoke, her eyes half closed. Would Frank be able to cope with her?

Mrs Hawkins squinted at Frank as if she was trying to recognise him. Maisie felt her stomach drop. She hadn't warned Frank about her mother's drinking. This was going to be a disaster.

'Well, you're a handsome one!' her mother declared, touching her hair as if to make herself more attractive. 'Are you a soldier? No uniform, but of course my lovely daughter here could make you one.'

Frank cleared his throat before he answered. It was a tiny clue that he was nervous, one Maisie was to get to know. 'Not a soldier.

I'm a mechanic for the trains. My dad did the same. It means I have to do shifts but I enjoy the work. I like fixing things. And I do the odd shift at Maisie's factory to earn a bit of extra once in a while.'

'Mum, we're...' Maisie tried to interrupt.

Her mum ignored her. 'A mechanic?' Mrs Hawkins went on. 'Good job that. Let me tell you, if you're interested in my daughter you'd better be a good man. A man worthy of being part of this family.'

Maisie almost choked. 'Oh, for goodness' sake.' She went into the hall and fetched her coat and hat. Anything to get away from the embarrassment she felt when her mum was in her cups. 'We're going, Mum. The kids have gone to get some sweets.'

'Sweets?' Her mother's posh voice was forgotten. 'Where'd they get money for sweets?'

'I gave them thruppence each,' Frank said. 'You have lovely children. They're a credit to you. Now, please excuse me if I take Maisie off. I've got to do some errands for my mother but have time for a quick cuppa with her if we leave now.'

As they stepped into the street, Maisie sighed heavily. 'Frank, I'm so... sorry about her. I hoped she wouldn't come back while you were there. She's lovely when she's not drinking, but...'

He held her hand. 'Don't worry, love. I thought she was interesting.'

'Interesting? There's a good word. Could mean anything.'

'Well, let's say memorable, shall we?'

Maisie laughed despite her embarrassment. 'You're a good man, Frank. I can tell that already.'

'Good enough to be part of your family then? Your mother would be delighted. But after only meeting once it's a bit soon to be thinking like that.'

But Maisie had a feeling he was the right man. Time would

tell. The trouble was with all her commitments and her mother's drinking, would she ever feel able to put her own happiness first? It seemed as if she was always looking after other people. Sometimes she just longed to let her muscles relax and have someone look after her.

But would it ever happen?

7

The steps up to Mrs Cohen's terraced house were scrubbed clean and inviting, a *Room to Let* sign in the window. Amanda counted the steps as she walked up, six steps. Six steps to freedom if she could get this room. Six steps to sleeping without a chair jammed under the bedroom door handle. Six steps to avoid having to hide her money from her gambling father, hearing his whistling when he had a rare win, hearing his temper when he lost. Six more days until her next payday when she would have enough money for a deposit the landlady needed.

She'd started saving and hiding her money when she found her mother crying over the bill from the corner shop. Like many women, her mother shopped there daily, buying food on tick and paying the bill at the end of the week. The trouble was there was nothing left in the kitty to start the next week so the whole cycle began again.

'Your dad's taken me housekeeping to bet on a horse,' she sobbed when Amanda asked her what was wrong one time. 'Now I can't pay the bill at the corner shop.' She blew her nose and wiped her face. 'Miss Pearson won't give me tick next week. What'll we do for food?'

That week they were lucky. Her dad won so the problem was solved, although getting a penny of his winnings out of him was a struggle. But the familiar story rarely had a happy ending. Amanda was determined not to live her life like that. She was going to learn how to start and run a business or get a better-paying job. Find somewhere to live away from the stress of her father's gambling.

As she tried to pluck up courage to knock on the door, she noticed something was missing that she'd seen in signs on the windows of many houses where rooms were to let – *No blacks, Irish or dogs*. She hated those signs. Their absence gave her a glimmer of hope. Perhaps the landlady was someone kind, someone who didn't see the world in such cruel divisions. Somewhat reassured, she knocked and footsteps soon told her the landlady was on the way.

Determined that her life would be different, she had plans. First she would move out, renting this room if it was any good. Then she'd raise every penny she could. She'd work with Bethan and Maisie somehow, take in alterations for local people, do overtime, anything to have a future. She imagined it as she waited for the door to open. She'd be living independently, not rich but able to pay the bills. No tick. No man would ever have a penny of her money. It seemed like heaven to a girl brought up in the East End surrounded by hardship and poverty.

'Are you Amanda?' The woman who opened the door had grey hair pinned back in a neat bun. She wore a black skirt and a white blouse with a grey cardigan, and knitted stockings slipped into slippers. In her apron pocket keys jangled. 'Welcome to Wentworth Street. It's nice to have someone arrive when they say they will. My last tenant, a nice girl, mind you, married now in

Golders Green. She was always running late, always with an excuse ready as a warm loaf.'

She let Amanda in, chatting all the while. 'It's a nice room, not too small and of course, we're just round the corner from Petticoat Lane market. People like it here.' Her chatter went on and on, talking about the area, the house, the neighbours and her cat, Snowy. 'The room's got a good bed, and the wardrobe is solid. I remember you said when you phoned that you sew so the table in the corner should be ideal for you.' She glanced at Amanda's coat. 'Make that yourself?'

'I got it in a jumble sale,' Amanda said, wondering how they'd manage for clothes without jumble sales. 'It was miles too big, so I had to take it apart and remodel it.' She couldn't resist twirling round to show it off. Several girls in the factory had admired it.

'Well, you did a good job. Come upstairs and see the room,' Mrs Cohen said, leading the way. The stairs were covered in brown linoleum and the walls painted cream with a few paintings of London scenes. 'Here we are.' She opened the door with a flourish. The room was average size, but bright with light good enough to sew by. In one corner was a single bed with a bedside table next to it. A single wardrobe was opposite and a chest of drawers with a mirror on top. But the most important thing for Amanda was a little table, big enough for a sewing machine. There was a gas fire. 'You'd have a meter for the gas,' the landlady said. 'But electric is included in the rent. You'd share the bathroom with two other girls and you can use the kitchen when I'm not in there. But,' she warned, 'if you leave it in a mess, I'll stop that privilege. Come and see the kitchen. You and my other tenants would have a shelf each for your food.'

Finally, she asked Amanda to sit down, questioning her about her family. Not expecting this, Amanda didn't know how much to say. Her parents weren't actually cruel or criminal, but her father's gambling and her mother's inability to deal with it caused strain. Quickly she assessed the situation and decided she didn't need to go into any of that. 'We're a close family,' she said, 'but it's time now for me to make my own way in the world. I love your room and hope you'll be willing to rent it to me. I'm clean and tidy and honest.'

She remembered how often she'd cleaned the house when her mother's low mood meant she wasn't capable of doing it. She never blamed her. Living such an uncertain life with a gambler for a husband meant she never knew from one week to the next how she could pay her bills. It would get anyone down.

'Now about the kitchen rota,' Mrs Cohen began but her slipper caught on the edge of the rug. She threw out her hands to catch herself, but instead her arm caught the sharp edge of the draining board. Blood welled immediately through her cardigan. 'Oh, my Lord,' she whispered, her face going pale.

Amanda acted quickly, pulling a clean handkerchief from her pocket. 'I do first aid at the factory. Let me help.' She eased Mrs Cohen into a chair and rolled up her sleeve. 'It's not a deep cut, but let's clean it under the tap and I'll bandage it with my hankie.' Mrs Cohen watched her silently, feeling shaky but glad someone so capable had taken charge. She decided on the spot that if this girl wanted the room, she'd let her have it.

'There, all done,' Amanda said a few minutes later. 'Are you okay? Do you need a glass of water or anything?'

Mrs Cohen continued to sit, not trusting her legs for a minute. 'No, I'm fine. Do you have any questions about the room?'

'I've got one question. Can I have a lock for my room?'

Mrs Cohen raised her eyebrows. 'A lock? No one's ever asked for that before. This is a safe house.' She was beginning to bristle. 'And I don't allow any male visitors, so if you've got a young man you'll have to meet him somewhere else.'

Amanda smiled. 'No, no boyfriend, I'm far too busy for romance. I suppose I'm just being cautious.'

'Tell you what.' Mrs Cohen gently rubbed her cut arm. 'I'll keep the room until Saturday. I've got two other girls interested but I like you so you can have first refusal. But if you're not here with the rent by midday Saturday I'll have to let it go.'

When she left the house, Amanda felt hope in her heart. It was a comfortable room, she knew she could turn it into a home and Mrs Cohen would be a great landlady. As she walked, she imagined how she would rearrange the furniture. She could make a pretty cushion out of some old fabric she'd been keeping and maybe start a quilt for the bed, although she couldn't imagine ever having enough time to finish one.

She just had to wait until payday, and she'd have enough money to secure the room. But would her money be safe until then?

8

Back at home, Amanda found her mother sitting at the kitchen table with her head in her hands. 'His dog lost,' she groaned. 'All my housekeeping gone. I'll have to pawn my wedding ring again.'

'Oh, Mum.' Amanda put her arm around her mother's shoulders. No one had much fat after years of rationing but she noticed how bony her mother's shoulders were and wondered if she skipped meals to save a bit of money. 'That's awful. I don't know why you stay with him.' But she did know. Her mum, like so many women, had little choice. They earned very little, rarely managed to save and would have trouble trying to rent somewhere on their own. Landlords could turn them down just because there wasn't a man 'to look after things'. Not for the first time, she wondered who made these rules. Whoever it was had never met her dad, that was for sure.

'Was he like this when you met him?' She couldn't believe her mother would have married him if he was.

'Not really. He did the pools like we all do, and once he had a little win so he started filling in more lines after that. The only other time he bet was on the big horse races like the Derby. Then once he got lucky and won fifty pounds. After that, there was no stopping him.' She sighed. 'He was a changed man. Wouldn't listen to reason. They say there's no way to change an addict and I reckon he's a gambling addict. I don't even know if that's a thing.'

Amanda shook her head. 'If only he'd stop...'

Even as she spoke, she remembered her savings. She'd hidden her money all around her bedroom: some under her mattress, some on top of the wardrobe, some tucked inside her underclothes and some in her spare shoes. But she felt her blood go cold remembering how often he'd found her money in the past.

She took the stairs two at a time, heart hammering. At her bedroom door she hesitated, hand on the knob, dreading what she might find, yet somehow she just knew.

Everything looked untouched. Her hairbrush and comb lay exactly where she'd left them on the dressing table, the bedspread still a little crooked from her haste making the bed before going out that morning. Relief flooded through her – until she noticed the corner of the bedspread was slightly turned up. The kind of detail he would probably miss.

Her fingers trembled as she lifted the mattress. The familiar envelope she'd used for her savings was still there, but now it was empty. She turned her room upside down, knowing she was being silly. She remembered every place she left her money. There was no money anywhere, all her savings gone.

He must have spent ages attempting to make everything look how it had been, probably hoping she wouldn't notice before he had a win and would put it back. Not that he ever would, but like all gamblers he was good at fooling himself. She dropped onto the edge of the bed, the empty envelope dangling limply from her fingers. Without much hope, she checked all the other hiding places again but of course every penny was gone. All her planning. Why had she been so stupid as to believe he wouldn't find her money and steal it? Her own father. Her throat tightened and she struggled to hold back tears. But she wouldn't cry for him. Not this time. Instead, she'd find a way to make sure he never had the opportunity to rob her again. She had to save enough to get a room and get away from this unhappy house.

Then she paused. Could she get it back before he gambled it away? He'd be at the pub, that was certain. That's where his bookie was, standing smugly at the bar no doubt, counting the money he took from suckers like her dad. Enough. Gritting her teeth, she decided she'd go and have it out with him.

Five minutes later, she burst through the pub door breathing hard, having run all the way. The sudden wall of cigarette smoke and male voices assaulted her senses. Heads turned, conversations stopped as if cut by a knife. In the far corner, hunched over a pint, sat her father, his head down. He was drawing a circle in spilled beer on the table. In front of him were betting slips, all torn in half. She'd seen enough of them in her life to know what that meant. It meant his horse or dog hadn't won.

The sound of the door opening got his attention. Looking up from his pint, he spotted her and glared, his eyes cold as steel. 'What're you doing here? This is no place for a girl!'

She strode over to him, ignoring the wolf-whistles and comments from men at the bar. 'Where's my money?' She kept her voice low, but heads turned anyway. Her father's face flushed dark red, then his eyes blazed even more and his lips twisted with anger. His mate Billy, who was sitting next to him, suddenly found his almost empty glass fascinating, while the other two round the table pushed back their chairs, muttering about getting in another round.

Within seconds her father sat alone, but Amanda knew the whole room was listening.

'I've been saving that money for something special...' She didn't get to finish the sentence before the bookie, a man she recognised as Ben something or other, interrupted. 'Something special, ay. Fancy yourself for a night on the town? I'll come with you, sweetheart. Give you a good time.'

Amanda whirled round. This was the man responsible for taking her father's money. Without thinking, she picked up an almost empty beer glass from the table and flung the contents at him.

It was only a dribble and most of it missed. He was still smiling as he wiped the small amount of beer off his face. The smile was a cruel one. 'I think your old man'd better do 'is betting somewhere else from now on.' His voice was harsh enough to make nearby drinkers instinctively lean back an inch or two. 'We don't like scenes like this here, do we?' He looked at Amanda's dad. 'You! Out! Now! And take her with you! Silly bitch.'

Not caring if he followed her or not, Amanda stormed out, ignoring the cat calls and crude comments from the men at the bar. They could all go to hell. Bastards.

Outside the pub, her legs finally gave way. She slumped against the wall, her hands shaking, gulping in clean air. From inside she could hear the men laughing and hated every one of them. Taking some deep breaths, she pushed herself upright again. She wouldn't cry. Not here. Not where her father might see her.

She walked back home dragging her feet, not seeing the familiar chippie, the newsagents, the bombed buildings. But memories of how her father used to be forced themselves into her consciousness. He used to take her to the fair, show her how to ride her bike, boast about her achievements to his friends. But the drink and gambling had taken that man away. Bit by bit, year by year, until all that was left was this selfish stranger.

And she remembered too how she got her interest in making clothes. Even from a young age, probably about five, she used to sneak into her parents' bedroom and try on her mum's dresses, turning this way and that in the mirror, admiring not just herself but the outfit. And as she got older she and her friends did the same, sometimes with their mum's clothes, sometimes with their own. It didn't matter. They just play-acted having a fashion show, putting on a swanky walk, shoulders back and head high like they'd seen on the Pathé News. One would pretend to be the reporter. 'And Amanda is modelling this season's new day dress made of finest quality cotton.' Best was if they could use a white nightie and pretend to be a bride. Funny, now that it was the last thing she wanted.

But her dad had dashed her hopes of a home of her own, of the start of her own fashion business which was her secret dream. She'd stay in her home with her parents with all their fights and problems. Back to square one. Perhaps she could get some extra shifts at the factory and start her savings again. This time she'd open a post office savings account. They'd give her a book which showed every penny she saved, no matter how small. She would never let that book out of her sight.

9

Maisie's attic bedroom was so cold that even with their coats on, the friends shivered as they talked. The gas fire in the corner spluttered, its warmth a cruel tease against the winter cold. Maisie's eyes darted to the meter, dreading the moment when it would clink empty and plunge them into darkness. The blackout curtains, held together with a peg, blocked the light but not the draught that slithered through the cracks like a thief in the night, stealing warmth and comfort. They rubbed their hands together to warm them. Hands that had worked all day making uniforms for the troops.

The market below Maisie's house was long closed, but two men were still clearing up with their big brooms and loud voices. A tram going past shook the house to its poor foundations. *Dig for Victory* and *Careless talk costs lives!* posters were gradually curling away from the walls opposite Maisie's house. It might be dark outside, but East End life carried on regardless. The air-raid warden was shouting to someone in a nearby house, 'This is your last warning. Close those damn curtains or I'll report you.' A horse and cart trundled by. Despite the cold, Miss Kelly and Mrs

Harold next door either side were standing outside gossiping about another neighbour, 'You'll never guess what she's gone and done!' and complaining about the shortages, 'Can't get a bit o' ham nowhere!'

The three friends were discussing how hard up they were again. 'You know we're all pretty good dressmakers,' Amanda said. 'And I told you I sometimes do alterations for people. Can't we turn that into a business?'

'What, and give up the factory?' Maisie gasped. It sounded like an impossible dream.

'No, keep our jobs there, but let it be known what we can offer. We talked about it a bit before. Between us we've got a load of skills. We can do alterations, even make clothes for people.'

Bethan shook her head. 'I can see two problems with that. No one round here's got any money and with clothes rationing, not many want new dresses even if they had enough clothes rations left.' She twiddled one of her curls through her fingers as she spoke.

Amanda nodded. 'You're right, but we could advertise in an area where they've got more money. We thought about that before. With clothes rationing I bet more people want what they've got updated, given a different look. We do that sort of thing all the time with stuff we get at the jumble.' She looked at her friends and could see they weren't convinced. With a sinking heart, she reached into her bag and pulled out some sheets of paper.

'What do you think of these?' Amanda spread three sketches of beautiful wedding dresses on Maisie's bed. 'I've been really careful to design each of them to use as little fabric as possible but still look special.'

Bethan sprawled across the end of the bed, making the ancient bed springs creak. She leaned on one elbow as she studied the designs. 'They're lovely, cariad,' she said. 'But who's going to ask us, girls they don't know, to make wedding dresses for them? They'd never do it.' She looked at the designs again, running her finger over them. 'There's lovely, they are. You're a real clever clogs. You know your numbers and can design dresses too. You'll be charging us sixpence to talk to you soon.'

Amanda put the sketches back in her bag. 'I know we can't start with something like these, but people always need alterations and repairs. We can do that standing on our heads.'

Downstairs they could hear Maisie's brother and sister fighting over who had eaten the last piece of bread and dripping. Maisie groaned. 'Never stop, them two, they're enough to drive anyone to an early grave.' She paused to check they weren't actually killing each other. 'Never mind them, I don't think we can get started with something like this. We'd need money for posters and time to hang them up, not to mention working out where would be best to try. Why don't we just think about it for a while and maybe mention to the girls at the factory that we do alterations.'

Sadness weighing her down, Amanda knew Maisie was right but she was going to hold on to her dream. One day... 'You're right...'

She'd no sooner spoken than they heard footsteps thundering up the old creaky stairs. The door flew open, banging against the wall. 'It ain't fair, Mais!' her sister Rose said, her eyes blazing. 'Ron hid my beads. I been collecting them to make a necklace for Mum.'

Maisie groaned, they never gave her a minute's peace. 'Leave it for a while. I'll come and sort it out when my friends have gone. Go on, shoo!'

After sticking out her tongue, Rose vanished as fast as she'd arrived.

'Never mind them silly kids,' Maisie said. 'I want to know what's going on with you, Bethan. You seen that Buddy again?'

A knowing smile spread across Bethan's face. 'I have. He's very keen. Took me to the pictures to see a film with Robert Grainger in it and then we went to a swanky pub for a drink.' She sat up and reached for her bag. 'And...' She paused for dramatic effect as she reached into her bag. 'He came bearing gifts... like one of the three wise men!'

She laid three pairs of stockings on the bed like a magician producing something out of thin air. 'There you are, one pair for each of us. Never let it be said I'm not generous. I got a bar of chocolate as well, but I've eaten it all!'

'Pig!' Maisie said. 'But thanks for the stockings, won't say no. Did he kiss you?'

Bethan's face went pink. 'Well, it's like this, see, the pub had these sort of alcoves where you were a bit private so we...'

Amanda and Maisie were aghast. 'You didn't go all...'

Bethan's head shot up. 'No. I didn't go all the way, thank you very much. But he certainly knows how to kiss. I had to push his hands away a few times but he took no for an answer. He's a real gent.'

Amanda groaned. 'He sounds too good to be true, if you ask me. And I'd bet a penny to a pound he'll want something in return for his presents. He's just biding his time. You just keep your hand on your ha'penny and your mind on Jesus or you'll be altering clothes to make them bigger!'

Bethan grunted and pulled a face. 'What sort of girl do you think I am?'

'One who could easily get her head turned by a rich, handsome GI, that's who,' Maisie replied.

Bethan looked at Maisie. 'Did you ever see that bloke you met at the dance?'

'Frank? Yes, he called in the other day out of the blue. I was doing the housework and I looked a right mess, but he didn't seem put off. We went out to the café for a cuppa. He seems like a good man, helps look after his gran who's a bit, you know. Forgets everything.'

Amanda nodded. 'Not all men would do that. My dad wouldn't, that's for sure. He wouldn't look after me or my mum, never mind his mum.'

'Still playing up, is he?'

'You could say that. But more importantly, have you noticed how Mrs Duncan is even more bad-tempered than usual? She's got the whole workshop trembling in fear.'

'Nothing new there then,' Maisie said. 'But never mind her, we're gonna have a trip to Petticoat Lane on Saturday. I've got some coupons and I want to see if Big Sal has some material cheap enough for me to make myself a new dress.'

A loud crash downstairs made Maisie flinch. She guessed it would be her mother, home from the pub, drunk enough to stumble into the furniture.

'Mais!' her mother shouted. 'Get down 'ere! Where's me tea, you lazy cow? Get your boat race down 'ere now!'

Maisie's face went red and she plucked an invisible thread off her sleeve. 'Mum's not very well at the moment,' she said. She knew her friends would have to be stupid to believe her mother was ill, but she wasn't going to say more. The smell of booze would probably knock them sideways as they went downstairs.

The other two began getting ready to leave, pretending nothing was amiss.

'Your mum still doing the night shift at the hospital?' Bethan asked Amanda, putting on her coat.

'Cleaning? Yeah, won't be home until morning. Sometimes I've already left by the time she gets in. Dad's on fire watch at the factory.' She didn't mention she was glad of that fact. She never relaxed when he was home.

There was no avoiding Maisie's mum as they headed for the front door. She was leaning against the kitchen table, making an effort to stand upright, unaware of a beer stain on her blouse. ''Ave you had a lovely evening up there, gels?' she asked, trying to sound upper class. 'Do give my love to your dear mother, Bethan,' she continued with a hiccup. 'I 'aven't seen her for ages. We simply must get together to take tea one afternoon.'

Amanda pretended to cough to disguise a titter. Everyone knew Mrs Hawkins never made it any further than the Salmon and Ball at the end of the street.

Next door's cat Ginger wandered in and wound itself around Mrs Hawkins's feet. 'Bugger off, you rat!' she hissed, then remembered there were visitors. 'I mean, this animal probably has fleas and it's important that our home is always spotless.'

The booze was winning over her attempt to act sober, but she kept trying, much to Maisie's embarrassment. 'Perhaps I shall retire to my boudoir,' she slurred. 'The evening air is becoming somewhat chilly, don't you think. Somewhat...' They all knew the boudoir was the tiny box room over the dustbins.

'Inclement?' Bethan offered, but the irony was lost on Mrs Hawkins as she staggered to the stairs.

Bethan and Amanda waved goodbye and went their separate ways. But Amanda's head had moved on from boyfriends to making some money. She was good at figures, as Maisie had said. So good, she realised something dodgy was going on at the factory. But who was involved and how could she prove it?

10

Two days later, after their shift, the girls went to the Old George pub on Commercial Street. It was a well-known pub with lots of action, but importantly no reputation for fights. They guessed they would see people they knew in there, and Maisie knew it wasn't a pub her mother frequented. The buildings either side had been flattened during the Blitz but as sometimes happened, this one was spared as if it had a protective magic spell around it.

'Evening, girls,' the landlady said as they walked in. 'What'll it be? And don't ask for anything fancy. We've got a limited choice here these days. You'd think there was a war on or something.'

Maisie looked at the other two. 'I'm having a shandy, what about you two?' They nodded and she turned to the landlady who was already serving an older man who was sitting propped on a stool in the corner of the bar as if he owned it.

'Shandy, is it, girls?' he said. 'Last of the big drinkers, are you? Tell you what, let me buy them for you. No strings attached.'

The landlady overheard. 'Go on, girls, let him buy it, he's harmless.'

That didn't stop each of the girls going over and giving the old man a peck on the cheek. He touched his cheek where they'd kissed and his smile was all the reward they needed.

The pub was crowded, mostly with after-work drinkers as they were. They looked around. There was a darts match in the other bar, a table with three men playing dominoes, another with men playing cards and sitting next to the fire, two old ladies knitting. They still wore their tea cosy hats and looked quite at home.

'Blimey,' a man at a nearby table said as they walked by. He pinched Bethan's bottom. 'Three princesses straight from Buckingham Palace, no less.'

'Princesses, is it?' Bethan said with a twinkle in her eye. 'Then you must be a frog and I don't kiss no frogs so you're wasting your time with me, bach.'

'Oh, a Welsh beauty,' the man replied. 'I hear them Welsh girls are hot.'

'I wouldn't even get lukewarm for the likes of you!' Bethan swiped him round the head and walked on. She looked at her friends. 'Come on, girls, let's play darts. Show these blokes how it's done.'

If only they had. It was like a competition to see who could throw the worst. They barely hit the board, never mind the bullseye.

One man stepped behind Amanda, put his arms around her tighter than necessary, held her hand and tried to guide the dart. Instead, she used it to gently stab his arm. 'Down, Rover,' she said with a grin. Then she threw the dart on her own and got a twenty-five, having hit the outer bullseye. 'See!' she said, laughing. 'I don't need no man to win.'

Two young, handsome black GIs walked in and the room momentarily silenced, then with an almost perceptible shrug most people carried on with what they were doing. People were getting used to the sight of the tall, well-dressed men in their midst. But it didn't stop the girls overhearing a few mutters about darkies. They were well aware of the segregation in the US armed forces, and black and white soldiers were never in the same pub, dance hall, or cinema. The men ordered two beers. 'No chance of a cold beer, is there? We gotta be on our way soon.' Americans never got used to the warm, weak drink that passed for beer since the war started.

'It's proper mad, it is,' Bethan said when they were talking about it later. 'They're all putting their lives on the line, lots of them are doing repairs around the East End too, and they're all men. Seems to me their personality is a damn sight more important than the colour of their skin. Tamping I was when I first heard about it. In Swansea, see, where I comes from, we all mix together. I went to all the religious festivals when I was a nipper, we all did, and we didn't take no notice of people's skin colour neither.' Her eyes went dreamy for a few seconds. 'I remember lighting candles for Hanukkah, and following a saint's procession. Us kids, we loved it all, we did.'

But before they had time to introduce themselves the two GIs bid a polite farewell to the barmaid, and said goodbye after leaving her a tip. She looked at the ten-shilling note. 'Blimey, they can come here more often!' She tucked the note in her pocket.

The girls spent the rest of the evening flirting with the men playing darts, talking to the old ladies about the knitting they were doing, and wondering what was up with Mrs Duncan.

'Maybe it's the change of life,' Maisie said, dropping her voice. 'Makes some women go bonkers, they say. The curse is a damn nuisance but maybe that's worse.'

One of the old ladies overheard her and caught her eye. 'Old age is not for wimps,' she said with a toothy grin.

11

It was a few days later and not much had changed. They were still broke, Mrs Duncan was still being a tyrant and the war showed little sign of ending.

'Let's have a cuppa.' Maisie wiped her hands on her apron. 'My horrible horde will be home soon.' She pushed her chair back and started towards the kitchen.

'There's something I want to talk to you both about,' Amanda said, reaching for her notebook out of her bag.

'Some juicy gossip, I hope, butt.' Bethan's eyes sparkled at the idea.

'You should know she doesn't do gossip,' Maisie shouted from the kitchen. 'Kettle's on, won't be a tick. Bet those little buggers have eaten all the biscuits, not that we had many.'

When they all had cups of tea in front of them, Amanda tapped her notebook in a gesture the others recognised. Maisie caught Bethan's eye and raised an eyebrow.

Amanda's fingers tapped on her notebook again. Twice she made as if she was going to speak then stopped, wondering if the others would think she was imagining things. Her tea was untouched, a thin skin forming on it. She glanced at the window and then at the door. Her hands shook slightly as she pushed her hair behind her ears.

Maisie put down her cup with a bang. 'Come on, out with it. You're making me nervous with all this stopping and starting.'

'Sorry.' Amanda's voice was lower. 'Maybe we should check... the others will be back soon...'

'Oh, for heaven's sake.' Bethan sounded ready to throttle her. 'There's no spies here, you daft thing.' Without warning she leapt up, strode to the front door, opened it and peered in all directions. 'Nope, no spies wearing masks and black hats. No spivs. No secret police. Just get on with it.'

Ignoring that, Amanda told her to sit down again. 'It might be a sort of gossip, because I'm not sure if I'm imagining it, but I think there's something dodgy going on at the factory. I hinted at it once before if you remember.'

The other two looked at her, wide-eyed. 'Dodgy, is it?' Bethan leaned forward. 'What sort of dodgy?'

Amanda put her head in her hands. 'I don't know if I should even be talking about this. You need to both promise not to repeat what I'm saying to a soul.' She looked up at each of them in turn. 'I need you to promise.'

'Here's me!' Bethan said. 'I can keep a secret, honest.'

Maisie looked worried. 'It's not something that'll get us into trouble, is it?'

'I hope not.' But the truth was that if they investigated further the people behind the problem wouldn't be very happy. There was no way of knowing. 'If anything looks like it will cause trouble, I won't involve either of you. I won't even tell you about it.'

Bethan clapped. 'It's like *Inspector Scott Investigates* on the wireless!'

Amanda glared at her. 'This is serious, Bethan. I think

someone is fiddling things at the factory. The records for fabric going in and uniforms going out don't match.' Maisie's spoon clattered against her saucer. Bethan sat up straighter.

'By how much?' Maisie whispered.

'That's it, I'm not clear yet. Have either of you noticed anything a bit odd?'

Outside they heard a tram trundle by and a rag-and-bone man shouting, 'Bring out your old rag and bones! Best price today!'

'He'll be lucky,' Maisie muttered. 'We use our rags for cleaning clothes or for a quilt I'm making if they're good enough. And bones! We use them in soups like everyone else.' She stopped. 'Not to mention when the curse comes to visit. Using rags is horrible, isn't it? I'm always worried the damn thing will fall out of my knickers. I'd die of shame!'

'Me too,' Bethan said. 'The curse, on the rag, Aunt Flo, time of the month. There's a hundred names for it. And washing them rags! I'm not going to lie. What a horrible job!' She shuddered. 'Let's talk about something else. What was we on about?'

'Dodgy doings at the factory. Keep up, girl!' Maisie slapped her arm.

Amanda sighed, glancing at her untouched tea. 'This isn't just a bit odd, girls. If I'm right and someone is stealing fabric, it could be big trouble. Whoever's doing it could end up in prison.'

Bethan's eyes grew as big as saucers. 'Prison?'

'Yes, prison. The army doesn't take kindly to things like that. There's a war on, after all. They'll want answers. You know how they are.'

Her friends looked at her as if waiting for instructions.

'So what I want you two to do is let me know if you notice anything unusual. Unexplained meetings, or empty boxes that should be full...'

Maisie frowned. 'But we don't see the boxes.'

'Okay then, perhaps see if you can find a way to walk round a bit more in your breaks. Pretend to have a headache and need fresh air or something. You're smart girls. You'll think of something.'

'I bet it's that warehouse man. The supervisor bloke. Shifty he is, hanging about, gives me the creeps. Eyes too close together. And handy! I've had to slap his hands away more than once.'

Amanda laughed. 'I think we need a bit more evidence than his eyes are too close together, Bethan. But it's good to keep your eyes open. I'm sure someone's up to something. That cloth the uniforms are made of is good stuff and I've heard of people dyeing it to disguise it. Don't take any risks but let me know if you spot anything.'

The three of them sat in silence for a moment, the weight of Amanda's words heavy in the room. Maisie reached for her now cooling tea and took a sip, as if to steady herself. 'Okay,' she finally said. 'We'll help. But it if gets too dangerous, Amanda...'

'I'll stop. I wouldn't risk you two. Or myself, come to that.'

12

The factory canteen was crammed with tired workers at the end of a long shift. The tension in the air was palpable. The long tables were crowded with women still in their work aprons and scarf turbans. Some sat with their arms crossed defensively, others knitted with quick practised fingers, not even looking at their work, and some chatted to the woman next to them. Most were impatient to get away. There were always queues at all the food shops and by this time the best of everything would be gone.

The three friends sat together at the back. Bethan was biting her thumbnail. 'Think this'll do any good? I've never been to a union meeting before.'

'Well, it beats just moaning day in, day out and doing nothing, doesn't it?' Amanda quipped.

Maisie said nothing. She stared at the edge of the table, her stomach twisting. She didn't want to admit it, but she was as worried as Bethan. What if they got sacked? What if this whole thing made things worse and Mrs Duncan was on their backs more than ever?

Her thoughts were interrupted when a tall, broad-shouldered

woman in her thirties tapped on the table in front of her. 'Can I have your attention, please, ladies?' Belatedly the woman noticed the few men present. 'And gentlemen.'

'Right, everyone.' Her voice was clear and determined. 'I'm Mrs Pain and a lot of employers think that's a good name for me. I aim to cause them pain to get workers' rights, your rights.'

A ripple of laughter broke through the room and even Maisie smiled faintly. Amanda leaned over. 'She sounds just what we need. I like her already.'

Mrs Pain waited for the women to settle down. 'I'm the union representative from the National Union of Tailors and Garment Workers. We all know why we're here. The factory owners have been pushing you to work longer hours for poor pay and with poor working conditions. In a factory not three streets away we got better working conditions and shorter shifts in just three months. What's expected of you, it's not right, and it's certainly not legal. But we have to fight this together. All for one and one for all. Okay?'

A few women nodded, one or two called out, 'Too right,' but many stayed silent.

'Do you think this'll do any good?' Bethan whispered to her friends again. 'Won't they just sack us?'

'How will they find skilled workers like us in time to meet the Ministry's quotas?' Amanda whispered back. 'Let's just listen to what she has to say.'

Mrs Pain was still speaking. 'I know what they'll tell you, I've heard it a thousand times. You're doing your bit for the war effort. That it all helps the lads at the front. That's all true but it doesn't mean you don't deserve fair treatment. Helping the lads at the front doesn't help you feed your kids or pay your rent, does it? Those lads at the front would want you to be paid properly for what you do.'

Joan, one of the older machinists, put her hand up. 'It's not just the hours, it's the fluff from the cloth. We all cough, and some people what've been here a long time have really bad chests. They go on at us all the time to meet targets, but the machines keep breaking down. They don't service them regular, neither.'

'That's right,' someone else said. 'And if the machines break down we get blamed for lower output. It ain't fair.'

'And we don't get paid nearly as much as them men in the warehouse. Our job is much more skilled.' The woman next to Joan had years of pent-up anger in her voice. 'And most of us have bad backs from sitting hunched over the machines for hours on end. And if we ask for a break, well, you'd think we'd asked for the moon! We all gotta go for a wee sometimes!'

The three friends listened to the familiar complaints. Money was the main issue for each of them. Amanda needed more to get a place of her own and pay for her course. Maisie thought about her useless dad expecting her to hand over part of her wages each week despite everything she did. And Bethan, well, Bethan wanted more money for a good time. One thing they all agreed on. Why should they get paid less than the men? Why should they work in unsafe conditions?

Once the women had started complaining the noise in the room rose as each had a story to tell, their voices often overlapping each other.

Mrs Pain held up her hand and waited for the room to quiet down. 'I believe everything you've said.' She paused and tried to make eye contact with as many women as possible. 'Now, it's high time something was done about this. But I need you to join the union so that I can work on your behalf. And it means being prepared to take action.'

'What, go on strike?' someone shouted. 'I can't afford to lose money!'

'I hope it won't come to that. There's a lot we can do without striking.'

'Won't do no good.' One woman called Doris stood up. 'They won't listen to us, they'll just fire us, and this place is handy for me.' She began weaving her way through the tables towards the door without looking back.

Mrs Pain waited for her to go. 'I know that's a worry for many of you, but I can tell you this union has had success in three other factories in the East End and no one lost their job in any of them. The East End is a small place, you probably know some of them.' There was murmuring as the women shared stories of people they knew in other garment factories.

'Now what I need,' Mrs Pain went on, 'is two things. First and foremost, I need you to join the union, it's a very small amount each week, and I need some volunteers to help me.'

'What would we need to do?' Amanda called out.

'Good question. Things like organise meetings, get petitions signed, encourage people to join the union, note any infringements of safety in the factory, that sort of thing.' She looked around but no hands were raised.

'I know it's hard to volunteer, especially when you all work so hard. But think of your rights – better pay, healthier working conditions, more breaks, all the things you've just told me about. They've gone on for years. Nothing changes unless we take action.' She paused and looked around again. 'Come on now, let's have a show of hands, who's willing to help?'

Amanda immediately put up her hand and after a brief hesitation Bethan did the same. They both looked over at Maisie but she bit her bottom lip and shook her head. 'I can't. I just can't.' She felt as if one more responsibility and she would crumble, fall apart and be no use to anyone. If nothing else, she had to hold it together for Ron and Rose.

But three other women put up their hands and Mrs Pain looked satisfied. 'That's wonderful. Five volunteers, plenty to share the load. Please stay behind after this meeting's finished so I can tell you more. Now, if you don't already belong to the union, there are forms on the table by the door for you to sign. It's a very small weekly amount and, if I may say so, money well spent.'

13

The rain was lighter as Maisie got off the bus after a tiring day at work. Nothing seemed to go right. Her sewing machine had seized up several times and Mrs Duncan tried to blame her. 'You must be doing something wrong!' The machines went wrong all the time, not just Maisie's. That union woman was right, she thought, as she bit back a rude retort.

The bus ride had been as bad as usual. Another building had collapsed somewhere so the bus had to take yet another diversion. How the driver knew where to go was beyond understanding. Maisie rubbed her temples. Her head ached from the constant noise of the factory, the clatter of machines and Mrs Duncan's sharp voice. She hadn't even had a moment to herself on the bus. As usual, they were packed in like sardines, the air thick with sweat and tobacco. All she wanted was to go home and relax. But that wouldn't happen. Ron and Rose would be at each other's throats as usual and her mum either in the pub or slumped in an armchair, glass in hand. Her father would probably be out somewhere. Some days it felt as if Maisie was the only grown-up in the family.

She thought about getting off the bus and walking the rest of the way just to clear her head, but she was too tired. In any case, walking in the dark even with a shielded torch was dangerous since the blackout. She'd read in the paper about how many deaths were caused because vehicles couldn't see pedestrians. Over one thousand additional road deaths a year she'd read, and that didn't even take into account people who fell into rivers or canals, or household accidents caused by using candles. It was all very well telling people to wear white, but most people didn't have white winter coats.

When she got home, rain dripping down her neck, she had to grit her teeth before turning her key in the door. From outside she could hear her brother and sister arguing. Nothing new there. Surely her mum would be home. She still hadn't found a job. She should be sorting Ron and Rose out but the chances were slim.

It wasn't only the sound of her siblings rowing that hit her when she opened the door. It was the smell of boiled cabbage, dirty dishes and damp laundry that hadn't dried properly for weeks that greeted her. She stood for a moment with her back to the door, shoulders slumped, her mood as gloomy as the weather. But there was one good thing. There was an envelope on the doormat with her name on it. Drying her hands on her hankie, she opened it and it was from Frank arranging to see her in a few days. She kissed the note and tucked it in her bag.

Before she'd even hung up her coat, little Rose hurled herself at her legs. 'Mais, Ron is being mean to me. He pinched my drawing and tore it up!'

'Well, it was rubbish,' Ron said, coming up behind her. He was only ten but sometimes he seemed much older.

'Right,' she said, pushing her shoulders back. 'You, Ron, go and do the washing-up. Don't break anything either. And you, Rose, dry up. And if I hear one word of an argument between you while you do it I'll tell Mum not to let you have any sweets for a week.'

Ron sneered. 'Like she gives us money for sweets anyway. She spends it all on booze, don't she?'

'Enough of your cheek, and don't speak about Mum like that, you little so-and-so. Go on, wash up now!'

She followed them into the living room, making sure they went into the kitchen where they were soon causing a lot of clattering noises. Her mum was half-asleep in the armchair by the fire which was nearly out. 'Mum,' Maisie said. 'It's cold as the grave in here.' She bent down to scrape a shovel full of coal onto the fire, giving it a stir with the poker. A spark flew out and landed on the rag rug in front of the fire. She absent-mindedly stamped it out.

Wearily she fell into the other armchair and looked at her mum properly for the first time. She looked even more worn out than Maisie felt, although Maisie had done a full day at the factory and her mum didn't even have a job. She did no more than give a little wave of her hand. In her hand was a glass of something she shouldn't be drinking. Probably her favourite cheap gin she got at the offie. That was where a lot of the housekeeping money went.

'Mum,' Maisie said. 'Are you okay? Your skin looks a bit yellow. I read that too much booze can give you jaundice. You've gotta give it up.'

Her mum raised the glass with a shaking hand and took a long swig. 'I can give it up any time I want, girl, and you don't get to tell me what to do. I'm the mum around here.' Her words were slightly slurred and her eyes weren't quite focused. It was a familiar sight to Maisie.

'If you can give up booze whenever you like, why don't you

then? Your skin'll look at lot better, you know, and you'll feel better too.'

Her mum just laughed. 'Mais, you don't have to worry about me. Some bloke in the pub was only telling me yesterday how lovely I was. Bought me a sherry he did too.'

Yes, and he was probably trying to get in your knickers, Maisie thought. She knew that people in her area all knew about her mum's drinking. She was so often in the pub and sometimes rowdy when she was staggering home, it was hard to hide. Maisie had seen the pitying looks of women down the street and heard their comments. 'Just look at her.' 'No wonder 'er 'usband's never at 'ome.' 'She should be at 'ome looking after 'er kids, not down the pub all the time.' 'Really let 'erself go, ain't she.' 'Always smells of booze, don't she!'

Maisie felt ashamed to walk down their street, knowing what people were saying. She rarely had friends round apart from Amanda and Bethan, and nor did Rose or Ron. None of them wanted others to see the chaos they lived in. Instead, they'd learned young to give excuses for their mum. 'She's not well today.' 'She got that black eye when she fell over in the garden.' 'Mum's got a headache.'

'Mum,' she said, standing up. 'You don't have to keep on like this. I'll help you and I can speak to the vicar at St Mark's. He'll help you too. You wouldn't be the first one he's helped.' She began tidying the room as her mother murmured about not needing help. She dusted, wiped tops, brushed the lino and straightened the furniture. She really wanted to open the windows to let some fresh air in but it was too cold and in any case she couldn't let any light show outside.

Her mum was half-asleep again, her head lolling to one side, the glass balanced precariously in her hand. Maisie gently took it from her, although she knew she was wasting her time. Her mum would soon fill it again.

She glanced towards the kitchen where Ron and Rose were still doing the dishes. They were bickering, but more quietly. It was only a matter of time, Maisie knew, before open warfare broke out again. She sighed and rubbed her temples. She needed something to eat, but even the thought of peeling potatoes and opening a tin of Spam felt too much effort.

Crossing over to the window, she fingered the edge of the blackout curtain, tempted to let some air in despite the cold. It was suffocating in here, the smells of the house and the full ashtray on the arm of her mum's chair were overwhelming.

Maisie struggled to hold back tears, despising herself for her self-pity. Ron shouted when he didn't get his own way, and sometimes he threw things around. Rose had started wetting the bed again, and her dad – she'd seen her dad with another woman going into the Roxy. Arm in arm. Sometimes she wished he'd just go off with her.

She pulled her cardigan tighter around herself and looked at her mother again, struggling to avoid anger. People said anyone could stop drinking, but living with her mum it didn't seem that easy. When she was sober, she was lovely and swore she'd never drink again, but she always did. It was as if a demon had hold of her.

The sound of a plate breaking stopped her reverie and she walked into the kitchen, her shoulders sagging. 'Maisie!' Rose sobbed. 'Ron did it on purpose!'

Maisie closed her eyes, attempting to keep calm. 'Right, the pair of you. Go to bed. Now. I'll bring up some bread and dripping later but you are not to come back down here tonight. I don't want to hear another word from either of you.'

She squared her shoulders and bent down to pick up the broken pieces, bracing herself for whatever the evening might bring.

14

Bert's Café was never quiet. From dawn till closing, if they ever closed, the little place buzzed with voices, clinking crockery and the smell of frying onions that clung to the walls no matter how wide Bert threw open the windows. The lino floor was worn through, tables scarred with cigarette burns, and the fog of cigarette smoke hung thick in the air. But it was warm, and it was cheap. That's all the three friends asked.

It was Saturday lunchtime, and they'd finished a half-day at the uniform factory and although tired, they loved going to the Petticoat as it was known. There was always plenty going on there.

Amanda pushed through the door, shaking drizzle from her coat, followed by Bethan and Maisie. The place was crowded as usual: three dockers in flat caps argued over Millwall's chances of winning, a pair of American GIs lounged at the counter trying to charm the waitress with a packet of Lucky Strikes, and an old woman in a hijab was eating a single slice of pie as though it was manna from heaven. In a corner, three ARP wardens hunched over mugs of tea, warming their hands and swapping stories of the previous night's raid.

The three women were lucky. Just as they thought there were no tables free, the dockers stood up and left three empty seats. They'd been to Bert's often but even so they all looked at the menu written in chalk behind the counter. They knew it was a waste of time, the limited menu never changed.

'I'm going to have bread pudding for a change,' Maisie said, her stomach rumbling. 'I hope they have some custard to go with it.' The other two settled for egg and chips.

Despite how busy they were, the waitress soon came to take their order. 'Want any drinks with that, ducks?'

They all opted for tea. It arrived quickly because Bert's wife, Flo, always had the urn on the go and the smell of stewing tea competed with the frying onion smell most days.

Amanda cupped the mug gratefully. The tea was strong enough to stand a spoon in, but the heat seeped into her fingers. She flexed them to get them working properly after being in the cold outside. The wireless crackled on a shelf by the till, halfway through an Andrews Sisters number, 'Don't Sit Under the Apple Tree'.

Behind the counter, Bert himself never stopped. A big man with sleeves rolled up above his elbows and a grin that made his customers overlook the watery stew and sausages stuffed with who knows what. He had a tea towel over one shoulder, his apron was smeared with grease, and he moved with a cheerful urgency, shouting greetings as each new person came in as if they were long-lost friends.

'Do you think that union woman will get us any more money?' Maisie mused. 'Things are getting really tight, we're living on bread and dripping half the time. And the rent's going up again. Against the law that is, but what can you do?' She didn't say her mum was asking for more of her pay, and she knew it would go on booze.

Bethan gave a tired laugh. 'Time I got one of them Yanks to marry me and keep me in luxury. Everyone says they're rolling in it.'

'I thought you'd found one already. Buddy, wasn't it?'

'Hmm, I've had a couple of dates. Had a smashing time, gave you some stockings, didn't I? We'll have to see if it goes anywhere.' She went into the daydream she was famous for, then snapped out of it. 'Anyway, I'm seeing him again soon. But I gotta say, his house sounds just lush, it does. He talks about it all the time.'

'Even if he turns out to be the love of your life, that's a long-term plan,' Amanda said. 'But what else can we do? Let's throw some ideas around.'

'How about laundry service?' Bethan asked. 'Ease the load of overworked mams, it would.'

Maisie pulled a face. 'Where would we do it? In a tin bath? And how would we dry it on a rainy day? No, that wouldn't work.'

Bethan's bottom lip pouted. 'Well, I thought we were just throwing ideas around.'

'How about knitting? Scarves, socks and mittens?'

It was Bethan's turn to be critical. 'Show me an old lady who isn't already doing that and I'll give you a million pounds. Anyway, knitting is boring and slow.'

'That's right,' Maisie said, joining in. 'Wool's rationed and if we unpicked jumpers from the jumble we'd have to wash it, dry it and it would still be crinkly. No, we need a better idea.'

Their food arrived – two egg and chips, golden and greasy. Both had a doorstep of bread spread with a scraping of margarine. Maisie's eyes lit up when she saw her bread pudding did come with custard, albeit about half the amount she was hoping for.

Amanda dipped two chips into the golden egg yolk. 'There must be something. We're clever with our hands. That's worth more than a few bob a week in a factory.'

Bethan shoved a chip in her mouth. 'Sewing? Alterations? We talked about that before, didn't we?'

'Didn't your mum ever teach you not to speak with your mouth full?' Maisie said, nudging her with a grin. 'Not a bad idea though. With clothes rationing lots of people want their dress and coats remodelled. They get fed up with the old stuff.' She took a bite of her bread pudding. 'But where could we do it? Home is too difficult, it's not like any of us have much spare space.'

Amanda put some salt on her chips. 'We'd need somewhere public. A shop, perhaps.'

Maisie snorted. 'You're getting to be a dreamer like Bethan if you think we can afford a shop. But what about down the Petticoat here? I don't suppose we could afford a whole stall, but we could ask Big Sal if we could have a corner of hers.'

Bethan laughed. 'Big Sal? Maisie, she'd eat us alive. You know what she's like. It's bad enough trying to get a deal when I've tried to buy enough material to make a dress.'

'She's tough, I'll give you that, but she's got a good business head. She'd only let us have a bit of her stall if she thought she'd make a bit out of it. Let's ask her, she can only say no.'

Amanda's hands twisted as she thought it through. 'I suppose it's worth a try. We've all had experience of repairs and alterations and some of them look damn good too. I get most of my work, modest as it is, through recommendations.'

But Big Sal could be scary. Would she help?

15

'Come on then,' Amanda said, finishing her tea. 'There's no time like the present. Big Sal'll be on her stall now.'

It had got colder while they'd been in Bert's Café, or perhaps it was the contrast as they stepped outside, coats and scarves pulled tight around them. The market was always bustling, with wartime restrictions everyone was looking for a way to make ends meet. And there were plenty of shady characters selling stuff on the black market out of suitcases. Stockings, watches, cigarettes, even jewellery. There was no way of knowing if the stuff had been stolen by the spivs. There were plenty of stories in the papers of men stealing jewellery and handbags off people who had just been bombed and were lying dead or dying in the ruins. According to the papers, it wasn't unknown for them to cut a finger off a dead body to get at a ring. The thought was enough to make anyone shudder. They had to risk being out during an air raid to do their dirty work, but must have thought it worthwhile.

The friends made their way through housewives clutching their ration books, soldiers on leave strolling arm in arm with their girlfriends and children darting from stall to stall, hoping to find something that had dropped on the floor.

Big Sal's stall was impossible to miss. She stood behind it like a general, a vast woman in an ancient fur coat and matching Russian-style fur hat. On her stall was everything anyone doing dressmaking could want – rolls of fabric, accessories like lace and zips, thread and dressmaking patterns. It was a sewer's dream.

Her booming voice competed with those of other stallholders trying to get the shoppers to part with their money. 'Lovely material 'ere, girls, you won't find none better!'

The friends stood a little way down watching her work, intimidated by the way she confidently handled everything and everyone. 'Come on,' Amanda finally said. 'Let's give it a try.'

''Ello, girls,' Big Sal said when they stopped in front of her stall. 'Making yourself something new to get the boys' eye, is it? You'll need coupons though unless...' She let the rest of the sentence hang and they knew she had some 'under the counter' fabric if the price was right.

'Not today, Sal, but we wondered if we could have a word.'

Sal eyed them, raising an eyebrow. 'You'll 'ave to be quick. Got a lotta customers to see to.'

Amanda swallowed, but her voice stayed steady. 'We work at the uniform factory. But we sew a lot more than that. We're handy with a needle.' Despite the cold she took off her coat and pirouetted to show off her dress underneath. 'This was an old lady's dress I found in the jumble, you'd never have recognised it.' The dress was elegant and modern, not a trace of the original old lady owner. 'We do alterations, remodelling and repairs and we do it well.' Shivering, she hastily put her coat back on.

Big Sal frowned. 'And you're telling me this, why?'

'We want to get more business and we wondered if we could

have a little bit of your stall on Saturdays to let people know what we can do.'

Sal raised an eyebrow again. 'You all do all this? You any good?'

Maisie stepped forward, looking more confident than she felt. 'We're skilled, Sal. You know as well as we do that people never have enough coupons or money to buy the clothes they want. They want them mended or remodelled to look different.'

'It would bring you more business too, like,' Bethan chipped in. 'People would come to your stall to talk to us but they'd probably buy from you too. And we only need a small space. We'd pay you a cut.'

Sal laughed. 'Too right you will if I give you a space. I can't afford to do something for nothing.' She studied them in silence then stopped to serve a customer who wanted a zip and some buttons before talking to them again.

'You've got cheek, I'll give you that much.' She might be jovial but her eyes were as sharp as knives. 'Three slips of girls, asking me for a slice of my pitch. But you're right, folk do need mending done. They ask me sometimes to recommend someone.' She leaned closer. 'You'd be here every Saturday? You'd need to be reliable. Can't 'ave customers come looking for you and you ain't 'ere. Makes me look bad.'

'We'll take it in turns, one of us each Saturday, and we're reliable.'

Sal stopped talking and tidied her goods while she thought, then she turned back to them. 'All right, you can 'ave that corner there. Saturdays only, mind. And I'll take 15 per cent of whatever you make.'

Bethan gasped. 'Fifteen per cent?'

'Take it or leave it, ducky. Plenty of others'd jump at the chance.'

Amanda nudged Bethan. 'We'll take it. And we're honest. We won't fiddle you. We can probably do some small repairs while we're here, but some bigger jobs we'd have to take home.'

'Makes sense. So one of you come 'ere next Saturday, no later than eight. The Petticoat starts early. Bring your needles and thread and stuff and we'll see 'ow it goes.' Her smile was wolfish as she shook hands with each of them to seal the deal. 'Look forward to doing business with you.'

They stepped away, hardly believing their luck. 'I thought she was going to tell us clear off at one point,' Maisie said. 'Not sure how we could cope with being in the cold for a whole day. Three vests and jumpers, I suppose.'

'And hands too cold to hold a needle!' Bethan said. 'Still, it's a start. And we've got our corner.'

They headed back to Bert's Café to celebrate, the door jingling as they stepped in from the cold February day. The place was as lively as ever, shoppers with their purchases on the floor near their feet, a little boy drawing on a scrap of paper, two stall-holders who had come in to thaw out after hours in the cold and drizzle.

The familiar smells of frying onions wrapped round the three friends and within minutes the waitress came over with three mugs of tea. 'Remembered what you 'ad from earlier,' she said. 'Want anything to eat? We got a bit of bread pudding left and some buns. Fresh they are, nothing stays long enough to go stale 'ere.'

The girls held up their mugs and clinked them together as if they were toasting with champagne. 'Here's to our new venture. It's modest, but it's a start. And if we take it in turns to man the stall, we'll still 'ave time to do repairs at home.'

'And look after my horrors at home,' Maisie said with a smile that covered up her worries about them. 'But 15 per cent. Sal drives a hard bargain. Let's hope it's worth it.'

Bert had overheard their conversation as he walked past. 'Sal? Big Sal? Blimey, if you've got a deal with her you must be on to something. She wouldn't waste her time with daft ideas.' He leaned closer. 'And between you and me there's plenty who'd pay for a bit of good sewing. Make them look like the cat's whiskers again and you'll never be out of work.' He stood back again, hands in his apron pocket. 'Tell you what, girls, if you make a poster, like, I'll put it up in the café. How about it?'

'That'd be wonderful,' Bethan said. 'And you know we'll always be regulars in here too.'

They lifted their mugs again. 'Here's to us. We're on our way, making do and mending.'

16

Amanda and Bethan looked around Maisie's living room. 'Where's your brother and sisters at?' Bethan asked. 'Never known it so quiet, bach.'

Maisie took their coats. 'They've gone to the flicks and I gave them enough money to go to a café for a drink after, so we should have a bit of peace and quiet.'

To their surprise, her mother, Mrs Hawkins, appeared from the kitchen looking sober and tidy. 'Hello, girls. Sewing this morning? I used to work as a seamstress for a fashion house years ago. I made the most wonderful creations. I might have a tip or two for you. Show me what you're doing.'

Amanda and Bethan looked at Maisie for confirmation. They'd never seen her mother sober before and couldn't quite trust her. Maisie gave a little nod and whispered, 'It's okay.'

Checking the table and surroundings were spotless, they unpacked the dress, one that had been brought to Sal's stall the previous day for some alterations. It was a beautiful evening dress, unlike anything else they'd ever worked on. 'Lush it is.' Bethan smoothed the fabric over the table and opened the sewing box. 'I never thought we'd be asked to work on something as special as this. She just needs a few alterations. I've noted all the measurements.'

Mrs Hawkins wiped her hands on a tea towel to make sure they were dry before touching the dress. 'It's lovely. It reminds me of when I was sewing before…'

No one asked her what before was. Maisie knew and the other two could guess. They'd seen the way Mrs Hawkins's hands trembled a little, the way she kept licking her lips and kept looking at the clock. The slight yellow tinge to her skin. They guessed she was waiting for pub opening at midday.

'Mum, you said you used to do some really special dresses where you worked.' Maisie looked at her mother with pride. 'What tips have you got for us?'

Mrs Hawkins tapped her teeth with her fingernails. 'Well, the back is going to be your challenge if you're going to make it a bit shorter. Put weights in the hem, tiny flat lead ones, sew them into the lining. It'll stop the skirt moving about too much when she sits and stands. We had to do it for when our ladies curtsied.' She smoothed her hands over the fabric. 'I often worked with gowns even lovelier than this.'

'There's posh for you.' Bethan was imagining ladies being presented at court. She'd seen that on Pathé News and felt jealous. Some girls had all the luck, she thought as she considered her own modest, often patched, clothes. She sighed and shook her head. 'But we can make one girl feel like a queen with this dress, can't we? I wonder what sort of do she's going to.'

Maisie watched her mother as she discussed the dress. For a moment she glimpsed the woman she'd been before the booze got a hold – confident, skilled, proud. She wished there was some way she could keep her like that forever.

Her mother interrupted her thoughts. 'About them weights.

We had proper ones. You won't be able to get them, but you could use farthings. Just wrap them in white fabric so they don't show. They should do the trick just as well.'

Mrs Hawkins picked up a sketch of the dress that Amanda had made of a wedding dress. 'You do this, Amanda? Getting married?'

Amanda laughed. 'Married? Me? Not on your nellie, but I love the dresses and often sketch some I'd like to make one day.' She sighed. 'But that's years away if it ever happens.'

Mrs Hawkins tapped the sketch. 'You've got real talent, there, Amanda. I remember when I was courting Maisie's dad. He bought me a dress. Lovely it was, but it didn't fit quite right. I made a few little changes. He never noticed but said I looked like a film star when he saw it first time.' She looked over at Maisie. 'I used to make all your clothes. Do you remember?'

'I do. I loved that red velvet dress you made. I thought I was the bee's knees in that one. You must have taken me to the flicks, 'cos I used to parade up and down the living room pretending to be one of those girls being presented to the King.'

'Your father took a photograph. It must be here somewhere. You were standing by the front door, looking like you thought you were a princess or something. We'll look for it later.'

Maisie nodded, struggling to hold back a tear. For once her mother was thinking of something beyond the next drink.

Amanda quietly pushed the box of beads towards Mrs Hawkins. 'How would you arrange these? The lady wants a few round the neckline so it looks a bit different. I bet you'll have better ideas than we have.'

Picking up the beads, Mrs Hawkins began arranging them. 'I had to do beads like this for a dress for... for...' Maisie saw panic cross her mother's face. The booze was affecting her memory. The clock struck the half hour, distracting her from what she was doing.

'I'll be going soon.' Mrs Hawkins put down the beads. Maisie knew it was only half an hour until pub opening time and her mother always wanted to be there for the whole two hours it was open over midday.

'Mum,' she said softly. 'Would you like a cup of tea?'

But the attempt at distraction failed. Picking up her coat, Mrs Hawkins waved them goodbye. 'I'd better be off. Don't want to be late, do I?'

As the door closed behind her, the three girls sat in silence. Amanda reached over and squeezed Maisie's hand. Bethan busied herself with the sewing box, giving her friend a moment to compose herself. Neither mentioned the tears Maisie quickly brushed away. Work was the thing that would get them through.

Her mum would get better one day, wouldn't she?

17

Bethan had been giddy with excitement all week. She'd got another date with Buddy, the GI she'd met at a dance. She'd been boring Amanda and Maisie with talk of it all week, her cheeks flushed.

'A real GI,' she said. 'Handsome as a film star like Clark Gable. He's taking me to the pictures Saturday. I'm glad it's not my turn at Sal's stall or I'd be too tired to enjoy it.'

Maisie's lips tightened. 'Hmm, I remember him from the dance. Second date, is it? You want to be careful, Bethan. Some of them are charming until they get what they want, then they get girls in the family way...'

Amanda nodded. 'And then they're back on a ship, halfway across the Atlantic and you're stuck with the baby and no way of getting him to do the decent thing. From what I've heard, their army won't help you. Watch yourself and if you go to a pub don't drink too much.'

Bethan tossed her curls. 'You're just jealous. He's different, I can tell.' She buried their warning behind her daydreams of sunshine and palm trees.

By Saturday evening she was ready. Her best frock, midnight blue with a crisp white collar, looked perfect. No one would notice the neat patch near the side seam. She'd curled her hair overnight with rag rollers and dabbed on a little of her mother's lipstick, blowing a kiss at herself in the mirror.

Her mother watched her, a frown showing her concern. 'I'd rather you went out with a local lad, Bethan. You can't know anything about these Yanks, can you? And don't be late. I'll be waiting up and worried about you if you are.'

Bethan was used to her mum being protective and knew it was her way of showing she cared. She hugged her briefly and with a quick, 'I'll be good!' went out the door.

Outside, Spitalfields was as dark as ever, the blackout making everything unfamiliar and sometimes a little threatening. The streets were dim even with a full moon, the dreaded bomber's moon when it was even easier for the German planes to bomb their targets. Like everyone else she had a shielded torch but they didn't illuminate much and it was easy to fall over, especially after a bombing when everything was changed. The ruins of those bombed houses crouched like broken teeth, and the smell of damp and smoke lingered in the air.

Buddy was waiting outside the Odeon, holding a Lucky Strike, looking as gorgeous as ever in his neat khaki uniform. As soon as he spotted her his grin spread wide.

'Bethan, honey! Gee, I'm so glad you could make it.'

No boy had ever called her honey and she felt her stomach flutter as she slipped her hand through his arm. 'I hope we don't have to queue long for the tickets, it's cold as charity tonight.'

He squeezed her arm. 'I queued already, sweetheart, got the tickets here.' They went inside and chatted while they waited for the film to start. The cinema was thick with cigarette smoke and the smell of damp wool.

As before, Buddy was full of stories of his life in California. 'Our house is big, eight bedrooms, my old man built it. Got a pool out back, oh, and orange trees in the garden.' As he spoke Bethan could see it all in her mind's eye, bright and clear as day. It seemed like a dream come true. She didn't spot the knowing looks of a couple behind them who heard everything.

A newsreel came first showing Allied bombers soaring across the Channel, and Prime Minister Churchill raising two fingers in his familiar victory sign. The audience clapped and cheered and a woman next to Bethan wiped her eyes with her hankie.

The main film was *The Gentle Sex*, a film about women in the ATS. Buddy seemed surprised. 'I didn't know your gals did all that,' he whispered. He stretched his arm round her back, fingers creeping lower. Bethan's breath caught, but when his hand pressed boldly against the side of her breast, she stiffened.

'Stop that!' Her voice was quiet but serious. 'Stop it now!' She moved so she could push his arm back.

He grinned, sheepish but unapologetic. 'Aw, don't be sore, honey,' he whispered in her ear, his tongue grazing it. 'You're prettier than any of the girls in the film.'

She was flattered but still pushed his hand away. He sat back but settled for threading his fingers through hers. She was happy to let him, her heart racing.

When the lights came up, the harsh glare startled her. They'd been lucky and had no air-raid warnings which sometimes interrupted films. He helped her on with her coat, his fingers brushing against her neck lightly.

Outside it was so cold there would be ice on the inside of Bethan's bedroom windows by morning, but that wasn't on her mind with Buddy being so close.

'Say, do you fancy a drink like we did last time?' He took her hand and tucked it under his arm. 'We've got time for one before time's up.'

Bethan was torn. She wanted nothing more than to go for a drink with him, but her mother's warning rang in her ears. But Buddy's lips nuzzling her neck weakened her resolve. 'Just one then.'

The pub was packed, blackout curtains drawn tight, the air dense with smoke and chatter. There were several other GIs there and two of them had local girls looking at them with stars in their eyes. The wireless crooned a Bing Crosby song but could hardly be heard over the noise of the crowd.

Buddy swaggered to the counter without asking Bethan what she wanted. She noticed him looking at his money before paying and supposed like most GIs he hadn't got used to English money. When he returned, Buddy put down a pint for himself, muttering, 'Warm, weak beer in this country.' Bethan looked closely at her pint glass. It wasn't beer, that was certain. 'What is it?' she asked before she took a sip.

'Cider,' Buddy said with a smile. 'The barman said it was the best they had.'

Her eyes narrowed. 'Do you mean the strongest?'

He shrugged his shoulders. 'Maybe, he didn't say. Have you ever been to the seaside, Welsh lady?'

'Of course I have. In Wales we have wonderful beaches and we lived near The Mumbles...' As she spoke, she remembered her happy childhood days with her family near the beach. Their house overlooked the promenade of the small seaside town often crowded with visitors in the summer. Those summers seemed blissful, full of sunny days, yet the winters could be cruel with lashing rain and strong winds that sometimes turned into gales. Then her father got this job in London and they had to move. She still missed their old house and being so close to her aunts, uncles and cousins.

'Mumbles? What's that? Beaches that speak badly?' Buddy speaking brought her back from her reverie.

She nudged him and took another tiny sip of her cider, resolving not to drink even a half a pint. 'No, silly, just wonderful wide sandy beaches.'

He nodded then went back to telling her about his amazing life in California. 'And film stars live in our part of town too.'

'Really? Have you met any?'

He took a long draught of his beer before answering. 'I haven't met any but Cary Grant lives nearby. I see him sometimes around town, and Clark Gable.'

'Cary Grant? Clark Gable?' She was breathless at the thought.

'You should come see, a lovely girl like you. You're the prettiest girl I've met since I got off the boat.'

'Do you mean it?' She could imagine herself getting married before he left the country then joining the other GI brides on the boat going to join their new husbands and start a wonderful life.

'Sure do, honey. A peach like you deserves to be somewhere sunny, not in this gloomy country where everything is so old and bombed to pieces.' She looked around at the pub, the tired wallpaper, the ceiling stained brown with cigarette smoke, the worn seat covers. There must be better places to be.

Buddy took another long swig of his beer and she noticed his glass was almost empty. He reached his arm round her shoulders again. 'I was wondering if you'd like to be my girl.' He hesitated. 'Or is it too soon to ask you that?'

She was so amazed she could hardly speak. This amazing man wanted her for his girl! 'Really? You want me to be your girlfriend?'

He squeezed her tight, his fingers just brushing the side of her breast. 'Sure. Will you? Say you will.'

She didn't need asking again. 'I'd love to.'

They were interrupted by the landlord ringing the bell for last orders, and the spell broke. Bethan suddenly remembered the time. 'Oh, I'd better get home, I'll be late. My mam will be worried.'

Buddy drained his beer and set it down with a flourish. 'Sure thing, honey, I'll walk you.' He held her coat as she stood up, nuzzling her neck again, sending a shiver down her spine that did strange things to her stomach.

It was cold enough now for their breath to rise in clouds. An ugly crater yawned where houses had stood, now a heap of bricks and splintered beams, someone's life in so many pieces.

'Tough luck,' Buddy said, looking at it, then linked arms with her again.

At her door, he bent low and kissed her more firmly than she was comfortable with, but when she backed off a little he behaved like a gentleman and made the kiss light. 'I'll see you again soon, won't I? I'm often busy at base but I promise I'll be in touch soon to arrange something.'

Her hand shook as she tried to get the key in the lock, then once inside she leaned her back against the door, trying to calm herself. Her mother's voice floated from her bedroom. 'That you, girl?'

'Yes, Mam,' she replied. 'All well, I had a lovely evening. I'm going straight to bed. See you in the morning.'

In her narrow bed, her mind went over the evening, her head full of palm trees, soft sand and sunshine. And she was Buddy's girl! She couldn't wait to tell the others. She thought of Maisie going out with Frank who seemed dull and dreary compared to

Buddy, and Amanda, who didn't want a man at all. They might be cynical, but the evening had been just perfect.

18

The factory smelled of oil, wool and secrets. The scents hung thick in the air, clinging to every surface and settling into the workers' clothes like an invisible shroud.

Amanda sat at her desk, shivering. The warehouse men had left the door open a sliver and the cold air rushed through like a flood. To anyone watching, Mrs Duncan the supervisor especially, it looked as if Amanda was writing figures in the log, her pencil scratching across the page with a steady rhythm, a perfect disguise for a mind focused elsewhere. Every roll of khaki that came in was accounted for, yet somehow, when the uniforms were packed up to be sent to the army depot, the sums didn't add up.

How could she find evidence? If she did, what would she do? Report the factory to the police or the military? She had no idea if they would take her seriously. And Mrs Duncan seemed to be stopping by her desk more frequently as if she was checking up on her. It made her tense all day.

She must ask Bethan and Maisie if Mrs Duncan was watching the sewing machine girls more often too. If she was on the take somehow, the last thing the supervisor would want was the factory girls having time to notice anything amiss.

The morning seemed endless, with only a ten-minute break. Just enough to nip to the WC where there was always a queue. Finally, the midday whistle shrieked through the air, loud enough to be heard above the clatter of the sewing machines. Instantly, they stopped, chairs scraped back and the weary women moved towards their chosen break spot.

'Why can't we have a nice canteen like the munitions factory?' one woman grumbled, heading towards the room where they could buy a small selection of refreshments and tea.

But the three friends usually brought sandwiches with them. They had flasks of tea at the ready. But before they could find a warm spot in the canteen, Bethan pleaded with them. 'I'm dying for a fag!' Bethan groaned, pulling the other two towards the door. 'Come with me!'

'But it's too cold,' Maisie said. 'We'll freeze to death.'

'I'll be quick, just half a fag,' Bethan promised. 'We can keep warm with our tea. And Amanda, you wanted us to go outside more in case we spot anything dodgy, like.'

'Why do we only get half an hour at midday?' Maisie grumbled, pulling her scarf closer round her neck. 'Those people in the munitions factory get an hour. It's not fair.' She stretched her arms above her head, wincing as her shoulders popped and her back groaned. 'My fingers feel like they'll fall off any minute.' She rubbed her hands together energetically, trying to warm them up and get them moving. 'I don't know how they can expect us to work on days like this.'

'It must be illegal when it's so cold, surely.' Amanda was rubbing her hands too, but also looking around for anything amiss. 'We'll ask that union lady. She'll know.'

Outside the wind was sharp and fierce. The yard was uninviting, wide and grey with ugly concrete. Bethan had to shield her cigarette with her cupped hand to light it.

'Ssshhh,' Amanda whispered. 'Come over here.' She led the way behind a low wall where the wind wasn't so strong. 'Let's see if we spot anything.'

Bethan groaned. 'Like what? A film star, a fairy, my future husband? There's lovely that would be.' She shivered. 'Remind me why we're outside instead of getting a cuppa in the canteen.'

'Because you wanted a fag, you daft thing!' Maisie said. 'And I bet Amanda is sleuthing, looking for clues. Anyone would think she was Miss Marple.'

Amanda didn't answer immediately. She was busy scanning the yard, looking between the warehouse and the vans. 'If someone's stealing fabric, this is where it'll happen.' Behind her concerns was a worry that if stock went missing she might be blamed as she kept records. What if she was wrong? Perhaps she was imagining things. But no – she'd checked and double-checked. Figures don't lie.

'So we're looking for some toerag nicking stuff, is that right? We're freezing our bums off just in case they choose right now to do it.' Maisie was glad to see Bethan stub out her cigarette. 'Come on, let's go inside.'

They had to walk past two vans on their way back in. It was so cold they almost ran, wrapping their arms around their bodies in an attempt to get warmer.

As they passed the second van, the door was slightly open although no one was inside. Her curiosity piqued, Amanda stepped towards the opening. Inside were rolls of fabric, not wrapped in brown paper as she would expect for a delivery into the factory. And no deliveries were due that day.

'Oy! What do ya think you're doing?' A harsh voice made her jump back. She turned around, expecting to see one of the warehouse men, but it was no one she recognised. Whoever he was, he wasn't wearing the usual thick cotton coat the warehouse men wore either. He was tall and skinny, with black hair slicked back with some sort of oil.

Maisie and Bethan instinctively stood either side of her for support.

'Not doing nothing, see,' Bethan said. 'Just on our way back by 'ere after our break and there's no need for you to be so rude, neither!'

'Leave her alone!' Maisie added.

The man's scowl deepened. Muttering swearwords under his breath, he jumped into the van. The sound echoed off the brick walls. His movements were rushed, agitated. He fumbled with the keys and looked around nervously before slamming the door shut. The van spluttered twice, then roared into life. He sped off, leaving a faint trail of exhaust fumes in the cold air.

'You're late, girls!' Mrs Duncan's voice snapped them to the present. She was standing in the doorway, arms folded across her chest. 'You've got one minute to get back to your stations or you'll be docked fifteen minutes' pay.'

They hurried past her, but only Amanda heard her say, 'Keep your nose out of other people's business.'

She swallowed hard. There was no way she could go around making accusations without firm proof. At this rate, the war would be over before she found it.

19

The church door opened, releasing a burst of Glenn Miller music into the rainy night. 'Quick, come in and close the door or we'll freeze to death.' The girls hurried in, shaking their umbrellas, the dance music drowning the sound of their footsteps on the wooden floor.

Their first stop was the ladies' toilet so they could repair damp damage to their hair and touch up their make-up, giggling all the time. On the walls several posters advised them to *Keep mum*, *Dig for Victory*, *Buy war bonds now*. They'd been around so long, no one noticed them any more.

'Pity your Frank couldn't come,' Bethan said. 'Where's he to tonight?'

'He's visiting his grandmother. She's sick, so he's going to keep her company again to give his mum a rest.' Maisie knew Bethan would think it more evidence that he was dull, but she thought it simply meant he was a good man. The more she knew of him, the more optimistic she felt about the relationship. 'What about your Yank? He coming tonight?'

Bethan's face fell. 'No, he's on duty, see. Pity, but he won't worry if I has a few dances. He can't expect me to join a nunnery when he's not about, can he?'

Satisfied they would pass muster, they went into the hall. 'Look, they've got flowers! They're out early,' Amanda said, pointing to jam jars filled with daffodils on the windowsills. The blackout curtains had been decorated with red, white and blue bunting, and a few paper chains swayed gently from the ceiling. It cheered up the simple room.

'Hey, looks like half the girls from the factory are here,' Maisie said, waving to a couple who waved back, calling out a greeting. After getting soft drinks, the friends joined the others, looking around to see who they fancied.

There were several men in uniform, both British and American, along with a postman who worked in their street, a boy from the butchers' shop and other familiar faces they saw around Spitalfields.

'Seen anyone lush?' Bethan asked Jean, who worked the same area as her.

'Nah,' Jean said, sipping her orange squash, 'but the night is young yet.'

The band, local boys, weren't the best, but no one cared. The atmosphere in the hall was already buzzing even though the dance hadn't been going long. There were more girls than boys inevitably but unlike the boys, they didn't mind dancing with each other.

'Jersey Bounce' started up and Amanda grabbed Bethan's hand. 'Come on, let's show them how it's done!' They whirled onto the dance floor, their skirts swishing as they jitterbugged. Mrs Green from the church guild shook her head disapprovingly at their energetic steps but the girls didn't notice. They were far from alone.

Exhausted after two dances, they went back to join the others, managing to sit on the edge of the stage to rest their feet and sip some lemonade. The air was filled with cigarette smoke, making it hard to see without their eyes watering. Despite blackout regulations, someone opened a window a crack, waved the blackout curtain about, then pulled it back in place.

'I need a wee,' Bethan said. 'I'll be back now in a minute.' Finishing her drink, she headed off. Seconds later, a group of GIs came in. At first Amanda took no notice. She didn't know any and she wasn't looking for love so it wasn't important to her. But then she noticed they were passing a flask to each other. It was obviously alcohol and some of them looked as if they'd already had a few. She was no prude. She enjoyed a shandy or a cider, but hated to see people drunk, and there was no alcohol being sold that evening.

Maisie nudged her and brought her back to the moment. 'Mand, I think that Yank over there is Bethan's Buddy. She's showed me his photo enough times. And look, he's flirting with that girl. I thought he was on duty tonight.'

Amanda's eyes opened wide. 'Buddy? Surely he wouldn't be daft enough to come here... oh, but perhaps Bethan didn't mention where she was going.' She plonked down her drink so hard some spilled over the top. 'He doesn't know me from Adam. I'm going to go over and stand near them. See what I can find out. Try to keep Bethan away till I get back.'

But it didn't work. Maisie did her best to distract Bethan when she came out of the ladies' toilet, but Buddy's laugh made her look in his direction. Her eyes widened and her face went white. 'On duty, is he? Duw, duw. There's lovely for him, isn't it.' Her Welsh accent got stronger with every word. 'The... the... lying mochyn. I'll have his guts for garters, the bastard.' She paused for a minute, noticing he had put his arm round a blonde girl's shoulders and was obviously trying to chat her up.

Bethan squared her shoulders. 'Right, girls, you and me, we're going to go and listen to what he's telling her, now in a minute, see. You with me?'

With so many people dancing, it was easy for them to make their way behind Buddy and his friends unnoticed.

'Sure thing, sweetheart,' Buddy was saying to the blonde. 'My place in Palm Beach is massive, has a pool out back. Everyone loves it.' He stopped to take another swig from the flask.

'A swimming pool?' the girl said, giggling. 'It sounds great.'

'And my kids love it. Little Denise is already...' His voice faded as he realised he'd said too much. The blonde didn't notice but his friends tugged at his arm. 'Thought we'd agreed not to mention family, Buddy-boy. Your wife'll kill you if...'

Another muttered, 'Palm Beach? First I've heard of it.'

Bethan looked at her friends open-mouthed. 'His wife? He's married?' She couldn't believe she'd been taken in by such a rat. 'He's nothing but a damn wide-boy. And there's me believing he had a fancy place with a white picket fence.' She put her hands on her hips. 'Right...'

Amanda touched her arm. 'Bethan, love, don't...'

But it was too late. Bethan shook off Amanda's hand and marched around so she was facing Buddy and the blonde. At that moment the band stopped playing one number and there was a lull in the hubbub.

'Hello, Buddy-boy,' she said, watching his face turn from surprise to guilt then settling on practised charm. 'I thought you were on duty tonight, darling,' she went on. She turned to the blonde. 'This here toerag is a lying bastard. Tried to get in my knickers, he did, with his talk of a flash house. Not in Palm Beach but California or somewhere.'

'Baby, I can explain...' Buddy started.

'Don't you baby me!' Bethan's Welsh accent grew even

stronger and quite a crowd was watching now. 'You talk nothing but lies.' She looked at the blonde. 'This man wouldn't know the truth if it bit him on the bum. He's a bloody liar.'

The blonde paused for a second, looking from her to Buddy, then threw his arm from her shoulder and strode off.

'Baby...' Buddy tried again. 'It's not what you think.' He ran his fingers through his hair. 'I didn't want you to find out like this.'

'Didn't want me to find out, is it?' Her voice rose higher. 'So you thought you'd string me along, making promises about taking me home to America, all the while keeping quiet about the wife and kids back home. What kind of man does that make you?'

Buddy took a step towards her, his eyes pleading. 'Bethan, please, sweetheart, it's complicated.'

'Complicated now, is it? What's complicated about a lie?' She was unaware of the growing number of people nearby watching the scene with interest.

He touched her arm and indicated to go a little way from the others. 'I didn't mean this to happen.' He spoke quietly so she struggled to hear him over the music which had started again. 'I didn't mean to... I really care for you, but...'

'But what?'

'I thought it would just be a laugh going out with you, but I... sort of fell in love... I didn't plan this to happen. When I was with you, I somehow forgot everyone else.'

'But you didn't bother to tell me, just came to a dance tonight hoping to pick up some other poor girl, I suppose. Never mind the wife and kiddy at home.' For a minute Bethan was taken aback by his words. He loved her? She didn't expect that. But then reality kicked in. She didn't believe a word of it. Anyway, it didn't alter the fact that he was a two-timing rat. Thank goodness she had never gone all the way with him.

Buddy went bright red and stuttered. 'Bethan, I may be a

soldier, but I'm a coward when it comes to relationships. I should have told you at the start.' He reached out for her hand, but she snatched it back. 'I'm so sorry. My mates dragged me here tonight because I was so low. They think I'm a real bastard for not coming clean.'

'Well, they're right, aren't they!' Bethan didn't give him time to answer.

Her slap across his face reverberated across the room. A few people nearby began clapping and shouting, 'That's it, girl, show 'em 'ow it's done!'

'Come on, bach,' Maisie said. 'Let's get you home and have a cup of tea, is it?'

'Tea? Not bloody likely. I've got pennies burning a hole in my pocket. Let's go to the Crown and drown my sorrows.'

As they fetched their coats, they caught snippets of conversations. 'These Yanks think they can...' 'She gave 'im what for, good and proper...' One patted her on the back. 'Well done, girl!'

Bethan didn't stop to listen. She walked out, head held high, muttering, 'All those weeks I wasted on that... that...'

As they put on their coats, they heard the band start up 'Little Brown Jug' and the unmistakable sound of the blonde giving Buddy a piece of her mind. But they didn't look back. The friends linked arms and stepped out into the rain, their heels clicking in unison on the wet pavement.

Bethan didn't really like getting drunk, especially if Maisie was with her. She knew about the problems with her mother. But tonight she was going to get as drunk as she wanted. Anything to cover her embarrassment and anger. How could she have been so stupid? As they walked, her mind went over the conversations she and Buddy had had. Had she missed anything that would have given him away? And all that rubbish about falling for her. Did he think she came down with the last shower of rain? Flirting with another girl and expecting her to believe that!

By the time she reached the Crown, Bethan's hands were shaking. She didn't know if it was the cold or anger or maybe the shame.

'How could I be so stupid?' she muttered, more to herself than the others.

'You're not stupid,' Maisie said firmly. 'He's the one who lied. That's on him, not you. You have nothing to feel bad about.'

Bethan shook her head and yanked the pub door open. The smell of beer and the warmth hit her immediately but didn't make her feel better. If anything it made her feel more alone, even though her friends were with her.

'Maybe I wanted to be lied to,' she said, her voice barely audible over the chatter inside. 'Maybe I was so desperate for that fairy tale I didn't bother to look for the monsters...'

Maisie and Amanda both put their arms round her shoulders, pulling her towards a table in the corner. 'No one would blame you for wanting a fairy-tale ending,' Amanda said. 'We all want that. It doesn't make you stupid. Just human.'

20

It was Maisie's first Saturday at the Petticoat and the cold had teeth as if winter hadn't noticed it should have been gone. It bit into her cheeks, pinched her nose, making her look like Santa's reindeer, and nipped her fingers raw. The fog from the river had rolled in early, leaving the market slick with damp and glittering with frost patches. 'Wear layers to keep out the cold,' everyone said. So Maisie had two vests on and her childhood Liberty bodice, too small now, but she squeezed herself into it. Then she had a blouse and two jumpers. No wonder she could hardly do up her coat.

Big Sal's voice thundered above the hubbub of the market.

'Come on, ladies, don't be shy. Look here for all your sewing needs. We've got everything.' Even though she hadn't made a joke she roared with laughter, the kind that shook her whole body and made Maisie feel more cheerful.

She was standing at the end of Sal's stall, where a little space had been cleared for her and her friends, for their new sideline. A bit of sacking showed where her bit of the stall started and Sal's finished. On it she had a pair of scissors, a biscuit tin full of threads, and a roll of newspaper for taking measurements. Amanda had made a sign in her neat writing with little sketches of sewing accessories surrounding the words.

NEED A STITCH, A NIP OR A TUCK? WE CAN HELP – DRESSES, TROUSERS, COATS, JACKETS. FAST, RELIABLE SERVICE

Maisie read it again for courage, though the cold made her eyes water. She was happy chatting to people she knew but worried that she couldn't compete with Sal to get customers to notice her. She wasn't as confident as Amanda nor had the sort of bright, cheery manner that drew people to Bethan. But it was her Saturday, and she wasn't going to let the others down.

Sal clapped a meaty hand on Maisie's shoulder. 'Cheer up, girly. You look like you're at a funeral and who wants to go to them? Make them feel like they're going to 'ave a good time just talking to you. You'll soon get the 'ang of it.'

Rubbing her hands, already frozen despite having gloves on under her mittens, Maisie pulled a face. 'Hard to be cheerful when you're freezing to death.'

'You'll soon get used to it, sweetheart, and we can take it in turns to nip off to Bert's Café for a nice hot cuppa and a warm-up. You'll be surprised 'ow quick the day goes if you get some business.'

Maisie listened to her patter and resolved to be braver. A paper-thin man walked by, weighed down with a bag of potatoes. She took a deep breath, determined to get their business started.

'You, sir, the handsome man with the string bag of spuds! I can see your pocket is half off. I can repair that for you in a jiffy. Make you whole again. How about it?'

The man grinned a toothy smile and walked towards her.

'Handsome, am I? How much will you charge? Mind, I'm not paying if you don't do a good job. Still, me ciggies keep falling out when it's like this. Lost ten Woodbine yesterday.'

They came to an agreed price and he went off to get a bit more shopping while she got on with it. 'I won't be long,' she shouted after him. 'You'll be warm again in no time!'

'See, girl. You just gotta grit your teeth and pretend you've got a mouth on you as big as mine.' Sal's face split in a grin. 'And you might be as pretty one day, too.'

Maisie selected the thread of the nearest colour to the man's jacket, then found her fingers were so cold she struggled to thread the needle.

''Ere, let me do that. Me fingers is used to this weather. Yours will be soon before you know it.'

The trick was to work neat but quickly, double the thread for strength, get the jacket back to the man before he had time to get cold. Around her, the market carried on as usual, unaware she had her first customer. Hawkers called out their wares, women bartered for everything, children darted like sparrows between legs.

Sal carried on her patter, not just drawing attention to what she was selling but to Maisie's skills as well. 'Come over 'ere, ladies. See this girl's hands. They're like magic, faster than your money disappears!'

Maisie was grateful and gave her a smile of thanks. The man with the torn pocket was soon back. He inspected the mend as if he had a couture jacket costing hundreds. He handed her the agreed amount, and gave a nod. 'Not bad, not bad at all. I'll tell me mates about you. Some of 'em ain't got a woman to do for 'em.'

Her first sale. Maisie tucked the coin away in her small purse and let herself feel more confident. Maybe this business idea would work after all.

As the morning wore on, each hour colder than the last, Maisie mended a sleeve for a woman who'd ripped it on something, she took two orders for hems, one pair of trousers to be shortened, the other lengthened. Her fingers were stiff, the skin split near her nails, but she felt a quiet satisfaction. Still, she was having to pretend to be confident, bluffing it.

'Maisie!'

She looked up from the sewing she was doing, and there was Frank, her boyfriend. He wore his railway cap, tilted back, and his scarf was tucked inside his greatcoat. He wasn't a traditionally handsome man, but his lovely personality shone on his face. It lifted Maisie's heart just to see him.

She reached out and grabbed his hand. 'I'm so pleased to see you. You weren't sure you could get away.'

He smiled and touched the side of his nose. 'Did a deal with one of the other blokes to swap. Couldn't miss a chance to see you, could I?' He looked around at her bit of the stall. 'That's a good poster. Looks professional.'

'Amanda did it. She's a great artist.'

'Still, she's probably somewhere in the warm while you're freezing your toes off out here.' He reached for her and kissed her cheek. 'I'm really proud of you, Maisie.'

She swallowed hard, fighting back the sudden tears that had nothing to do with the cold. There were few compliments in her home, she wasn't used to them. 'I've had a few customers,' she said. 'And I'm learning to shout out like Sal does. You wouldn't know me. I hardly know myself. Bluffing, that's what it is.'

He squeezed her hand. 'I'll go and get you a cuppa. I've just got time before I'm due back at work.' He looked over at Big Sal. 'Want a cuppa, Sal? Warm you up.'

'Is the Pope a Catholic?' She laughed. 'I always want a cuppa even though they make me pee all the time.'

A woman approached, holding a dress. Maisie straightened up and smiled at her. 'See you in a minute, Frank.' The woman wanted the dress shortened, but it would take longer, so Maisie offered to do it for the following Saturday. 'It won't be me here next week, but I'll do the sewing. You'll be pleased with it, I guarantee.' They agreed a price and the woman gave Maisie half now, the rest to be paid on collection. When Maisie looked up again, Frank was there holding two steaming mugs of tea.

'Two teas for two lovely ladies,' he said. 'I saw you with that customer then. You're a natural.' Maisie and Sal took the drinks, warming their hands on the thick white ceramic mugs.

Frank reached into his pocket and took out a small parcel. 'Something else to warm you up.'

Maisie's eyes lit up when she saw what it was. A Cornish pasty.

'Where's mine then, 'andsome?' Big Sal said with a laugh. 'Ain't I pretty enough?'

'Sorry, Sal. Next time.' He kissed Maisie on the cheek again. 'Gotta get back. See you soon, love.'

She nodded, her mouth full of pasty, and then he was gone, swallowed by the market crowd.

Maisie barely had time to brush the crumbs off her coat when a sudden shout split the air.

'Oy, stop 'im. Stop that man!'

A figure darted through the crowd – short, wiry, with a bulging sack over his shoulder. He bowled past their table, sending Maisie's thread tin crashing to the ground, reels of thread scattering across the cobbles.

'Mind yourself!' Sal bellowed, putting a protective arm across

Maisie. 'That's Ernie Smithers, biggest rogue in the Petticoat. He'd steal your knickers off your bum given 'alf a chance.'

Two policemen barged through the crowds after him, whistles shrieking. The crowd parted, like the Red Sea parting for Moses. Children, excited by the disturbance, chased anything that had been knocked off stalls, an apple, a pair of gloves, a tatty necklace.

Shouts and jeers followed the excitement, then it was all gone, swallowed up in the noise and chaos of the Petticoat.

Maisie's heart thumped. For one startling moment, Ernie's eyes had locked with hers as he rushed by. She saw the desperation in them, half terror, half defiance. Then she crouched down, gathering her threads with shaking hands. 'Nearly knocked me over,' she muttered.

Sal sneered. 'I've 'eard about 'im. Bomb chaser 'e is. Goes out during a raid nicking stuff. Even cutting fingers off the dead to get their rings. Bastards! 'Anging's too good for 'em.'

Maisie had seen plenty of news reports in the papers about the ghouls. Like everyone else, she sometimes bought some black-market stuff, a pair of stockings, say, or some cigarettes, but she'd never buy anything she thought was stolen. Sal's words made her think again. Perhaps she'd been too innocent.

Luckily another customer distracted her from these gloomy thoughts, a woman who wanted a tear in her best dress fixed. 'That'll take a while, love,' Maisie said. 'Would you be okay coming back next week?' She knew if she rushed the job it wouldn't be as perfect as she wanted it to be. The woman moaned a bit but finally agreed. Maisie notched up another sale, another small victory.

By the time the light began to fade, Maisie's purse held a satisfying clink of coins and a few ten-bob notes.

'You might as well pack up, girl,' Sal said. 'You done good. But before you go let's see what you've earned so I can get me cut.'

Turning their back on the people walking by, they counted the money and Sal worked out her commission like a professor of mathematics. 'There,' she said, patting Maisie on the back. 'Looks like you and your mates got a good business idea there. You coming back next week?'

Maisie was dog-tired and very glad it wouldn't be her every week. She couldn't understand how the stallholders, many of them old, did this day in, day out. 'Not me, it'll be Amanda or Bethan. Not sure which but I might pop by and say hello.'

As she packed her stuff away, she felt proud of the money in her purse. They'd agreed that each Saturday whoever was at the Petticoat would keep what they earned. It was a great incentive. And that, she thought as she trudged homeward in the drizzling rain, was worth every frozen finger.

21

'Does this dress look okay?' Bethan twirled in front of the mirror, her mother watching with a smile. The dress was a very old one of her grandmother's that she had remodelled. Grey and white with tiny pink zig-zags, it flared out at the bottom and Bethan knew it would be great for dancing.

'There's lovely, it is, cariad.' Her mother turned her round to check if the seams she had drawn down the back of her legs were straight. 'Perhaps one of them Yanks can give you a pair of stockings. You'll freeze to death with bare legs like that.'

Bethan laughed. 'But you know what you always say – vanity will keep me warm! Anyways, Joe's taking me to Rainbow Corner. It's lush in there, it is. If I can I'll try to bring you something back.'

Her mother's smile vanished. 'Joe? A new one, is it? I want you to be careful. There was that Buddy. You thought he was the one. Almost packing your suitcase you were. It's not that I think all GIs are secretly married or even rotters. But if you goes out with a local lad it's easy to check him out, like.'

'But Mum,' Bethan said, twirling around to make sure she looked good, 'there was Josh, that other GI I had a few dates with.

He was a decent bloke. Pity he got sent abroad. Still, plenty more fish in the sea. I'll keep trying. Find someone to take me to Hollywood or New York, or California, or Chicago. And all the other places I've read about that sound so lush.' She pretended to look around. 'Gotta be better than dodging bombs in the East End, isn't it? And I'll be more careful next time. No more Buddy for me!'

Her mother's smile didn't reach her eyes. 'I worries about you. Don't be alone with anyone, some boys won't take no for an answer. And take those small pointed sewing scissors with you. Keep them handy and if you have any trouble, stab them in the thigh. Show 'em what Welsh girls are made of!'

Bethan kissed her goodbye and hurried all the way to the underground station. It wasn't just Yanks who could be too handy, she thought, she'd had to deal with a few groping hands on the underground. All of them Brits as far as she could tell. She'd developed a way of dealing with them. 'Touch me once more and I'll pull the emergency cord and have you arrested,' she would say loudly. It worked every time. The offender would probably like to give her some lip back, but to do that in front of others would be to admit guilt. But she liked her mother's suggestion and had her scissors in her hand ready as she got onto the train.

Changing at Holborn, she finally got to Leicester Square and walked to Rainbow Corner with minutes to spare. Joe was already waiting outside, looking dashing in his GI uniform. And he held a flower in his hand. How romantic! Bethan couldn't imagine any East End lads doing that.

Joe smiled and kissed her cheek. 'Come on, let's get something to eat and then go dancing! And boy, I just can't wait to show you off. You look pretty as a picture.'

He took her into the self-serve café. 'Have anything you want, sweetheart,' he said, squeezing her hand. 'Try something you haven't had for a while. I know all about the rationing you folks here have to put up with.'

The area was much more relaxed than she'd experienced at the British Restaurant at the Petticoat. With rationing they had to make do with what they could get, although they still turned out decent meals for only a shilling. But she'd been told everything had to be accounted for. Here at Rainbow Corner, food seemed endless. They had so much of everything. Proper coffee instead of that awful acorn drink, sugar, eggs that weren't dried. The smell was different too. At the British Restaurant it was all boiled cabbage. Here though, the air was rich with the scent of coffee, bacon and fresh baked treats.

She walked along until she found something familiar. 'I'll have one of those, please, with some chips if they have them.'

'Chips?' he queried. 'Wouldn't you prefer fries? They'll be hot and you'll love them.'

She coloured up when she realised he was talking about the same thing as her. She'd heard people say that their common language divided them and began to understand it.

They sat at a table in the corner, and she picked up her knife and fork. 'No, honey,' he said with a smile. 'We eat food like this with our fingers.' He demonstrated, opening his mouth wide and taking a huge bite of hamburger. Mustard and ketchup dribbled down his chin and he wiped it off with his handkerchief.

'You call this a hamburger.' Bethan picked hers up. 'My mam makes these when she can get the meat, rissoles we call them. We don't have the fancy bread though.'

'Yeah, but ours are better.' Joe handed her the bottle of ketchup. 'Go on, knock yourself out – have some of this.'

'What is it?' She felt herself colouring again.

'You don't know, honey? My, you Brits have been deprived. It's ketchup and that there is mustard. Have some of each. You'll just love how it tastes.' He took her bun from her and piled on both along with so many onions they kept sliding off. Back home, she thought, onions were hard to get and such abundance and extravagance would be considered unpatriotic. Her mother could make a tiny bit of mince last three days.

But her critical thoughts flew away when she took the first bite. It was a revelation – not just the meat itself which tasted moist and richer than she was used to but the combinations of flavours – the soft white bun, the casual way of eating.

She groaned with pleasure as she chewed through the mouthful. 'Mmm, that's lush, that is.'

He laughed. 'I love seeing you enjoy your food, so many girls are picky. And I've just gotta ask about your accent. Us Yanks can't tell one from the other. You don't sound like a Londoner though. What part of England do you come from?'

Her eyes opened wide. Here we go. 'England? England? I'm not English. I'm from Wales, mon. Gotta be honest with you. It beats England any day.'

He frowned. 'Whales? Isn't that some sort of big fish?' He saw the look she gave him. 'Guess not. You're Welsh then. That's in England, right?'

'No, Wales is a country. We're joined on to England but a separate country. We have our own language and everything.'

He blinked hard. 'Well, I'll be... you mean you don't speak English?'

She slapped his arm. 'I'm speaking it now, aren't I? Most of us speak both, like. Clever we are.'

She spent the rest of the meal educating him about her country and naming famous Welsh people but he'd never heard of any of them. Then she realised she was monopolising the conversation. All the advice columns in magazines said girls shouldn't do that. 'I'm sorry, my mouth won't stop when I talks about home.' She looked around. They'd finished their burgers and Coke. 'Is it time to dance now?'

They'd only had one dance when she noticed a change in the dance hall. The band had just finished 'Pennsylvania 6-500' and the GIs who'd been lounging against the walls suddenly straightened up. More came in and a buzz of excitement seemed to go through the whole building.

Joe was looking around. 'Well, I'll be damned!' He grabbed her arm. 'It's really him!'

'Who?' Bethan followed his gaze to a doorway where a uniformed officer had appeared. He looked like every other American officer to her.

'That's Glen Miller! Greatest band leader in the good old US of A.' Joe was so excited he could hardly speak. 'I saw him in New York a while back. What a night that was...' He looked like a child on Christmas morning. 'You know who he is, right?'

She nodded. 'I do, of course I do, but I didn't know what he looks like. Fancy him being here.'

The way the room changed reminded her of something Amanda had said about missing fabric. 'I've noticed,' she'd explained, 'often there's some drama or other when fabric goes missing. It's like they create a fuss at one end of the factory so we don't look at what's happening at the other end.' Bethan hadn't paid much attention before, but she had been looking out for that ever since. Amanda was rarely wrong.

The factory worries fell from her mind when the band struck up 'In the Mood', played with great enthusiasm. When the number had finished, the officer – Miller – smiled and made his way towards them, stopping to shake hands with several GIs. The rhythm filled the air, sweeping around like a gust of warm wind. The crowd responded with claps and cheers, worries about their future momentarily forgotten.

Bethan couldn't help but sway to the music and clap in time too.

When the number finished, the crowd erupted into more applause, some stamping their feet with approval. Miller took a bow then began weaving his way through the room, having a word here and there, shaking hands with some, patting others on the back.

Bethan's pulse raced as she realised he was walking in their direction.

'Come on.' Joe tugged at her arm. 'We gotta get close. I'm gonna try to talk to him.'

Bethan was feeling overwhelmed. The room was hot and she felt sticky. It was thick with the smell of the Camel cigarettes the Yanks smoked and the smell of sweat from so many people dancing. 'I don't think...'

'Hey, Captain Miller!' Joe called out, waving. To Bethan's embarrassment, Miller actually walked in their direction. 'Great night,' he said when they were near. 'This place is certainly a home from home for you boys.' His accent was different from Joe's, softer somehow, but Bethan had no idea what part of America he came from.

He didn't stay long. 'Well, excuse me, guys. Must go and say hi to some more people.'

The opening notes of 'Moonlight Serenade' filled the air and Joe turned to Bethan. 'Dance, pretty Welsh lady? This is his signature tune.'

Although she'd spent time with Yanks before, for the first time Bethan felt the gulf between her world and Joe's as he talked about home, about New York, Broadway and Times Square. They were places she'd only ever seen on film. She realised that moving to America might be harder than she'd thought. There was a lot of difference between the two countries.

'You've really been to all those places?' she asked.

'Sure have. The lights, the buzz, the people, the music. You'd love it. Maybe I'll take you there one day.'

But she was wiser now. She'd heard promises like that too often to take them seriously. She swayed to the music, letting Joe hold her a little closer, but only a little.

'Penny for them.' He'd noticed her distraction.

'I was just thinking that... there's a world of difference. Your country sounds so huge and grand compared to mine.'

He laughed. 'Everywhere's different from somewhere else. It's the people what make it home, that's what my ma always says.' The number finished and he asked if she wanted to dance again.

'Can we sit this one out? I'd love another Coke.' She watched him go, thinking about what her mother had said. Be careful. She liked Joe well enough and didn't think he'd try to take advantage of her, nor did she think he was the man for her. She'd drink her Coke and make an excuse to head off home before long. But she couldn't completely push aside the thought of being a GI bride. Not yet anyway.

22

As always, the railway station was alive with the usual wartime hustle, the sharp whistle of trains departing, the heavy clatter of boots on the paved floor, the incomprehensible announcements from the crackly loudspeakers. Civilians in well-worn coats hurried along the platforms alongside soldiers in their neatly pressed uniforms and polished boots. The air smelled of smoke from the trains and cigarettes as well as oil and the cologne the Yanks often wore.

Above all hung the ever-present tension of wartime – hurried goodbyes, stolen moments, nervous joking and kitbags slung over shoulders nearly hitting people behind.

Bethan stood on platform eight at Victoria station, wrapped up in several layers of clothing with her best coat over the top. She'd spent extra time getting ready that morning after curling her hair the night before. Amanda had teased her when she told her about her preparations for the date. 'Anyone would think you were going to meet the King instead of spending a day in Brighton with a Yank. Mind you, there is a palace there!'

Amanda didn't understand. No one did. This winter day trip

to the seaside wasn't just a day out, it was the start of something bigger. After three dates, she was getting fond of Jim. He was tall, dark, handsome with a dimple that gave him film-star looks. Her gloved hands toyed with the catch on the handbag she'd borrowed from her mother. Glancing at the clock, she saw she still had ten minutes to wait. Her heart fluttered with anticipation, and she instinctively drew her coat more closely around herself. Much longer and her nose would be as red as Rudolph's.

She lay in bed last night picturing it – the two of them walking along the Brighton promenade she'd seen in books in the library. It would be cold but that would be an excuse for him to hold her hand and walk close together. She knew there was barbed wire along that part of the coast, but the town still had plenty to offer. 'It's a favourite spot for us Yanks wanting a change of scenery,' Jim had assured her. 'You'll love it.' She imagined them stopping in a cosy café, leaning towards each other, gazing into each other's eyes. The war would feel a million miles away.

But as the minutes ticked by, she began to feel uneasy. Had she come to the wrong platform? She scanned the soldiers on platforms either side, annoyed that they hadn't arranged to meet in the station café or even at the front of the building. He might well be waiting somewhere else, thinking she had stood him up.

Twenty minutes went by. No sign of him and doubt began to crowd into her mind. *I bet he's just running late*, she told herself. *Maybe something happened at the base so he couldn't get away.*

The whistle blew again, sharp and decisive. The porter, an elderly man carrying a whistle, shouted, 'Train to Brighton! Last call for train to Brighton!'

Bethan stayed where she was, nearer the entrance to the platform so she could catch him when he came running, out of breath, delighted to see her waiting. The crowd thinned as people got on board, saying goodbye to their loved ones and lugging suitcases or pulling children's hands. She still had hope. He'd arrive breathless, full of apologies for cutting it close. She'd laugh it off, just thrilled to see him.

But the train doors slammed shut, the engine let out a great hiss of steam and she struggled to hold back tears. There were a few last stragglers and a porter hurrying to offload some parcels, but that was all. She let out a sad breath, still hoping he had merely missed the train but would arrive and they would spend the day together in London instead.

But she really knew better. He wasn't coming.

She stood immobile, watching as the train began to move, its wheels clanking against the old tracks as it slowly pulled out of the station.

But another thought forced itself into her mind. *What if he never arrived at all? What if he never intended to, but just made promises he had no intention of keeping?*

The excitement she'd felt that morning began to drain away, still buoyed up with a smidgen of hope. He'd seemed like a decent Yank, kind and thoughtful. After her experience with Buddy, she thought she'd got better at avoiding the bad ones. Had he pulled the wool over her eyes too?

Bethan went to the station café where she could see people coming in. He could still arrive. They could get the next train or spend the day in the West End. Warming her hands on a cup of tea, she never took her eyes from the entrance, her heart jumping every time a man in US uniform came in. But after forty minutes she had to face the truth. She'd been stood up.

Shoulders slumped, she set off for home. The sky was grey, heavy, leaden. A light shower of rain soon began but she didn't bother to raise her umbrella, so unhappy she didn't even notice it.

As she walked away from the station, a GI and his girlfriend walked past, arm in arm, giggling at something, looking so in love that just seeing them pierced her heart like a knife. She hated the way it made her feel, the jealousy, the way she resented the girl without any good reason. *Why can't that be me and Jim?*

By the time she reached home, she was soaked through. Her mother greeted her in the warm kitchen, wiping her hands on her apron. She took one look at Bethan. 'Oh, love, you're drenched. Didn't he turn up? You poor thing. Go on, get some dry clothes on and I'll make you some hot chocolate if we've got any left, then you can tell me all about it.'

Bethan found her mother's kindness too much and tears began to roll down her cheeks. Angrily she wiped them away with the back of her hand. Upstairs she got a towel and dried herself, changing into dry clothes and putting her wet ones to dry. Would she never find the man of her dreams? Was there something wrong with her? Should she do what her mother said and only go out with local lads?

But then she'd never get to America.

Her mother brought her watery hot chocolate up and sat on the edge of her bed. 'Want to talk about it, cariad?'

Bethan's eyes were red from crying. She blew her nose and took a sip of the chocolate without answering.

'You know,' her mother said, 'I never told you this, but before I met your dad I was engaged to someone else. Reggie his name was and all my friends were so jealous. He looked like Cary Grant. I loved him so much I almost... well, I don't need to go into that. I thought he was the love of my life.'

She had got Bethan's attention. 'What happened?'

'He only got another girl in the family way, didn't he? While he was engaged to me! Worse, he tried to deny it, saying she was, well, a slag. But her dad knew better and he was round to Reggie's mum's house double quick. They got married two weeks later. I thought I'd die of heartbreak at the time, I'd never find a man to love me.' She paused and bit her lip, remembering that painful time. 'But Reggie led that girl a merry dance so I got off light.' She squeezed Bethan's hand. 'You'll find the right one yet, bach. You're young and pretty. Lots of nice men will want you.' She went to the door. 'Come down when you're ready, love. I'll make us some sandwiches. Only fish paste, I'm afraid, but we can sit and chat if you want to.'

Her mother's words stayed with her as Bethan drank the hot chocolate. For a while she stayed in the warm under her blankets, still wearing her dry clothes. Maybe her mother was right. But for now, she told herself, she had to let the dream of a day in Brighton go. Her mum had warned her more than once that going out with a GI would mean she wouldn't know anything about him. Wouldn't know if he was married in America or was just being nice to get what he wanted. Plenty of girls had got in trouble that way.

'Find someone local,' her mum had said with a sad smile. 'Then you can check him out. Every girl should do that. It'd save a lot of heartache, and I don't want you to be heartbroken. You deserve better.'

The more she thought about it, the more Bethan realised how stupid she'd been. Had she learned nothing from her experience with Buddy? Had she been too trusting? But surely not all GIs were untrustworthy. She knew of several girls who were happily engaged to GIs with no sign of trouble. She decided she'd need to be more cautious in future, although how she'd tell the good ones from the bad ones was beyond her so far. There was no magic sign that she could work out.

Or could there be?

23

Bethan and Amanda trudged along in the heavy gloom, the gibbous moon providing almost no light against the blackout. Their footsteps were heavy after another tiring day at the uniform factory. The smell of the sewing room still clung to their clothes and Bethan could almost hear Mrs Duncan's piercing voice barking in her ear, pushing them to 'sew faster, be more careful'.

'You still looking for somewhere to live?' Bethan asked as they struggled to see where they were going in the mild March evening. She circled her arms, trying to relieve the tension in her neck from hunching over a sewing machine all day.

She suddenly yelped as a man on a bicycle rode at speed so close to her that his sleeve briefly caught her hair. 'Oy, stupid!' she shouted after him, but he was gone and she was wasting her breath.

'This blackout'll be the death of me,' Amanda muttered, squinting through the gloom. No streetlights lit the way and the white paint that was put on lampposts and kerb edges at the beginning of the war had long since faded. 'My neighbour's cousin got run over last week in the dark, broke his leg, poor man. That's him off work for weeks.'

They got no further when the air-raid siren went off with its low mournful hum that quickly swelled into a deafening wail, echoing down the street.

Amanda grabbed Bethan's hand. 'Quick, this way.' She knew of a brick and concrete shelter nearby, just off Roman Road. As always, they looked into the sky for the feared German bombers but were puzzled when none appeared, nor were the searchlights criss-crossing the sky as they usually did.

'That's strange,' Bethan started, but she got no further as Amanda dragged her towards the shelter. With several others they went inside. The air was damp and heavy and they'd only just got to the door when there was another noise, much louder than the air-raid siren.

'What the...' Bethan gasped.

The noise ripped through the air – a high-pitched screech like a jagged flame followed by a crack like thunder which shook the ground beneath their feet. They instinctively ducked, hearts pounding. It was over in seconds, but it split the air, making everyone freeze. Even though it was short-lived, echoes of it bounced around the tight-knit Bethnal Green streets.

'Get inside quick,' someone shouted. 'Must be a new type of bomb.'

The two friends wasted no time hurrying inside, yet for a moment they still imagined they could hear that noise, unlike anything they'd ever heard before. Within the shelter you could almost taste the fear. People spoke in hushed tones, their voices trembling as they speculated what the new and awful noise might mean. Mothers clutched their children tighter, couples sat so close there was no space between them. There was always a worry that a direct hit could destroy a shelter and a bigger fear of new types of bomb.

There was no electricity, but someone had brought in an oil lamp and a few candles were lit too, relieving the gloom but making spooky shadows. A mother was cuddling her toddler, trying to tell her a fairy tale over the noise. The little girl clutched her mother's coat as if terrified she might vanish any moment. An elderly couple sat hand in hand on the bench on one side of the shelter, looking resigned. A single woman sat and shook. She was dressed up for an evening out with a victory roll hairdo, a tight red skirt, an equally tight woollen jacket and scarlet lipstick. Her eyes roamed around the shelter as if searching for something.

'Right,' the elderly woman said. 'New type of bomb or not, let's make the most of it. Let's have a right old sing-song. Who's with me?'

Her suggestion was met half-heartedly but when she began singing 'Roll Out the Barrel' more than half the people there joined in. They sang two more songs, 'It's a Long Way to Tipperary' and 'My Old Man', when someone hammered on the door.

The singing faltered then stopped altogether as people looked at each other frowning. *What now?* was the unspoken question.

People looked at each other. 'What?'

'There's been no all-clear,' someone said. But the woman nearest the door opened it and an ARP warden, his face pale and lined, shouted, 'Come quickly. Problem at the underground! We need helpers *now*!' For a second no one moved, the meaning of his words sinking in, then Bethan stood up, pulling Amanda with her.

Almost running, they followed the warden round the corner and what they saw stopped them in their tracks.

24

At first Bethan and Amanda couldn't understand what had happened. The blackout was in operation, although they could see the waving lights of shielded torches. The sound of emergency vehicles was getting nearer. Lots of them.

'What is it?' Bethan asked the warden as they ran.

'Accident, crush on the steps...' he gasped, struggling to hold back a sob.

As they got nearer, they heard a cacophony of sounds – shouting, screaming, calls for help. 'Where's my baby?' 'Help me!' 'Get off me!' The cries overlapped and echoed off the surrounding buildings, and the girls didn't properly understand what had happened until they were very near the scene. The flickering torchlight played tricks on their eyes, casting moving shadows over the tangled mess of bodies in the station entrance, a chaotic knot of limbs like some macabre knitting gone wrong. The cries for help and shouted instructions of the wardens seemed to come from every direction, pulling the friends towards the steps like magnets. The scene was difficult to comprehend, made worse by the darkness and moving torchlights. But as they got nearer, the full horror of what was in front of them became clear. And it was a sight they would never forget. It was a nightmare come to life.

The entrance to the station was choked with people – some standing like statues in stunned silence, others sobbing or shouting for loved ones. A man was on his knees nearby praying, 'God help us, help us, please.'

In the dim light of the torches, and a couple of oil lamps, they could see the pile of bodies completely filling the station entrance – a tangled, writhing heap of arms and legs, some moving feebly, others heartbreakingly still. The sound of muffled cries came from some in the entrance and from people still trapped further down the stairs to the underground. ARP wardens barked orders, trying to bring some semblance of order to the chaos as ambulances arrived. 'Get those stretchers over here!' 'Put the dead over there!'

The air was thick with dust, sweat, fear and the metallic tang of blood that clung to their throats like smoke. Bethan, her breath caught, paused for a second then grabbed Amanda's arm. 'Come on, we've got to help.'

'Get those kids out first!' someone shouted, their voice hoarse with urgency. Nearby a man shouted, 'My wife's in there. My wife!'

'Get out of the way.' A fireman pulled the man out of the melee. 'We'll get everyone out as quick as we can. Wait over there!'

The closer the two friends got to the station, the more disorientating it became. Flickering torchlight illuminated pale, terrified faces and the glint of tears on cheeks. Someone, perhaps another ARP warden, took blankets out of the ambulances that had just arrived and covered the bodies of the people who had already been pulled free and who didn't move. Two men moved them to one side, lining them up. They stretched out in a solemn row, like a silent landscape of small, uneven hills, each one marking the end of someone's life. A breeze caught the blankets, and they moved in the cold night air. For a moment people nearby felt hope, but the blankets soon settled unmoving again.

The scene on the underground steps was chaos. Following instructions from the wardens, Bethan and Amanda worked frantically, their hands reaching into the crush of people as they tried to see who they could move. Who was not too partially buried under other people. Bethan's pulse thundered in her ears as they fought to work out what they could do. Her hands landed on a man's shoulder, and for a moment she thought he might be alive. But when she tried to move him, his head rolled back unnaturally and even in the dim light she could see his eyes were blank, staring into nothing. Her breath caught in her throat, the world around tilted and she thought she might faint.

It seemed impossible to go on, to reach for another body, when she was surrounded by death. Then she felt Amanda's shoulder press firmly against hers, a small welcoming touch in the turmoil. 'Keep going,' Amanda urged softly, her voice cutting through the fog of Bethan's panic. 'You're doing well.'

'Let me move him,' a warden said gently, seeing Bethan's struggle, his face grim but determined. 'Concentrate on finding the living.'

Amanda knelt nearby, feverishly trying to free a boy whose leg was pinned beneath a tangle of lifeless limbs. His wide, tear-filled eyes locked on hers, yet he said nothing. 'We'll get you out,' she promised yet couldn't help but wonder if one of the bodies pinning him down might belong to his mother.

Every movement was a struggle, every limb they shifted bringing waves of pain to someone. Amanda winced at the boy's cries as they finally freed his leg. It was obviously broken. She cradled him against her, moving his hair away from his forehead, kissing his cheeks. 'You're safe now, love,' she whispered again and again.

'This one needs help,' she said to a nearby ambulance worker, her words letting him know the boy was alive.

Around them people worked like ghosts, faces smeared with dirt and blood, taut, holding tight to their emotions to get the job done.

They lost track of time. The hours blurred in an endless cycle of pulling, lifting and passing. The cries of the injured grew fainter as the pile of bodies thinned, yet the silence was worse. It was the silence of those who would never speak again.

By the time the last person was pulled from the steps, it was almost midnight. Every person had been moved on, some to hospitals, others to temporary mortuaries set up in nearby pubs, churches and public buildings. The ambulances and fire engines had all left, leaving the rescuers empty, alone but for people who had just heard of the tragedy and came looking for news of loved ones. They had no answers for them.

Some volunteers drifted off, but most just sat where they were, too numb to do anything. A WVS van arrived and was distributing tea and sandwiches which no one tasted. The taste of death was too strong.

Bethan sat on the cold pavement, her hands wrapped around the hot tin mug of tea she couldn't bring herself to drink. The taste of death still lingered in the back of her throat, stronger than any tea or sandwich could mask. Amanda was beside her, staring in the distance, not seeing anything but horror, her mind too traumatised to think clearly. They were both covered in dirt and blood, clothes ripped and hair awry.

Neither of them spoke. What good would words do? Around

them, they barely noticed the low murmurs of the other workers or the distant rumble of trains and trams.

'You lot want a drink?' The voice of the landlord of the Cow and Cat pub nearest the station brought them back to the moment. 'I've got permission to stay open a bit longer. Come on in out of the cold. First drinks are on me.'

Like zombies, the workers rose and headed to the pub with only occasional hushed conversations between them. They hardly noticed the warmth of the pub that on any other March night they'd have been grateful for.

Bethan and Amanda hesitated at the doorway, the smell of spilled beer and smoke mingling with the reek of sweat and blood still on their clothes and hands. The pub was dimly lit, the gentle glow of the lamps casting long shadows on the walls and tables. The landlord waved them in with a nod, his face pale but kind. 'Come on in, girls. You've earned a drink.'

He'd lined up pints of beer on the bar. 'Come on, grab a drink. Anyone want anything different?'

Amanda grabbed two pints and handed one to Bethan, who stared at it as if she'd never seen one before and had no idea what it was. They sat near the fire, took a sip of their drink but didn't taste it. A man in an ARP uniform leaned back against the wall near them, his hands still shaking as he lit a cigarette. No one spoke above a whisper.

Bethan finally broke the silence between them. 'What do we tell people, Mand? Do we say we were here?'

Amanda clasped her hands and looked down at the floor. 'I suppose we do whatever feels right. But I know I wouldn't want to describe what we've seen. No one else wants those images in their heads if they don't have to.'

Bethan sighed. 'All those people tonight... they just wanted to get home to their families. Mothers, fathers, children, just going about their lives. So many gone or their lives changed for ever. And here am I, chasing dreams of a country I've never been to. It seems so unimportant after what we've seen, insignificant. Maybe I'm a bit crazy wanting travel and adventure. Does it count for anything in the end?'

Amanda nodded. 'It's not wrong to have dreams, Bethan. Those people we helped tonight, or couldn't help, they had them too. Sometimes dreams are what motivates us, pushes us to keep going every day.' She wiped tears from her face. 'But it makes you think how fragile life is, doesn't it? What's really important in life.'

Bethan took another sip of her drink and sighed again. 'It's not where you are that's important, is it? It's who you're with, it's who you help every day, who helps you.' She struggled to suppress a sob. 'Love and friendship. Those people in the underground, they didn't want adventure or to escape their lives, they just wanted to live them. They just wanted to feel safe.'

The landlord interrupted their musings with a tray of sandwiches, offering them around. 'Go on, eat something. They'll do you good.' A few people took them but neither of the girls could eat a thing.

'Did we do enough?' Amanda asked quietly, but the ARP warden overheard.

'I saw you two girls. You did everything you could. You worked as hard as any man.' His words were reassuring, but his voice was as shaky as his hands. 'You can be proud of yourself, girls.'

'Do you know how many died?'

The warden shook his head. 'I don't suppose we'll know for a while, but well over a hundred. Nearer two hundred, I reckon.'

That news, overheard by several other people, silenced everyone. Some would be wondering if people they knew were amongst the dead and injured. They couldn't be everywhere at all times, and might have missed something or someone they knew.

As the minutes dragged slowly by, someone suggested a toast. 'To those poor people. Those that will never see tomorrow and those who survived.'

Bethan and Amanda clinked their glasses, and a murmur spread throughout the room. 'To them.'

25

The sewing machines droned on, their rhythmic clatter filling the factory floor as usual. March sunlight struggled to find its way through the blast-taped windows. Amanda and Bethan slipped in through the side door well past clocking-in time, their faces taut and pale. Neither had slept much and when they did their dreams were haunted by scenes of broken tangled limbs and life-less bodies. They moved towards the clocking-in machine like ghosts, their usual energy missing, replaced by a terrible weariness.

No one noticed them at first, but as they punched their clock-ing-in card they became aware that one by one the sewing machines stopped as the women looked at them.

'What time do you call this?' Mrs Duncan glared at them as she spoke, pointedly looking at her watch. 'You'll be docked an hour and a half. And I'll expect you to work late...'

'Oh, shut up. Just shut up, you stupid woman! You have no idea...' Tears streamed down Bethan's face, but her voice, trem-bling with fury, rose enough to be heard over the machines still working. 'You think clocking in late matters after what we saw last night? After what we went through? Bodies broken, dead babies, little ones crying for their mams – do you have any idea?'

Amanda's quiet grief contrasted with Bethan's anger. She stood frozen, dark rings round her eyes, her hands clutching her clocking-in card so tightly it bent. She wanted to speak up like Bethan but the words stuck in her throat.

Mrs Duncan's head jerked back as if she'd been punched. 'Why, you...'

But several women had left their sewing machines and crowded round Bethan and Amanda. They looked shocked at Bethan's outburst, whispering to each other and looking back at Mrs Duncan to see how she would respond.

'Were you there?' No one had to ask where. News of the tragedy was all everyone was talking about. Several women were missing from their machines, having lost loved ones themselves. No one was unaffected.

They were silent, waiting for the two friends to respond.

'We... we... helped the emergency services...' Amanda struggled to hold back a sob. 'It was... it was...'

'I heard over a hundred died,' young Millie said. 'A hundred! I can't take it in. And why haven't we heard nothing about it? Not on the news, not in the newspapers neither.'

Another young worker spoke up. 'It's another government cover-up. My dad says it happens in every war. Treat us like idiots. "It'll ruin morale," my dad says that's their excuse. Like we don't deserve to know.'

Robbie, the old caretaker, had joined them. 'I heard the council asked three times to make them steps safer, a handrail and things. Never got the money. Bet it gets done now. Too late.'

'Closing the stable door...'

Millie's eyes were wide with curiosity. 'Did you see any...?'

The questions and comments came thick and fast until Ruth,

the oldest worker there, took control. 'Right, you lot. I think these two need a bit of peace and quiet, don't you?' She looked at Mrs Duncan as if daring her to interfere. 'I'm going to take them to the canteen to get a cup of tea…' She glared at the boss again. 'And I'm in the union now, so if I hear you've docked a penny out of the wages of these two girls, you'll wish you'd never been born.'

'Just who do you think you are…' Mrs Duncan stopped mid-sentence as if she thought better of the harsh words she wanted to say, then she spun on her heel and strode away.

'Come with me,' Ruth said, holding out her hands to Amanda and Bethan, her eyes full of sympathy. As they walked through the rows of machinists, the women looked up, murmuring kind words. One or two got out of their seats and patted them on the back and gently squeezed their arms.

The canteen was quieter than any of them had ever seen, although the two kitchen workers were setting up for the next break. 'You're early!' one, Enid, shouted. 'You'll 'ave to come back, ducks.'

Ruth told the friends to sit down and quietly went to speak to Enid. The friends heard a gasp as Enid's head turned towards them. Less than five minutes later, steaming cups of tea were in front of them, along with something very special, iced buns. 'I 'eard you two was right 'eroes.' Enid patted Amanda's shoulder. 'What a terrible, terrible thing to 'appen. Thank the good Lord there were people like you to 'elp out.'

Sitting next to them, Ruth held her cup between her fingers. 'My old man was in the Great War. He was in the trenches. Never talks about it, mind, but I think sometimes talking helps. But when you're ready, not before. Tell you what. I'll just sit here. Or tell me to go away and I'll go. I won't be offended nor nothing. We don't have to talk.'

The two friends sat warming their hands on their tea, the

buns untouched. Then Bethan spoke, so quietly Ruth had to lean forward to hear her. 'It's the children I keep seeing. Their little hands reaching out, their cries, calling out for their mams. I can still hear them now...'

'We tried to help,' Amanda whispered. 'We did our best, but it didn't feel like enough. The bodies were piled so high, they choked the entrance to the station like a heap of broken dolls, limbs, heads, faces all jumbled together. And it was dark... even with the torches, we couldn't see what we were doing properly, couldn't tell one arm from another to free people.' She began to weep, tears streaming down her face as if they'd never stop.

Ruth shook her head. 'You're right heroes, that's what you are. You went to help with no training and did all that. Some people would have turned away, but not you.' She sighed. 'It's gonna take a good long while for them memories to stop hurting. Maybe they never will, but they'll get fainter like an old photograph left out in the sun. Then you'll be able to remember all the people you helped, saved. Think on that, girls.'

It took another half an hour before the girls felt able to return to the factory floor. 'I think keeping busy will help,' Amanda said. 'What do you reckon, Bethan?'

Her friend nodded. 'Better than sitting around with them pictures going round and round in my head, like.'

As they entered the factory floor again, all the sewers stood and gave them a round of applause. The two friends didn't know what to do. They just stood there waiting for it to finish, then muttered their thanks and went to their workstations. Soon their hands were busy, but their minds were still stuck in the shadows of the night before.

26

Maisie headed towards her house, tired from queueing for something for their tea. She hadn't seen Frank for ten days, although he'd written to her twice. That made her smile because they lived so close, but both had so many commitments actually meeting was difficult.

As she got her key out, she could hear Ron and Rose arguing. 'You're not the boss of me!' Rose was shouting. Maisie was tempted to turn around and walk away.

And who knew what state her mother would be in. The lovely kind woman she was when she wasn't in her cups, or the embarrassing drunk who forgot she was supposed to look after her family.

Sighing, she turned the key in the door and pushed it open, wishing she was back with her friends.

'Mais!' Rose came rushing up and tugged at her arm. 'Ron is being mean to me.'

'Let me at least take my coat off, will you!' Maisie wondered how she could survive the rest of the evening – tidying up, cooking their tea, looking after her mum if she was around. All she really wanted to do was make a sandwich and go to bed.

She strode into the living room. 'Right, you two. Listen to me. Ron, you go and tidy your bedroom and do it properly. I'll be coming to inspect it. Rose, you come with me and help me make some soup.'

At least vegetables weren't rationed so she found a mix of them in the cool cupboard. Some were going a bit wrinkly but they'd do for soup. They had no bones, but she started the soup with some dripping to give it flavour. 'Right, Rosy, you peel those carrots and two potatoes. I'll do the parsnips. We'll get a nice soup going for our tea. Warm us up.'

They'd just put the saucepan on to heat when Maisie heard the front door open with a crash. She hurried to see what had happened, her heart thumping when she saw her mother collapsed on the floor. So this was how the evening was going to go, she thought angrily, me picking up the pieces yet again. Then she felt guilty, this was her mum lying on the floor.

For a second she stood immobile, her hand gripping the knife she was holding as her breath caught again. Her mother's face, an unhealthy yellow, was turned to the side, her cheek pressed against the floorboards, her hair a tangle of sweat and neglect, dribble hanging from the corner of her mouth. From where she stood Maisie smelled the sharp tang of alcohol, the sour smell of unwashed skin and even the sharp smell of urine. She stepped forward cautiously, afraid of what she might find.

'Mum?' she whispered.

'Is Mummy dead?' Rose asked, fear making her voice tremble.

'No, she's not, Rose. Go and turn the saucepan down. It'll be boiling too much. Go on, scoot!'

She reached out to touch her mother's hand and noticed a cut on the palm, dirty and ugly. How had she got that? Leaning forward, she checked her mother was breathing. Yes, there was a slight rise and fall of her chest, but only just. Worried her mother might vomit, she turned her on her side, hoping the movement might wake her. It didn't.

'Mum! Mum!' She shook her mother's shoulders gently. More gently than she wanted. She wanted to shake her until her teeth rattled and she got some sense and stopped drinking.

'What...' was all the response she got, and her mother's eyes closed again. Maisie was terrified. What if her mother died? What could she do? She had to do something, but her mind struggled to think clearly.

'Ron, come here!' she shouted so loudly her mother shifted her position slightly.

Ron strolled over and stood leaning against the doorpost with his arms folded, acting years older than he was. He stood looking down at his mother as if she was nothing to do with him. 'Drunk again,' he said with a sneer. 'Nothing new there.'

'Is that all you can say? Go and get Mrs Simpkins next door. Quick! And don't argue!'

He shrugged and walked slowly towards the door as if there was all the time in the world.

Rose came back. 'I turned the saucepan off.' She was struggling to hold back tears. 'Is Mummy going to die?'

'Not if I can help it. Go and get a cushion to put under her head.' Her mother was groaning gently.

'Go and get yourself a slice of bread and dripping,' Maisie told Rose, wanting to get her away from this frightening scene.

She got a damp cloth and wiped her mother's face, powerless to know how else to help her. It was a relief when the front door opened again and Mrs Simpkins bustled in. She was a kind lady but never hesitated to say what she thought.

'Drunk again, is she?' Mrs Simpkins took a bottle of smelling salts out of her pocket. The smell of ammonia it gave off made Maisie cough but it did the trick. Her mother came round and looked at them, bleary-eyed.

'What're you doing here? Let me sleep.'

She seemed about to doze off again, but Mrs Simpkins was having none of it. 'Oh, no, you don't, madam,' she said, her voice as sharp as the smell of the salts. 'Up you get and get some water into you.' She knelt down and put her arms round Maisie's mum's shoulders, trying to pull her into a sitting position. All she got for her attempt was a lap full of vomit before Maisie's mum became unconscious again.

She scowled and shook her head. 'Good job I've got a pinny on.' She wrinkled her nose as she took it off and screwed it up into a ball. 'But I think we're going to have to get the doctor. She's too far gone for us to deal with.'

27

Although she was expecting it, the sharp rat-tat-tat at the door made Maisie jump. It was Dr Kennings, his black bag in his hand, his face lined with years of concern for poor East Enders.

He looked past her and saw her mother on the floor. She hadn't moved since Ron left. Maisie had covered her with a blanket, not knowing what else to do.

'She collapsed there,' Maisie said. 'We tried to get her up and make her more comfortable, but we couldn't.'

Mrs Simpkins came back from the kitchen muttering something about, 'Shameful carry-on.' She stood watching the doctor as if she didn't trust him.

Dr Kennings knelt beside Maisie's mother, his movements practised and efficient as he checked her pulse and looked at her eyes closely.

Finally, he stood up, shaking his head wearily. 'Your mum's in a bad way, I'm afraid. She's dehydrated, and that and the alcohol have put her body under a lot of strain. I'm guessing this isn't the first time. Is that right?'

Maisie felt herself going pink as if she was responsible for her mother's condition. Silently she nodded. 'Will she... will she live?'

Dr Kennings was putting his things away in his black bag. 'She'll need to go to the hospital. They'll know what to do. They have experience with alcoholics. Someone will have to go to the phone box and call for an ambulance.'

Maisie was shocked at the word. Alcoholic. Deep down she knew it was true, her mother wasn't just a heavy drinker, she'd gone beyond that, but it was still terrible to hear her called that.

Ron had returned and once again had been watching the scene while leaning against the doorpost. 'I suppose that'll be me again. I'll need some pennies.' Although his words were harsh, his eyes flicked back to his mother lying prone and his jaw clenched.

Maisie hurried over to her purse and handed it to him. 'Dial nine-nine-nine and read the instructions how to use the box!'

Without a word, he grabbed his coat and went out, slamming the door behind him.

Mrs Simpkins frowned. 'That lad needs a good clip round the ear. Never did mine any harm. Brought them to their senses, I can tell you. Thinks he's all grown up, doesn't care, but lads like him, they're always the first to crumble when the worst happens.'

The minutes stretched endlessly as they waited for the ambulance. Maisie sat on the floor beside her mother, feeling helpless, sometimes holding her hand, sometimes wiping her mouth with a damp cloth and sometimes adjusting the cushion under her head.

Dr Kennings stood nearby. 'To tell you the truth, it's surprising your mother is still here, Maisie. Much longer without help and I dread to think what could happen.'

Maisie swallowed hard. 'What's wrong with her, doctor? Can it be cured?'

The doctor chose his words carefully. 'There is probably something wrong with her kidneys or liver. That's often the case with heavy drinkers. But as to a cure, a lot depends on her. If she survives this episode she'll have to stop drinking, and a lot of people in her situation find that very difficult. That can be harder to cure than the illness itself.'

Her mother was unlikely to stop. Maisie knew that so she didn't answer. The mere thought of trying to help her stop was exhausting. Her dad would do nothing. Ron and Rose couldn't take on that sort of responsibility. It would all fall to her once more.

The front door opened again. Ron peered round the door. 'It's on its way,' he said and stepped back out again without another word. 'Where's he off to now?' Maisie wondered. Something else to worry about.

The ambulance arrived sooner than expected, its siren warning of its arrival. Maisie watched helplessly as two ambulance men lifted her mother onto a stretcher. One of them muttered something about, 'I hate drunk women!'

'I'll come with you!' she cried, then she turned to her neighbour. 'Can Rose stay with you till I get back?'

Mrs Simpkins nodded. 'Go on, girl, I'll look after her. I can smell you've started a soup. I'll take it home with me, and me and her can share it when it's ready. I suppose Ron has a key and he's big and ugly enough to look after himself.'

At the hospital, Maisie was told to wait in the corridor while her mother was taken away somewhere. She sat biting her nails and worrying. What if her mother died? Ron and Rose would be heartbroken, although Ron would never show it. He'd just be angry all the time. Angrier. A nurse took pity on her after half an hour and gave her a cup of tea, promising, 'They won't be long now.'

Finally, a white-coated doctor appeared and stood in front of her. 'Your mother is stable for now.' He paused and rubbed his forehead. 'But her condition is serious. She's suffering from some-thing called alcoholic hepatitis. Her liver is struggling to keep going. We'll keep her here for observation, probably for a couple of days at least.'

Alcoholic hepatitis. The words were strange to her, foreign, clinical, like they belonged to someone's else's life, not her mother's.

'What is alcoholic hepat...' Her tongue struggled to say the words.

'It means your mother's liver is in a bad way. It's inflamed, not working like it should be. We often see this in heavy drinkers, and it can be very serious. We'll help her all we can but unless she stops drinking, it can quickly get worse.'

Maisie bit her lip to hold back tears. 'But will she get better now?'

He sat beside her, his hand on her arm. 'She'll get worse before she gets better. We won't give her alcohol in here so she'll have withdrawal symptoms, sweating, shakes and the like. They're not pretty to see. If you plan on visiting her, you must be prepared. But if she goes back to drinking, this will almost certainly happen again. Her body can't take it.'

'Can I see her?' Maisie didn't really know if she could face it but felt that she should.

'I suggest you wait until visiting time tomorrow. We've given her something to help her sleep now, so she wouldn't know you were there. Go home and get a good night's sleep.'

The night was cool as Maisie walked back from the hospital, her thoughts a tangled mess. She could have got a bus but wanted to sort things out in her head before she got back to Rose and Ron and perhaps her dad. If he'd reappeared from the pub and the bookie. Her mother was alive, but there seemed no way of knowing for how long. And if she recovered from this, would she be able to stop drinking? She'd tried before and each time Maisie had got her hopes up, only for them to be dashed a few days later when her mother began drinking again.

And what was Ron up to? He'd got in with some unsavoury older lads and she was worried they were leading him into mischief. And poor sweet Rose. All her life she'd lived with an unpredictable mother, and the strain often showed on her little face. Thinking about it made Maisie feel as if the weight of the world was on her shoulders. But she pushed them back and knocked on Mrs Simpkins's door. Time to pick up Rose and face whatever the rest of the evening brought.

If only Frank was with her, his calm presence would be sure to bring her comfort and he never judged, never said a bad word about her mum. She was grateful for that when so many other people had plenty to say. She hugged the thought of seeing him again soon, knowing it would give her the courage to carry on.

But she didn't know what the future held for them.

28

'Right, girls, let's get started.' It was a few days after the terrible underground tragedy and Amanda found keeping busy was the best way she could cope. The best way to keep the images and sounds of that night from overwhelming her.

But she'd promised Mrs Pain to get a petition going for better pay and conditions at the factory and Bethan and Maisie said they'd help.

It was the factory midday break so, clutching a pile of forms, they went around the room asking the workers to sign to take action. One question on the form asked if they were in the union or not and if not, would they like to join.

'That Mrs Pain doesn't miss a trick getting more members, does she?' Bethan said. 'But she's just what we need, someone who knows what she's about and not afraid to take action.'

They approached the first group of workers, two young women laughing over a shared joke. Bethan cleared her throat to get their attention. 'Hi, Lily, hi, Nora. We're going round asking people to sign a petition.'

Nora's eyes narrowed. 'A petition? I've never signed one of them in me life. What's it for?'

'Better pay and conditions,' Maisie said. 'Remember we were talking about it with Mrs Pain, the union leader.'

Lily shook her head. 'But neither of us is union members. I can't afford it, ducks.'

Maisie could well understand her situation. Most of them lived from payday to payday, like she did, with never a penny to spare. 'Don't worry about that.' She realised the forms were getting sticky in her hands. 'It won't cost anything to sign and you're not committing yourself to joining the union or anything like that.'

The two women looked at each other. 'Sounds okay to me,' Nora said, reaching for the form. 'I could do with more money, I'm always skint by the middle of the week. Them blokes in the warehouse earn more than us and their work is nowhere near as hard or skilled. It ain't fair. It annoys me every time I think about it.'

'But it sounds risky to me.' Lily was looking towards the door. 'Look, that bloody Mrs Duncan is watching to see who signs.'

'That's why we've all got to stick together. They can't fire all of us.' Maisie could have killed Mrs Duncan for sticking her nose in. She decided to tell Mrs Pain. She had no idea if the union leader could do anything about spying on the workers but it was worth trying.

'All right, I'll sign,' Lily said reluctantly, 'but I hope I don't regret it.'

As the friends moved amongst the workers, heavy footsteps got their attention. They turned and saw Mr Turnbull, the warehouse supervisor, striding towards them. His beefy arms were folded over his chest and his eyes blazed.

'What's going on here then?' he barked, his voice so harsh all conversations ceased.

Amanda stepped forward. 'It's a petition for better pay and conditions. We have every right to...'

'Right? Right? Your right is to do the job you're paid for, not stir up trouble. Management won't stand for this, I can tell you, and nor will I.'

Bethan's eyes blazed. 'You don't get to tell us what we can do, boyo. You're not our supervisor and you can't stop us.' Her Welsh lilt was strong and confident. 'We're not breaking any laws, see, so you can't stop us.'

He sneered. 'You'd better think carefully about what you're doing. The boss, he don't take kindly to rabble-rousers. If you know what's good for you you'll forget all this nonsense right now.'

They didn't budge an inch. They just stood looking at him, waiting for him to wind down like a neglected wind-up toy.

'Have it your way,' he finally hissed. 'But don't come crying to me when you're out on the street without a penny to your name.' With that he spun on his heels and stomped off, leaving a heavy silence in his wake.

Finally Mrs Grey, one of the older machinists, spoke. 'I gotta say, you girls got guts, I'll give you that, but guts don't pay the rent or put food in our kids' bellies.'

Bethan turned to her, her voice pleading for understanding. 'Mrs Grey, you've been here longer than anyone else. You've seen the working conditions get worse and the pay not go up like it should. Surely you agree something needs to be done.'

Mrs Grey raised an eyebrow. 'Don't get me wrong, girl. I'll sign that there petition, but I've seen plenty of girls come and go with ideas like this, love. None 'ave worked yet.'

Respected by everyone there, her words galvanised all but the most stubborn. They queued to sign up before the end of their break.

Later, as the shift finished, the friends huddled together outside the factory. 'Well, that was a right to-do,' Bethan said. 'I was trembling, hope it didn't show.'

'It did not,' Amanda said. 'You were brilliant. We all were and we've got somewhere. It's a start.'

'Tidy,' Bethan said. 'My dad'll be right pleased with me for sticking to my guns.'

Her words struck Maisie like a knife in the stomach. If only she had a father who would be interested. Or a mother, come to that. Her mother was slowly getting better, although the withdrawal symptoms still bothered her and her skin was still a bit yellow. The doctors weren't committing themselves to how long it would be before she could leave hospital. But there was just no way Maisie could discuss what had happened today with her mother. She'd never understand. But Frank was, he was a member of his union and understood how these things worked.

Amanda linked her arms through her friends'. 'We make a great team, whether it's getting well known down the Petticoat or getting petitions signed. I wonder what we'll achieve next?'

Bethan looked around to make sure they couldn't be over-heard. 'Have you found out any more about dodgy business going on in the factory, like?'

Amanda hesitated for a minute. She had found out more but didn't want to burden her friends with the knowledge.

It was just the day before. She had spotted two boxes marked 'Waste' in the warehouse and become suspicious. The waste had only been collected two days earlier and they didn't have that much. Her heart pounding, she looked around to see if anyone else was in the warehouse but they must have been having one of their long tea breaks. Her mouth dry and fingers shaking, she prised open the lid of the nearest box, almost ducking down when it opened with a click that sounded loud enough to be heard at the docks. She knew it was just nerves. It wasn't a loud noise. But she still paused and glanced around again, looking as guilty as any cat burglar. When she was convinced no one was nearby, she looked into the box.

It was anything but waste. It was a roll of good fabric, still with the label on it. She could hardly believe her eyes. There was no time to check though, she heard footsteps heading back towards the warehouse. Carefully she put the lid back on, almost dropping it on the floor in her haste. Then, on her toes, she ran back to the sewing room.

It was proof. She sat at her desk, struggling to calm her breathing and slow down her racing heart. She wished she'd never been so nosy, never looked in the box. She'd found evidence but didn't know what to do about it. It was sure to be moved soon. Who would she tell? She couldn't be sure that anyone she spoke to wasn't in league with Duncan and Turnbull. And she'd heard too many stories of police being on the take to see that as an option. She was stuck.

It was her secret for now. One she wasn't going to worry her friends with.

'Only more of the same,' she replied to Bethan. 'Mrs Duncan sometimes being shifty and looking like she's up to something when she speaks to that warehouse supervisor... That's not proof though, is it?'

'What, with Mr Turnbull who was just in here throwing his weight around?'

'That's right, him. I'm sure they're in it together but there's nothing I can prove yet.'

They had to go back to work, their break was up, but Maisie

just had time to ask Amanda, 'Why are you doing this? I don't understand what you'll get out of it.'

'That's right, cariad,' Bethan said. 'It could just lead you to a load of trouble.'

They'd reached the factory floor and had to split up and go to their workstations. Amanda knew they were right and couldn't really understand why she was pursuing this herself. But she hated dishonesty and if they were doing what she thought they were doing, they were harming the war effort.

But then, as she picked up her clipboard and pencil, she remembered them going to Petticoat Lane. All of them had treated themselves to a pair of stockings even though they knew they were black market. Did that make them as bad as what was going on here at the factory? Everyone had some dodge going on, she thought with a sigh.

29

Later that evening, Amanda arrived at the small union office tucked away on a side street in Poplar. It was about three miles from her home and in the past she would have gone on the underground. Not since the tragedy. Even the thought of going down the steps made her feel faint. No longer could she use the underground as an air-raid shelter either. She had to find public shelters instead.

The union office only had one room, a tiny kitchenette and a toilet shared with other organisations in the building. The walls of the main room were plastered with posters calling for solidarity and better rights for workers.

Amanda clutched the completed petition forms and a small envelope containing money she had collected from those willing to join the union. She was slightly nervous. She liked Mrs Pain but there was no denying she was business-like most of the time and Amanda found that a little intimidating. But she was greeted with a wide smile and she went in.

'Amanda, come on in. It's good to see you.' Mrs Pain indicated a chair next to her desk. Her face was lined with exhaustion but her eyes were as sharp as ever. Her thick cardigan looked like it had seen many winters, but Amanda felt sure Mrs Pain wouldn't think that was important.

She sat and placed the forms and envelope on the desk. 'I've got the signatures – well, me and Bethan – we worked together.' She pushed the papers towards Mrs Pain. 'I hope you'll think we've done enough.'

Mrs Pain picked up the petitions and flipped through the pages, a slight frown on her forehead as she concentrated. 'This is fine work, Amanda. Really fine. You have no idea how hard it can be sometimes to get people to understand the importance of collective action.' She paused. 'Did management give you any trouble?'

Amanda shifted in her seat, feeling a mix of pride and unease. 'Mostly it was fine but that horrible warehouse supervisor Turnbull caught us in the act and tried to intimidate us, to make us stop. And Mrs Duncan's been watching us like a hawk. It made some of the girls too scared to sign.'

'That's often the way,' Mrs Pain said. 'Management uses fear to keep the workers in line, always has, always will. That's why unions are so important. We're needed to remind workers that together, we're stronger than any one supervisor or manager.' She paused and stepped into the little kitchenette where the kettle was whistling. 'Just in time for a cuppa, Amanda. I presume you'd like one.'

She put the cups, milk and teapot on a tray on her desk. 'Let's give it a minute to brew. But I must remind you that this won't be quick, getting the management to change, to be more generous. These signatures are a great beginning, but that's all they are. Real change takes time. It's slow work, often really frustrating. But that's my worry and what you're doing helps a lot.' She stopped talking and poured the tea, passing one to Amanda.

'So what next?' Amanda asked. She felt deflated by Mrs Pain's words.

Mrs Pain took a sip of her tea before answering. 'The petition is a tool, an important one to show management that the workers are united. But it won't be enough to scare them. Strikes do, especially if the Ministry are demanding their quotas be met. Walkouts frighten them too. The threat of their factory grinding to a halt does. That's where this is headed eventually, but I'd rather you didn't mention that. We don't want to frighten off the girls who haven't got used to the idea of a union yet.'

Amanda's stomach knotted at the thought. She pictured the factory floor, the girls bent over their sewing machines, the pressure of quotas and everyday stress. Could she really ask them to risk their jobs? What about her own?

'But strikes are dangerous,' Amanda said quietly. 'They could fire us and hardly anyone there can afford to lose even a day's pay.'

Mrs Pain's expression softened. 'I know it's scary, love. Believe me, I've been through it more times than I can count. But this is for the future, yours and all the other girls at the factory. It's about thinking long-term. Management won't act out of kindness. We have to take what we want.' She gestured to one of the posters on the wall. It showed a crowd of women holding banners, the bold text reading *Equal pay for equal work*.

'I'm sure you know women have been fighting for equal pay since before the war. It's been decades of struggle and we're not there yet. I remember several girls saying they get paid less than the warehouse staff even though their work is more detailed. It's because the warehouse staff are men, of course.'

Amanda nodded slowly, her resolve hardening. 'I'll do my best to make people understand, but I don't suppose I'll win everyone round.'

Mrs Pain topped up her teacup. 'You never will, love, but you'll win round enough and you've already made a great start.' She tapped the pile of petition papers. 'You've got the fire and the brains to see it through. Never doubt yourself.'

As Amanda left the office, the weight of the conversation settled on her shoulders. She clutched her coat tightly against the evening chill, her mind buzzing with thoughts of what lay ahead. But, she reminded herself, it would be slow work and most of the time she wouldn't be required to do anything. Then she remembered the figures that didn't add up and sighed. There was always something to worry about.

30

It was Bethan's turn at the Petticoat, her first, and she got up early, peering out to check the weather. It might be almost April but winter was reluctant to leave. It was just getting light and she was relieved it wasn't raining. She'd been too excited to sleep, and lay awake planning what to wear, determined to keep warm but look good too.

She tied her turban at a jaunty angle, wound her scarf round her neck twice, put on her brightest lipstick and picked up her basket of sewing stuff.

'Dio'r mor!' she muttered to herself as she stepped into the bitter morning. *Good heavens!* It was cold enough to freeze her eyelashes together. Her breath came in white clouds as she hurried through the streets to the market, half running to keep warm. It was Saturday so, unlike a weekday, some houses and tenements showed no sign of life yet. But plenty of others never would, they'd been blown to bits in the Blitz.

Even though she was early, the Petticoat was in full swing when she arrived, a jumble of noise, smells and colour. Big Sal's stall was easy to spot. She was larger than life, dressed in outrageously colourful clothes and her voice could be heard from France. 'Roll up! Roll up! We got everything you need for sewing. Best bargains in London. If you don't come I'll sing you a song instead and you don't want that, do you!'

Bethan slipped beside her, breathless with excitement. She'd visited briefly when it was Amanda's turn, and met Sal again then, but this was her first proper day. 'Morning, Sal, bach. Got a corner saved for me?'

'Course I 'ave, you little firecracker,' Sal said, clearing a space. 'Go on, girl, set out your needles an' stuff. Let's see if you make as much money as your mates did.'

Spreading out the piece of sacking, Bethan laid out her things carefully. Amanda's sign, her threads, needles and scissors, her tape measure and notebook. It didn't look much. She'd have to make up for it by attracting customers with her patter. The previous evening she'd practised it in front of her family. 'Got a hole in your knees? Need a repair done quick?' Each thing she tried had her mam and sister collapsing in fits of giggles and her dad putting his hands over his ears, groaning. After five minutes she gave up. Perhaps Sal would help her.

No one would say Bethan was shy. The first group of lads that passed, three of them walking through like they were the big I-ams, got her attention. She whistled softly and earned herself a raised eyebrow and a laugh.

'Oi, boyos,' she called. 'Your mams'll be worried to death about you with the buttons hanging off your coat. Better than your bum hanging out though!'

Sal looked at her in surprise. 'You don't need any lessons on getting customers, girl.'

The tallest boy, one with red hair that stuck up as if he'd been frightened of something, came over. 'Ain't seen you 'ere before. Never forget a pretty face, me. But don't need any sewing. Pity.'

Bethan laughed. 'Boyo, you should look at the back of your sleeve. Coming undone it is. I can fix that for you while you go to the café. Only cost you thruppence.'

Sal roared with laughter. 'She'll 'ave your boots polished and your hair cut next!'

The other lads teased their friend mercilessly, while Bethan took his coat off his back, sewing faster than she'd ever done before. They tried to chat her up the whole time but she was concentrating on the job so she hardly noticed. Cutting the thread and inspecting her work with satisfaction, she handed him back the coat with a flourish. 'There you are, cariad. Fit for church tomorrow it is.'

The lad gave her a mock bow and pressed the coin into her hand, then kissed it. 'You're a good 'un. Thanks, miss.'

They went off laughing and teasing each other again. Bethan tucked the coin in her purse triumphantly.

A few minutes later she spotted an older woman whose coat hem hung down. 'Hello, Mrs,' she said, almost dragging the woman to the stall. 'The hem of your coat's hanging down a bit. I can sew it for you double quick, like. Can't let down your perfect image now, can you?' All the time she was sewing she flattered the woman, admiring her scarf. 'That colour really suits your skin, and it brings out the colour in your eyes. I wish I had one half as pretty.' The woman chuckled, flattered, and paid sixpence, twice what Bethan had asked for.

Sal patted her on the back. 'Gotta say, I reckon I could be learning from you, young lady, not the other way round.'

By mid-morning, Bethan's corner of the stall was rarely empty. She chatted, joked, flirted and scattered Welsh words into her speech so they sounded like spells. 'Bendigedig!' she cried after finishing a difficult hem. 'Wonderful, that is. Look at it. Strong enough to climb Snowden in!'

People laughed, and laughter drew more people.

Early afternoon, Sal leaned close to Bethan, her voice quieter than usual. 'Watch yourself, Bethan, girl. That Ernie Smithers is in the market, saw 'im sniffing around earlier. About time the law caught up with 'im.'

Bethan felt her mouth go dry. Maisie had warned her about the man and although she couldn't see why he'd want her sewing materials, she didn't want to take any risks.

'Will he come here?'

Sal growled. ''E'd better not. I'll 'ave 'is guts for garters, but keep your eyes peeled.'

Nothing happened for a while and Bethan went back to charming customers to come to her bit of the stall. She shouted to a man passing by, 'Sir, your trousers are hanging by a thread. Come and let me save your dignity!' The crowd laughed, making her forget her nerves. For the moment.

It was half an hour later when the uproar started. A cry went up from nearby. 'Stop! Thief! My bag!'

Heads turned. A man came pelting through the crowd, clutching a woman's handbag close to his chest with one hand, his other arm pumping. Behind him a middle-aged woman walking with a stick was crying out, 'He's got me bag! Help me!'

'It's that bloody Ernie!' Sal shouted and stepped neatly into his path, her arms spread wide. 'Oh, no, you don't, laddie!'

Ernie tried to dodge her, stepping this way and that in a parody of dance steps, but despite her size Sal kept pace with him. 'Drop it, Ernie!' Her voice echoed off nearby stalls.

But he hadn't given up trying. His eyes darted this way and that, but people had stopped walking and were surrounding him. For a minute it looked as if he would push Sal to the ground. He even gave a half-hearted attempt, but he was a skinny man and she didn't budge an inch. Then they heard a piercing whistle and, 'Police. Make way!'

Two uniformed police officers pushed their way through the throng. Desperate, Ernie tossed the bag aside and it fell on Bethan's stall with a thud. Then he darted sideways, ducked under the stall and vanished down an alleyway.

The police gave chase, but Ernie had melted away like butter on a hot day.

The woman snatched her bag back, almost weeping with relief. 'Thank you, thank you, Sal. I thought I'd lost everything.'

Sal shook her head. 'One day they'll catch the little rat, and I hope I'm there to see it. What a coward, running away from a pair of women.'

The crowd cheered, and Sal grinned and gave a mock curtsey. One good thing came of the event. People were more aware of Bethan and the services she was offering. One man asked her to mend a hole in his glove, and another asked her to give a price for making a dress for his daughter. Bethan was thrilled. That was the sort of business they wanted, making dresses. She hoped that once she'd made one, word would spread and they'd get more orders.

'You know...' Sal had overheard the conversation. 'My friend's daughter is getting married in a while. She's a nurse, ain't got much money and she's marrying a soldier. Shot down 'e was, in a wheelchair now, poor sod.' She shook her head thinking about it. 'Would you make 'er a wedding dress? It'd 'ave to be real cheap though. What do you think?'

A wedding dress. Romantic Bethan was thrilled at the idea. She still hadn't found her dream GI but she hadn't given up hope of a big white wedding herself. She'd invite all the relatives from Swansea and they've have a right good Welsh knees-up.

'I'd like to talk to Amanda and Maisie about that, but I'm sure we can help. Give me her address and leave it to me.'

'Right. Why don't you go and 'ave a break, warm yourself up? I'll go after you.'

Bethan had a sandwich in her bag, but knew it would be boring fish paste, perhaps with a bit of soggy tomato if she was lucky. She groaned at the thought of it. Then the smell of warm bread, yeasty and sharp with the faint tang of onions and vinegar got her attention. It pulled her towards the source like the Pied Piper calling the children of Hamelin.

Just along from Big Sal's stall, a short man in a flat cap stood behind his trestle table piled with beigels. They shone golden and were sprinkled with poppy seeds. His wife, wrapped in a woollen shawl over her coat, was slicing slabs of salt beef so thin you could see through them. A big bowl of pickled cucumbers was beside her, glistening in brine.

'Hot beigels!' the man cried, in his rich, rolling accent. 'Six for a shilling! Salt beef like you've never tasted in your life.'

Bethan felt the coins she'd earned burning a hole in her pocket. She'd treat herself, just this once. A flash of guilt at wasting her fish paste sandwiches went through her mind, but then there'd be no shortage of barefoot kids wanting a snack.

The man on the stall saw her hesitate. 'Ach, pretty girl! For you a special price. One extra beigel.' He held up a slice of beef, juicy and pink, steam rising from it. 'It melts in your mouth. Better than butter, better than gold.'

His wife joined in. 'And a pickle too. Always a pickle. It cuts the fat!' Bethan noticed how round she was and doubted the truth of that, but that didn't stop her mouth watering.

She picked a shilling from her purse and took her bag of beigels, the salt beef stuffed inside, pickle on top. Living in Spitalfields she was used to Jewish food, but this was the best she'd ever had.

'Oh, cariad, bach,' she murmured in Welsh. 'This is heaven.'

The vendor beamed. 'You hear that, Rivka? Heavenly. We're selling tickets to heaven for a shilling each!'

People nearby laughed, and Bethan, cheeks pink, turned back towards Sal's stall, determined to give Sal one of the beigels. She caught one of the lads eyeing her food. 'Don't look at me, you'll have to buy your own.' But she opened her bag, took out her fish paste sandwich and gave it to him. 'There you are, bach. Enjoy.'

By the time the market began to thin, Bethan had a tidy pile of coins in her purse and three garments to take home to work on. And the possibility of making a wedding dress with Amanda and Maisie. She was cold through to her bones but satisfied with her day's takings.

'You done well today,' Sal said, slapping her so hard on the shoulder she nearly fell over. 'Quick with your tongue, quicker with your needle.'

Bethan laughed, though her knees still felt weak. 'I thought my legs would give way when that Ernie came at us. You were a real hero.'

'Amanda's turn next Saturday, is it?' Sal spoke as she began to pack her fabrics away for another day.

'It is, and she's a brilliant dress designer. I'll talk to her about a wedding dress.'

Sal called her close and lowered her voice. 'Don't tell anyone, but I'll talk to her about some parachute silk I've got tucked away in the shop.'

Walking home through the fading light, Bethan remembered those words. Parachute silk! She knew it was perfect for a wedding dress, but not legal to buy. Still, she'd seen articles about wedding dresses made of it in the paper so it seemed like the law sometimes turned a blind eye to it. Sometimes it had been decommissioned because it was damaged. Perhaps that's what Big Sal had.

She felt exhausted and yet exhilarated. She thought of Maisie's honesty and troubles with her family, Amanda's cleverness, and her own short-lived romances. Together, they made a strange little group, stitching hems while London burned, trying to carve out something of their own.

She whispered to herself something her mum had always said to her. 'Bydd popeth yn iawn.' *Everything will be all right.*

31

The back room of Big Sal's shop smelled of fabric dust and the little paraffin stove in the corner. The place was a jumble with bolts of cloth piled like barricades, boxes of buttons and a long cracked mirror leaning against one wall.

Maisie, Bethan and Amanda sat side by side on three mismatched chairs, knees touching, cups of tea warming their hands. With the paraffin stove not up to keeping out the chill, they were glad of the hot drink.

Sal bustled in, her big frame blocking the light from the doorway. Her grin spread across her face, the one she wore each time she thought she had done something clever.

'Girls,' she announced, moving to one side. 'This is Grace. Grace, these are the sewing wonders I told you about. They could work in a hospital sewing up wounds, they're so good.' She caught herself. 'Oops, perhaps I shouldn't...'

Behind her stepped a young woman with auburn hair cut in a neat bob. She was pale and looked so tired they wondered if she had been working at the hospital all night. She smiled shyly and perched on the edge of the chair Sal dragged forward for her.

'I've heard so many good things about you,' she said softy. 'It's really kind of you to see me.'

'We're really thrilled to meet you,' Amanda said, getting up and shaking her hand. 'You must be excited with your wedding coming up.'

Grace's smile lit her face. 'I am, but at the moment I'm doing nights and I'm often too tired during the day to do much. With the bombing you can imagine how busy we are.'

'So you're going to be a spring bride.' Bethan's eyes sparkled imagining it, her Welsh lilt brightening the room. 'Well, early summer.'

A faint flush made Grace's pale cheeks colour. 'Yes. I'm marrying Robert. He was one of my patients at St Bartholomew's.'

Bethan leaned forward. 'A soldier then, is he?'

'Yes, he was injured in North Africa like so many other men. His spine was...' She faltered, folding her hands together. 'Let's just say he's in a wheelchair now and always will be. We didn't think he'd live at first and each time I went on duty I hardly dared look at where his bed was in case he'd died. But it turns out he's strong and he was determined to heal. Attitude has such a lot to do with how well patients do.'

'So it was a hospital romance, like those Mills and Boon books I gets from the library.'

Outside they could hear the market in full swing, vendors shouting their wares, footsteps, music. One of the other stall-holders was looking after Sal's stall for a while. She usually looked after the shop so she was well versed in selling fabric.

'Hospital romance?' Grace smiled. 'Well, he's not a handsome doctor like they are in those books. He's an engineer and we're strictly forbidden to have relationships with patients. If Matron found out we'd be fired immediately. But...'

'But you fell in love...' Bethan was off on one of her romantic daydreams, this time a hospital one where she did indeed meet a tall, dark handsome surgeon.

'Yes, we fell in love but we didn't do anything about it until Robert was discharged.' She laughed. 'We had our first date the very next day!' Grace continued, her voice firmer now. 'And if you agree to make my dress, you'll get to meet my mother...'

'Good luck with that!' Sal laughed.

Grace looked at her and frowned. 'She's not a bad person. But she thinks I should marry someone able-bodied, who can provide for me. She doesn't listen when I tell her he can get special training to use his existing skills in a new type of job.' She shook her head. 'I know it won't be easy but I love him. He makes me laugh even on the worst day. He makes my world feel safe.'

'Ah, that's lovely, that is,' Bethan said, a dreamy look in her eyes.

'He sounds like the sort of man any woman would be proud of,' Amanda said. 'Shall we talk about your dress?'

'Hear, hear!' Sal said, standing up. 'I told Grace you were the very ones to make it for her. Didn't I say? You showed me them wedding dress sketches you did, Amanda, and I was dead impressed. The best girls with a needle in the East End you are. And what's more, I might 'ave just the thing here...'

Sal vanished into the shop, where they could hear her moving things around then she reappeared carrying a canvas sack, tied tightly at the neck.

'Now, ladies, you gotta keep your mouths shut about this.' Her eyes twinkled with wicked fun. 'We don't want the law to know about this, do we?' She untied the cord and drew out a length of shimmering fabric. It slipped through her thick fingers like water, its pale cream colour catching the light with a gentle sheen.

The friends knew what it was, but Grace gasped. 'It's... it's...

parachute silk, isn't it? I've heard about it but never seen it. It's beautiful.'

Sal grinned like the cat who got the cream. 'That's right, Grace. Don't ask me 'ow I got it. I'd have to kill you if I told you!'

Grace got up and touched the fabric, running her hand over it with a sigh. It was soft as a whisper, warming under her fingers. 'It's lovely... I couldn't possibly...'

'Course you could. Your mum might be tough at times but once she did me a good favour. This is my chance to pay 'er back. You'll be doing me a favour. Mind you, I expect an invite to the wedding. No good me keeping it 'idden, is it? Better to see it on a pretty girl like you.'

Maisie reached out and touched the fabric. She thought of all the brides she'd seen in magazines, of women cobbling together dresses from sheets, or adapting their grandmother's wedding dress. They did a good job but this was something special.

Grace looked hesitant again. 'Sal. You're very kind, but I can't afford silk.'

Sal shrugged. 'I'm not daft, girl, I know that. But this ain't a perfect length. The bloke what used it must've landed in a field. He lived, so I 'eard, so no worry there. No, these girls'll 'ave to work 'ard to get the stains out and be clever cutting round those ones they can't get rid of.' She stood looking pleased with herself. 'So I'm gonna let you 'ave it at a knock-down price.'

Grace still looked uncertain. 'I'd love nothing more, but my mother... she can hardly keep us fed. I think you know my dad was killed in 1940, flying over France. Since then, it's just her, me and my younger brother and sister. I couldn't take food from their mouths for a dress, even with fabric as beautiful as this. Then there's paying these three lovely ladies.'

The room felt silent. Outside, the rattle of a costermonger's barrow clattered past.

Bethan leaned closer, her voice gentle. 'Cariad, your Robert deserves to see you looking even more beautiful than you do today. You deserve it too. And well...' She looked at her friends. 'I'm sure our charges won't be too much either.'

'Tell you what,' Amanda said. 'I've done some sketches of wedding dresses, just for ideas. Why don't we have a look at them and see if you fancy any. Obviously we haven't cut any fabric or decided on anything, so there's plenty of chance to get the dress exactly right for you.'

They spent a happy fifteen minutes studying Amanda's sketching, discussing style, length, sleeves, beads, neckline and more.

'I really want something simple,' Grace said, running her fingers over one of the designs. 'Something like this. I've always thought a simple design can look very elegant.'

Amanda clapped her hands. 'You know, as soon as I saw you, I thought of that design. It would be perfect for your slender figure and long legs, but I didn't want to sway you so I haven't said anything before.'

'Well, that's settled then,' Sal said. 'I expect these girls'll give you a price in a day or two, and so will I, then you can decide if you want to go ahead. 'Ow's that?'

Later, when Grace had gone, the three girls lingered in the back room with the fabric pooled on the table between them. Sal was back in the shop and they could hear her booming voice, but here they felt like they were in another world.

'I wonder if he really did live?' Maisie mused. 'She wouldn't say if he'd died, would she? Some people would be too superstitious. And she said it had been decommissioned but I'm not sure we can believe her.'

'Well, I'm not going to ask her again,' Amanda said. 'Let's just believe what she said. Anyway, I can't see any blood on it and that's a good sign.'

Bethan ran her fingers over the fabric again. 'She's broke. What're we going to do about charging her?'

Maisie nodded. 'Her mum's a widow and the husband-to-be is in a wheelchair. I don't think we should charge her. We can ask her for a photo so we can show it if we want to make any more wedding dresses. As far as I'm concerned that'll be payment enough.' She looked at the others. 'What do you think?'

Amanda sighed, but her mouth curved. 'So we do it for nothing then. But it'll be good for us too. We've never made anything like this. We'll learn a lot doing it.'

Bethan grinned. 'We'll love doing every stitch and I'm looking forward to seeing her in it. If we don't get invited to the wedding I vote we sneak in anyway, at least for the service.' She reached out her hands and the others took them.

'To our first wedding dress,' Amanda said. 'Who knows what it will lead to? But first, we have to find a place to cut out this lovely fabric.'

32

The door handle rattled and for one terrible moment the three girls froze. Amanda's scissors paused mid-cut, while Maisie held a piece of the silk so tight she screwed it up. Bethan's face went chalk white.

How could they explain to the police why they had RAF property, the parachute, spread across Mrs Duncan's cutting table at the factory?

They looked at each other, wide-eyed. There was no time to hide, they were going to get caught. What they were doing must be illegal, Amanda thought, though Big Sal never admitted it. Her hands holding the scissors shook.

'Damn. It must be stuck again,' came a man's voice. Billy from the warehouse doing his rounds. The friends sagged with relief as the footsteps moved away.

'That was a close one,' Maisie said. 'If only one of us had a room big enough to cut out fabric.' She sighed. 'Still, we can sew in Bethan's bedroom.'

'Shh,' Amanda said, whispering. 'We need to get this done and get out of here before we get caught.' She had spent ages at home trying to get the marks out of the fabric. She'd got rid of some, but others would have to be worked around.

'Here, hold this edge down,' she ordered the other two. Soon they were laying out the pattern pieces she had made, juggling them this way and that to avoid the stains.

'How's it going with your latest Yank?' Maisie asked. 'I can't remember who this one is. Has he taken you out somewhere this week?'

Bethan's face lit up. 'James?'

She closed her eyes for a minute and imagined again what life would be like if she married a handsome GI and moved to America. Somewhere glamorous. He'd be rich and sexy and fall madly in love with her. She'd only have to snap her fingers, and he'd do whatever she wanted. She sighed and shook her head. One day...

'You going to see him again?'

Bethan shook her head. 'Nuh, he was too handsy if you know what I mean, like a limpet, took some shaking off I can tell you. Their lads earn a lot more than our lads too. It doesn't seem fair, does it?'

'Enough of that,' Amanda said with a smile. 'Come on, let's get this done so we can get out of here before we get caught.'

Footsteps nearby made them all freeze again. Work stopped until the danger had passed. Bethan wiped her forehead. 'Nerveracking this is, mind. Glad we don't have to do it very often. I'm not cut out to be a criminal.'

'Pass me that pin,' Amanda said, determined to get the job done as soon possible. She stood back and looked at the spread of fabric. 'I think we can get the sleeves out of this bit if we're careful to avoid the marks.'

'"Ow you getting on with your Frank?' Bethan asked Maisie. 'How many dates have you had now? Nice lad, I'm sure, but his ears! So big I bet on a clear night he could pick up radio signals from Berlin.'

Maisie glared at her and thumped her arm. 'Less of your Welsh cheek. It's what's between those ears that counts. He's a good man and that's the important thing. We've been out quite a few times now. I like him a lot.'

Bethan rolled her eyes. 'There's nice, that is. Can't beat a good cwtch.'

'Girls, girls!' Amanda said. 'Let's get this job done then we can talk about your love lives.'

'Anyway,' Maisie went on, but working as she spoke now. 'I prefer a good man who won't get shipped out at a moment's notice. Or who won't get a girl in trouble and then bugger off.'

Bethan folded the fabric pieces they had cut and carefully wrapped them in some old wallpaper. With paper rationing, they had to use whatever they could get. 'Anyways, do you think you might have a future with him?'

Maisie moved the fabric across the table and helped Amanda place the next pattern piece. 'He's... a good man... steady... doesn't drink too much. Has plans to move somewhere a bit nicer and buy a house. Maybe one of those new prefabs they're planning. He'd like to keep chickens, but his mum's back yard isn't big enough.'

Bethan scoffed. 'Chickens? Wow, he's got big dreams! Not exactly California, is it?'

'And he's got a cat that's blind in one eye,' Maisie said, tongue in cheek. 'If our relationship goes anywhere, we'll have to have it live with us!'

'Stop that, girls,' Amanda said. 'We've got a dress to cut out, remember, and time's getting on.'

She nearly dropped her scissors when a sharp knock came, three quick taps that might as well have been gunshots in the silent room. Bethan squeaked and dropped her box of pins on the floor with a jarring thud, followed by an explosion of tiny, high-pitched pings as the pins scattered in every direction.

'Girls?' Frank's whisper came through the keyhole. He sounded urgent. 'Better get out of there. Some bigwig is doing the rounds, ready for something or other tomorrow. Ministry, I expect. You've got about ten minutes before they get here so wrap up whatever you're doing double quick.'

'What's he doing here?' Bethan said. 'He doesn't work here.'

'Not often, but he had a bit of time to spare so he said he'd keep an eye open for us and warn us if anything looked like going wrong.'

Frank's footsteps rapidly retreated, leaving the three of them looking at each other with dry mouths. The fabric, which had looked luxurious a moment earlier, now seemed like a burden.

'Quick!' Maisie ordered. 'Wrap all the bits up.'

'We need to make sure we get all the pins,' Amanda ordered. 'Old Duncan'll know they're not hers for sure. I'll do the pattern pieces and wipe down the table.' Heart in her mouth, she yanked her handkerchief from her sleeve, wiping away the silvery threads and shoving them in her pocket.

The voices grew louder – they weren't far away now. Bethan's hands shook so badly she dropped a piece of fabric. 'Damn, thick as mince, me!'

They were still wrapping the pieces when the lights on the stairwell clicked on. The voices grew louder.

'Window!' Amanda whispered, her head jerking towards it. 'There's a fire escape.' They knew it got used sometimes during air raids but had never used it themselves and never in the dark with trembling legs and a parcel of parachute fabric to carry. The metal stairs zig-zagged down the building like a giant's ladder. Below were dustbins where a dog was looking for a meal.

'I don't care what the Ministry say...' The voice was so close now. 'But we'd better check every floor, every room.'

A piece of fabric, a sleeve, fell to the floor as they climbed out of the window. Terrified, Maisie reached back in and just about managed to grab it, tucking it in her blouse. Then she tried to close the window. It squeaked louder than a mouse being chased by a hundred cats.

'Did you hear that?' The man's voice sounded louder than ever. 'Is there someone here?'

The evening air outside hit them like a slap, carrying the dreaded wail of an air-raid siren. Its timing couldn't have been worse. Or perhaps better. At least the men would give up their search for now and head for safety.

'Move!' Amanda shouted over the wail.

Clutching the fabric as if it were worth a king's ransom, they scuttled down the ladder as fast as they dared. White-knuckled and white-faced with fear, they thought every step would bring death. The stairs creaked, swayed and groaned in protest.

Searchlights were scanning the sky, and they could hear the ack-ack of the anti-aircraft guns in the distance. Below them people were running to their shelters, urged to hurry by the ARP wardens.

They hit the ground running, terrified they would drop the fabric. Amanda tucked it in her coat, making her look as if she was in the family way. Ahead was the underground entrance but both Bethan and Amanda stopped dead when they saw it.

Maisie looked at them in amazement. 'Come on, you two. Feet stuck to the ground, is it?'

To her surprise, Bethan let out a sob so loud, Maisie heard it over the siren. 'Oh, I'm so stupid.' She belatedly realised both her friends still wouldn't go down underground. 'The warden'll tell us where else to go.'

It was the basement of St Cuthbert's church, rapidly filling with people and cold as the grave. But they were glad to find it.

Maisie let out a shaking laugh. 'Blooming 'eck. That was too close for comfort.'

'Proper twp,' Bethan agreed, her Welsh accent thick with relief. 'At least if we get bombed down here we'll already be closer to God!'

Above them, the ceiling trembled with distant explosions. But down here in the dim light, their treasure securely between them, they finally felt safe.

But that didn't stop Bethan's mind giving her horrific flash-backs to that terrible underground tragedy. Would she ever forget the weight of the bodies? How they were packed together on the stairs, limp and lifeless or screaming in pain? Her hands had shaken as she pulled a little girl free, her fingers trembling with the strain of holding someone's leg out of the way. She remembered how the air was thick with dust and the dreadful smell of panic. Every cry for help cut through her like a knife. She'd done what she could, dragging people out one by one, slowly, painfully, but the silence that followed was worse. She had these daytime nightmares, whatever they were called, more often than she admitted to anyone and the silence punched her heart as much as the cries.

Amanda speaking brought her back to the moment and she let go of a breath she hadn't realised she was holding.

'The bride will have her dress after all,' Amanda said with relief. 'Let's hope she likes it.'

33

Maisie and her mother got out of the taxi that had brought them from the hospital. The breeze smelled of the docks and the grease and hot oil from the engineering factories. As they neared the front door, a neighbour spotted them. 'Good to see you 'ome, Elsie,' she shouted. But Elsie, Maisie's mother, hesitated on the doorstep.

'Will... will... I...' she murmured.

'You'll be fine, Mum,' Maisie said, squeezing her hand. 'We all want you home. We've missed you. Don't worry.' Her mother looked thinner than she had been for years, her skin still an unnatural colour, although not as yellow as it had been. She clutched Maisie's arm for balance.

'I suppose we'd better go in,' she said and forced a smile that never reached her eyes.

As soon as they got in the front door, Rose came running up and wrapped her arms round her mother's legs. 'Mummy, you're home, you're home.'

Elsie rubbed her hair. 'Never thought I'd leave that hospital, let alone get back here, but I'm glad to see you, Rosy Posy.'

'You're here now,' Maisie said. 'We'll just take it one day at a time.' Even as she spoke, the doctor's words echoed in her mind. *She can recover, but only if she stops drinking altogether.* The doctor's face had been sombre. *If she doesn't, it will kill her.*

Maisie settled her mum on the settee and went to put on the kettle. But her mother reached for her arm before she'd taken a step. 'I've made a mess of everything, haven't I, love?'

Maisie knelt beside her, holding her mother's hand again. 'You're here now, Mum. That's what matters. A new start, a second chance.'

Her mother rested her head on the back of the settee, her eyes glistening. For a moment, Maisie allowed herself to believe the new start would work. Yet deep inside, she struggled to believe it.

She'd got no further than putting the kettle on when her Aunt Betty came bustling in without knocking. 'Thought you could use a bit of help,' she said gruffly, setting down a few things on the kitchen table.

'Aunt Betty, that's kind of you.' Maisie struggled to hold back the tears that had been threatening since her mother collapsed. Funny how it's easier to hold yourself together during tough times, but kindness can lead to tears.

'You're a good girl, Maisie,' her aunt said, nodding an acknowledgement that she'd seen her mother, who seemed to be asleep. 'Your mum, and that useless lump of a dad of yours, are lucky to have you.' She got out the cups and saucers, milk jug and sugar bowl. 'I'll come around more often, sweetheart. You've been carrying this on your own for too long. It's not right. You should be out having a good time at your age, not being a nursemaid to a...'

Maisie placed the last plate on the drying rack and wiped her hands on the tea towel. Aunt Betty checked Rose and Ron and that Maisie's mum was asleep then quietly closed the kitchen door. She gestured to Maisie to sit down and sat opposite.

'She wasn't always like this, you know,' Aunt Betty said, her voice low. She sounded wistful.

'Mum? What do you mean?'

Betty nodded. 'Your mum, she was such a lovely little thing when we was kids. Always cheerful, singing, messing about, enough to drive you crazy but we all loved her. You wouldn't think it now, would you?'

Maisie shook her head, unsure what to say. Her aunt could be critical, but she'd never talked about their past before. Not like this.

Betty sighed. 'Dad, our dad, not yours, well, he wasn't up to much. He had a wicked temper on him, and when he drank, and that was almost every night, his mood always got worse. We soon learned to keep out of his way.'

She looked sad as if she was remembering times from their childhood. 'The trouble was, your mum was the youngest. She couldn't have been more than a toddler when he'd come in worse for wear and then if she as much as whimpered, much less ask for anything, well... I'll leave it to your imagination.'

'But what did he do?' Maisie couldn't imagine. Her dad was no angel but he'd never been violent.

'Don't get me wrong, there were worse dads. Some of 'em lived down our street, drinking was just a way of life to a lot of men. But our mum, your gran, she didn't do much, anything really, to protect us. If it got really bad she'd turn to drink too. No wonder your mum grew up thinking booze was the way you coped with life.'

They were interrupted by a knock on the door, making them jump. Maisie looked at the clock. 'That'll be the rent man. He's late.' She stood up and got the rent book and some money out of the kitchen drawer. 'I won't be a minute.'

When she came back, they continued the conversation as if it had never stopped. 'So Mum didn't stand a chance.' She paused and looked down at her hands. 'But you've never taken to the drink.'

Betty reached across the table and held her hand. 'Your mum was teetotal for ages when she met your dad. Happy as the day is long she was, especially when you were born. She was so proud of you. You were the best-dressed baby in the street even if most of your clothes did come from jumble sales.'

Maisie struggled to remember that but images of her mother drunk, trying to put on airs and graces, got in the way. 'What happened? Why did she change?'

'Life got in the way. It often does. Money got really tight, your dad began gambling and was hardly around. Worse than useless he was. Your mum did try, honest she did, she wanted to keep you all as a happy family but the booze won. It started with just one drink, but it never ends that way. That's why I never touch a drop of the stuff.'

Silence settled between them, heavy with emotions. 'It's not anyone's fault, you know,' Betty said. 'Not hers, not yours. But she's got to decide to stop and mean it or I dread to think what will happen.'

At teatime, the whole family gathered round the small table for their tea – Maisie, her mum, her dad, Aunt Betty, Rose and Ron. They'd been having simple meals for ages, bread and dripping, drop scones, potato cakes, but Aunt Betty had brought round some corned beef and they had corned beef hash and cabbage. It felt like a feast to all but one of them.

Maisie's dad grumbled. 'Hmm, what'd'ya call this then?' He

pushed the food round on his plate. 'I'm going to Joe's Café. Better bloody food there.'

No one was surprised. It was more surprising that he had been there at all. Not a word of encouragement for Maisie's mum or thanks to Aunt Betty.

When he'd gone, Maisie's mum turned to the others. 'I'll be better this time, I promise.' Her voice was so low, it was as if she didn't believe the words she was saying herself.

Rose, wide-eyed and hopeful, reached out to touch her mum's arm. 'We believe you, Mummy. We all do, don't we?' She looked around at the others for support and they all nodded. Luckily she was too excited to notice none of them looked convinced.

'I won't drink no more,' her mum said. 'I swear it. I'll be good, Rose, and for you too, Ron.' He merely shook his head.

Maisie wanted to believe it, she really did.

Later that evening, after everyone had gone to bed, Maisie found herself in the kitchen staring at the wall, seeing nothing. She heard a soft tap at the back door and opened it to find Frank standing there, his cap in his hand and a cautious smile on his face.

'I know it's late, but I just wanted to see how it went. I can't stay long.'

Maisie stepped aside to let him in. 'I'm sorry I haven't seen you much, Frank.' She reached for his hand. 'It all gets on top of me sometimes. All this stuff and everything else.'

He put his arms around her and rubbed her back as if comforting a child. 'You don't have to do everything yourself. I want to help, you only have to say.'

She stroked his cheek. 'I just... find it difficult to ask for help. I'm so used to locking all my worries inside and just getting on with everything.'

Frank let her go and picked up his cap again. 'Well, you don't have to carry the weight of everything on your own any more. I'm here and we can face everything together.'

At the back door they kissed and she clung to him, never wanting him to leave.

But for the first time in ages, Maisie felt a flicker of hope. Aunt Betty was going to help, so was Frank, and her mum really seemed to mean it when she said she would become sober. Perhaps things were going to get better after all.

Soon after he left she went upstairs, knowing she'd never sleep until she'd checked on her mother, so she gently opened her bedroom door and stepped inside. The dim light from the landing illuminated her mother's sleeping form. She looked so peaceful, her breathing even, and Maisie felt a little of her tension ease away.

Then, as she turned to leave, her foot nudged something under the bed. Puzzled, she crouched down and reached for it, her fingers closing on a horribly familiar shape.

A bottle.

She could make out it was the cheap gin her mother had favoured for so long. The bottle was nearly full, but it merely being there told its own story. All those promises, and that regret, the kind help from Aunt Betty – it all felt as if it could fall apart like a house of cards in a gale.

She wanted to throw the bottle against the wall, to shatter it into a million pieces. Instead, she carried it downstairs and emptied the contents down the sink. Then she put the bottle on the table where her mother would see it and went to bed knowing sleep would never come.

Next morning her mother came downstairs bleary-eyed. She stopped in her tracks when she saw the bottle. 'That's where it...' she began then stopped herself. 'I didn't drink it! I haven't touched a drop. It must have been there from before.'

Maisie knew it was a lie. When her mother was in hospital she had gone through the house checking everywhere where a bottle could be hidden. She emptied all she found and threw away the bottles. How on earth, she wondered, had her mother managed to get hold of it?

'Mum, you promised.' Maisie's arms were folded, her expression hard.

'I know, sweetheart,' her mum whispered, tears streaming down her face. 'I'm trying, Maisie, I swear it. I only had a little bit. You must have thrown the rest away. You did, didn't you?' This last part was almost said with hope.

'You know, Mum, it'll kill you. I don't want to be without a mum and Rose and Ron still really need you. If you can't stop drinking for yourself, stop for them.'

More promises.

But could Maisie trust her again?

34

There was a light drizzle as the three friends made their way to St Mark's church hall. The path was edged with daffodils, their cheerful colour a sure sign spring was on the way.

The air inside the hall was heavy with tobacco smoke and the sour smell of damp coats. Rows of wooden chairs had been set out, and every one was filled, mothers with children on their knees, old men leaning on sticks, people on crutches, two with plasters on broken arms. The atmosphere was electric. This was the first council meeting after the underground tragedy at Bethnal Green station and feelings were high.

'Come on,' Bethan whispered. 'There's seats at the back.'

They slipped down the side aisle, nodding to people they knew. Bethan's face was pale in the dim light. Like Amanda, she hadn't spoken much all day. Amanda leaned towards her and took her hand. She knew what Bethan was going through. The same as her. She had nightmares every night. Sometimes she was helping part of the rescue team, just like really happened. Those dreams were frightening enough, but worse were the other ones. The ones where she was one of the victims, falling down the steps and crushed beneath the weight of hundreds of bodies piling on top of her. Limbs snapping, breath squashed until she was no more. She'd wake up drenched in sweat, knowing she'd never get back to sleep.

Three people sat at a table facing everyone else. On it were papers, three glasses and a jug of water. The man in the middle, who looked vaguely familiar to Amanda, stood and tapped his glass. The sound got everyone's attention and the hubbub in the room died down so quickly it was as if it had been turned off.

'Ladies and gentlemen,' he said, his voice clear and crisp. 'Thank you for coming here this evening. I am Councillor Jones and with me tonight are two local people you'll undoubtedly recognise, Reverend Smith and Mrs Bateman. I'd like to suggest that before we begin we stand and have a minute's silence in remembrance of those we lost in this terrible tragedy.'

There was much shuffling of chairs as people stood and the sound of sobbing came from several people attending.

The silence was poignant, every person there remembering someone they had lost, or who had been injured, or like Amanda and Bethan, remembering being part of the rescue team. Yet beneath the grief there was anger. Fists clenched, jaws tightened, eyes narrowed. The sorrow in the hall was fathomless, but it was not gentle. It was edged with anger, a demand for answers and justice.

When the minute ended, the councillor spoke again. 'On behalf of the borough council I extend our deepest condolences to each and every one of you. As you know, the stairway to the underground station has been made safer now with the addition of handrails...'

'Yeah,' a man shouted from near the front, 'and why didn't we 'ave them before? We asked and asked but nothing ever bloody got done until it was too damn late!'

Around and behind him people muttered in agreement, a few shaking their heads or even their fists in fury.

Councillor Jones held up his hand for silence which was slow coming. 'I do understand your anger. As you probably know, we in the council asked the government on three separate occasions for funds to install the rails and better lighting but only now has that been forthcoming. Like you, I know it is too little, too late.'

He paused and looked around before talking again. 'Now, many of you want to know about compensation. It is being handled under the Personal Injuries Act of 1939. Claims are being processed but inevitably, with such a large number of claims, it will take time.'

'And 'ow am I supposed to feed my kiddies while I wait?' a woman shouted. She had a child on her knee and another sitting by her feet. 'My old man'll never work again.'

'I appreciate how difficult it is for you,' Mrs Bateman said, standing for the first time. 'As you know, many local charities and churches have been offering support and have been helping to identify the victims. Your local library will have a list of organisations to approach if you are unsure where to turn.'

Her words prompted a fresh outburst of chatter amongst those present.

A big burly man stood up, arms folded across his chest. 'We've 'ad to pay to bury our dead, bury our children, our loved ones. I'm a proud man, never asked for charity before in me life.'

Amanda's mind drifted for a moment, and she was back in the days immediately after the tragedy. She remembered the small Baptist church hall down the road, crowded with people who had lost loved ones. Parish volunteers moved quietly amongst them, offering small amounts of money, food, even a bundle of clothes and blankets. Friendly society representatives scribbled notes and wrote in their ledgers, handing out tiny sums to help pay for coffins and simple funeral arrangements. Amanda could see it wasn't much, enough for the basics, but it was something. Even in the middle of their grief, she saw neighbours pooling what little they had, women from the WI delivering tea, candles lit in windows. The memory of it made her throat tighten again, but it was warming too. East Enders were poor, but they often found ways to help each other.

The councillor tapping his glass once more brought Amanda's attention back to the moment. He was trying to reassure people that their claims for compensation would be dealt with, although he admitted he couldn't say how long that would take.

Shouts, cries, mutterings filled the room. Someone banged on the floor with his stick. The sorrow of the silence had changed to anger, and now it came spilling out.

'Why ain't the council paid us nothing, that's what I want to know,' someone shouted and others called out in agreement.

Councillor Jones held his hand up for silence again. Once more it was a long time coming. 'I'm afraid the council can't provide compensation without going through the normal procedures.'

The burly man stood up again. 'Procedures? Procedures? Procedures don't pay the bills, do they? And where were the procedures to get the lighting and handrails done? If it was Kensington or Chelsea, they've have sorted it double quick. But it's only Bethnal Green so we can all go rot.'

Amanda felt herself flooded with anger. Surprising herself, she stood up. 'He's right,' she called out, her voice ringing across the hall. Heads turned. 'We was there, me and my friend here. We saw it with our own eyes, we helped the rescue teams. No lamps, no handrail, just a black pit. People fell because they couldn't see, and there was nothing to stop the crush.'

Bethan stood up too, trembling. 'It wasn't an accident waiting to happen. It already happened. And what else have the council neglected that puts our lives in danger?'

The hall erupted once more, applause and shouts of agreement. The councillor looked dumbfounded, his notes clutched uselessly in his hand.

An older woman in the front row stood and raised her voice. 'Those girls are right. We need more than condolences. I lost two of my family in that crush. Gone forever.' She stopped and wiped her eyes with her hankie. 'We need safety for the living and justice for the dead.'

'You were wonderful, both of you,' Maisie said later. 'I've never seen you speak out like that.'

When the meeting finally broke up, the three friends stepped out into the cold night air. The blackout covered the streetlights, and their shielded torches only helped a little.

'We've got to do something,' Bethan said. 'How about we get together with the ladies at the WI and put on a charity dance? All proceeds to families affected. It won't bring their loved ones back, but it'll help, won't it?'

35

The delicate white silk draped over Amanda's arm seemed to shine in the light from the window, turning the salvaged parachute fabric into something magical.

The three friends had spent hours cutting and sewing the dress together ready for this first fitting. 'If we spend this many hours every time we might as well work overtime at the factory!' Maisie grumbled more than once.

'But it wouldn't be such fun, would it, bach,' Bethan said. 'Every time we make a dress I imagine myself walking down the aisle, see. Flowers everywhere, a handsome man waiting for me...'

'One with a white picket fence?' Amanda said with a grin.

Bethan glared at her. 'A girl can dream, can't she? I'm still going to find Mr Right. Mr American Right. He'll be tall, handsome, kind...'

'Not a liar...' Maisie chipped in, 'or have a wife back home...'

'Okay, you horrible pair. I'll be more careful next time. I wonder if that Buddy's found some other poor girl to go out with.'

The bride-to-be, Grace, was standing in her petticoat ready to try on the dress. Her eyes shone at she looked at it. Outside they could hear a tram trundling along Wentworth Street and somewhere a woman shouting to her kids to come in for their tea.

'Just think, not long ago someone was floating down from the sky in that,' Maisie said, stroking the fabric. 'Light as air it is.'

'Don't say that!' Grace's mother, Mrs Cooper, said. 'It's unlucky.' She had a mirror facing the door with a St Christopher charm hanging from it and a horseshoe above the kitchen door. On the mantelpiece was a four-leaf clover in a wooden frame.

'Oh, I should have said,' Maisie quickly replied. 'He got down safely.' Her fingers were crossed behind her back. She still had no idea if it was true. Big Sal said it was, but Maisie suspected she'd just made that up. 'You've got to admit it's a lovely bit of silk.'

'You be careful with them pins.' Mrs Cooper was worrying the edge of her apron. 'My mother always said a pinprick at the fitting meant tears at the wedding.'

Grace ignored her comments, stood on a chair and they helped her slide the dress over her slim body. 'We need to get this just right so it looks as good sitting down as it does when you're standing.'

Mrs Cooper sniffed. 'In my day brides stood at the altar...'

Grace sighed. 'Mum, I've told you. I want to be at the same level as Tom when I say my vows.'

Another sniff. 'And will he be able to be a proper husband to you? That's what I want to know. You never answer that question, do you, young lady.'

'Mum!' Grace couldn't believe her mother was talking about such things in front of strangers. She was wasting her time trying to stop her.

'And I want some grandchildren one day. All my friends have got them. I thought you was going to end up an old maid, going off and training to be a nurse like that.'

'Mum, we've got visitors. Save your arguments until they've gone, please. And I'm only twenty-four, hardly an old maid. Let me try this dress in peace.'

Her mother put her hands on her hips. 'I'm only trying to help. What sort of a life will you have being nursemaid to a cripple, that's what people will say, you know. Mrs O'Brian down the road was talking about it only the other day. She thinks he's marrying you to get a free live-in nurse. That's what she said.'

Grace shook her head. 'She's an interfering old bat who always sees the worst in everything. I'm marrying Tom because I love him. You'll have to get used to the idea.'

Her displeasure obvious in every step, Mrs Cooper stomped to the kitchen and they heard her putting the kettle on. They all paused when they heard a plane overhead, then relaxed when they heard the familiar drone of an RAF engine.

'Sorry, girls,' Grace said. 'She's just nervous. She wants everything to be perfect. Worries what people will say. Always has, always will.' She turned to look in the long mirror they'd brought downstairs from the bedroom.

'How did you and your boyfriend meet? I bet it was romantic.' Bethan wanted everything to be romantic.

Grace laughed. 'Anything but, I'm afraid. I think I told you he was a patient of mine. When I first saw him he'd just been admitted. He was hardly aware of where he was and I had to get him ready to go to the operating theatre. At that stage, they weren't sure if they could save his leg.' She went silent for a minute, remembering when he realised his leg had been amputated. 'It's so hard for a man, a soldier, to lose a limb...'

'What do they do with the spare legs and things?' Bethan interrupted. She wasn't known for her tact.

'Bethan!' Amanda nudged her so hard she almost fell over.

'Ignore that,' she said to Grace. 'So you got to know each other as he recovered. I suppose it gave you a chance to get to know the real him.'

'We nurses have a saying,' Grace said, twirling this way and that so her dress moved around her. 'We say a patient's charm doesn't last longer than his bandages, but his did. He is a good man, honest, and I know I can trust him with my life, our lives. But enough of that, let me have a proper look at this dress.'

Her eyes became soft when she saw herself. 'Oh, Amanda, I know it's not finished but it's just lovely. And I've never seen one like it anywhere. Thank you so much.' She smoothed the fabric over her hips and down her arms with pleasure. 'I'd have been happy with a quiet wedding at the Town Hall but now I've seen this I've changed my mind. Mum wanted Christ Church but it has steps. They'd be too difficult for Tom.'

'You look smashing,' Maisie said. 'You'll be the envy of everyone in... St Matthew's, isn't it? We've got some little scraps left over. If you like you can have them to make bows to put at the end of the pews. I've seen pictures of that in society weddings.'

Mrs Cooper came in with a tray laden with cups, saucers, and a blue and white striped teapot. She put it down and stood looking at her daughter, head on one side. 'Hmm. Gotta say it's looking quite pretty. Needs a bit of adjustment though.'

'Mum, this is the first fitting. They'll make sure it fits perfectly.'

'We will, Mrs Cooper,' Amanda said. She got out her pin cushion and began pinning here and there. The parachute silk, laundered three times to remove most traces of its wartime purpose, draped perfectly from Grace's shoulders as Amanda pinned and adjusted the bodice. Maisie knelt with her mouth full of pins, carefully creating hidden pleats that would make the dress work for both walking down the aisle and sitting during the ceremony.

Ten minutes later they suggested Grace look in the mirror again. It was a perfect fit and the silk made her lovely skin glow beautifully.

'Well, if that's done, come and have your tea,' Mrs Cooper said. 'It must be well stewed by now. You didn't ask about a veil, did you? Well, she's going to use my one.' She proudly produced her wedding photo. As a young bride she looked radiant, the harsh lines in her face nowhere to be seen. Amanda wondered what life had done to her to produce them. But this wasn't the time to comment on that. 'You looked just stunning, Mrs Cooper. It's a lovely photo.'

Mrs Cooper took it back, wiped it with her tea towel and put it on the mantelpiece. 'Yes, it was a good day. Can't say the same about the man or the marriage though...'

'Mum! Give over, will you!' Grace looked close to tears. 'Don't spoil this day for me.'

Keen to break the icy atmosphere, Amanda spoke softly. 'Mrs Cooper, would you like to see some buttons I got on the market? The man said they were from that bombed-out shop in Toynbee Street. We've been saving these for Grace's dress. Even she hasn't seen them yet.'

Carefully, she unwrapped several pearl buttons, laying them on a cushion. The buttons caught the light, gleaming like tiny moons. 'They're old, but so elegant. I think they'll be perfect for Grace's dress.'

Mrs Cooper smiled and she looked at her daughter. 'They'll be perfect and that dress looks lovely even if it's not finished yet. You'll be the talk of Spitalfields.'

Grace took off the dress which they gently folded back into its box.

'Next fitting on Sunday then,' Amanda said. Through the

window they saw a woman hurrying along weighed down with shopping, trying to keep a toddler off the road.

Mrs Cooper stood in the doorway watching the friends go, one hand pressed against a lucky charm bracelet she always wore. But when she turned back to Grace there was a kindness in her face that wasn't there before.

'I'm proud of you, you know. You're the best daughter anyone could have and you looked smashing in that dress.'

36

Next day Amanda was again reviewing her logbook and inventory records in the factory. She knew there were discrepancies but even after all this time she didn't believe her eyes. What she was sure was going on was so blatant, surely it couldn't be happening. Looking around to make sure Mrs Duncan wasn't near, she flipped back through older records. What she saw made her frown and look closer. Some records had definitely been altered. They were always made in pencil. Someone had rubbed out some of the figures and put in fictitious ones. The handwriting wasn't even the same. Whoever did it felt confident they wouldn't be found out.

Feeling conspicuous and like she would be challenged any minute, she walked into the warehouse, there she could cross-check the current figures against stock levels. If she saw any boxes marked *Waste* she'd leave them alone.

Although she'd been in there before, she noticed how dimly lit it was, the overhead bulbs casting long shadows across the towering stacks of crates and fabric rolls. The air was heavy with the smell of dust and cigarette smoke, and every creak of the wooden floor sounded ominous, making her heart quicken.

It's so blatant, she thought again, remembering what she'd seen before. *It's not just sloppy record keeping. They must be very confident of getting away with it.*

"Ere, what you doing?' Mr Turnbull, the supervisor who was so aggressive in the union meeting, had crept up behind her. His harsh voice made her jump and his tense shoulders and crossed arms matched his tone.

Amanda struggled to keep her voice steady. 'Just checking some figures.'

'Well, you know you don't need to do that, girly. I give you the figures every week, regular as clockwork.' He stopped and leaned forward so close she could smell his breath. 'Sure you're not snooping for that union of yours? Wouldn't put it past you. Always stirring up trouble, you are.'

'I'm just doing my job, same as you are.' She stepped back so she didn't have to breathe in his unpleasant breath. Although it was morning, it smelled strongly of beer. Turning her face away, she took a couple of deep breaths, needing to keep her anger and fear hidden until she was sure what to do.

Mrs Duncan had already made thinly veiled threats, so it might be dangerous to tackle her. So what to do? Amanda had gone over this in her head a hundred times, exploring the possibilities. Each one had to be weighed up against the likelihood of action being taken and her own safety.

Then a solution popped into her head. She would seek out Mrs Pain, the union leader, and talk to her about it.

She turned to leave but Mr Turnbull hadn't finished. 'You get on with your little numbers, girly, and leave the real work to the grown-ups. You keep poking your nose in and you'll find yourself out of a job quicker than you can say union. Got it?'

Not responding to his words, Amanda went back to her workstation, shaking but determined. *They think they can scare me into silence*, she thought. *But they're wrong. What they're doing is illegal.* She would go to Mrs Pain, the union leader. If anyone could help, it would be her. More importantly, she wouldn't be dealing with this alone.

She wasn't going to let them get away with it. As she sat down, her mind flew back briefly to that terrible night in the underground station. The memories still clawed at her regularly but they didn't overwhelm her like they had. She could feel it now, how the experience had changed her, how surviving that night had made her stronger. The fear was still there, always, but it had lost its iron grip on her. And planning the charity dance with her friends made her feel like she was doing something positive, even if she couldn't bring the dead back to life.

She clenched her fists, feeling determined. She wasn't just surviving any more. She was going to fight back.

37

The house was unusually quiet. Maisie stood at the kitchen sink, scrubbing a pot hard enough to rub right through the bottom. Ron and Rose had finally gone to bed after a day of bickering and driving her crazy, and Aunt Betty had retired early too. Being around two youngsters all day took it out of her, she said.

Outside, the early-evening air was crisp but mild, with a faint scent of spring blossoms on the few trees that had survived the bombing. A soft glow lingered in the sky, a reminder that the days were finally getting longer.

Maisie glanced at the clock. Half past eight. Frank had said he might stop by if he could get away from work early enough. With the wartime chaos on the trains, he could never rely on any sort of timetable for his job.

The knock on the door made her jump, and she dropped the saucepan with a clatter. She dried her hands quickly, and tidied her hair as she walked to the door. A gust of wind caught her skirt as she opened it, carrying with it the faintest chill of the fading day.

There he was, cap in hand, his hair slightly mussed up from

the wind. He held a bunch of spring wildflowers he'd no doubt picked from bomb sites.

'Evening, sweetheart,' he said with a warm smile.

She stepped aside to let him in, her heart lifting at the sight of him. 'You're a real sight for sore eyes. I wasn't sure if you'd be able to come.'

He shook his head. 'You know I come to see you every spare minute I get.'

'Sit yourself down and I'll get you a drink. I think there's a bottle of stout in the kitchen if you want it.'

He sat on the settee but looked awkward somehow, not his usual self. 'That'd be great. Why don't we share it?'

She fetched two glasses and the stout and went to sit beside him. 'Is everything all right?' she asked as she poured the drinks. 'You don't look yourself somehow.'

'Well. Yes and no. There's something I need to talk to you about.'

He didn't continue immediately, and she could see him swallowing nervously. She put her glass on the side table and turned to face him. 'What is it? Has something dreadful happened?'

He took a sip of his drink and paused to wipe his mouth with the back of his hand. 'It's nothing bad, Maisie, but you might think so. I do in some ways. The thing is, I've been offered that promotion I told you about. I thought with the war on I'd never get it.'

Her face lit up. 'Frank, that's wonderful! You deserve it. You've worked so hard...'

He held up a hand. 'Hang on, there's more and you won't like this bit. The thing is... the job's in Scotland.'

His words hit her like a slap in the face. 'Scotland?' she repeated, her voice barely above a whisper. 'Scotland? But that's...'

Frank nodded, his expression unreadable. 'So far away. I know. It's a big step up, Maisie. Better pay, more responsibility, more chance to go higher still.' He paused and put down his glass then took her hand in both of his. 'It's the type of opportunity I've been wanting for ages. But it means I'll have to move. At least for a year, maybe more.'

Maisie looked at him open-mouthed, her mind whirling. Scotland. It might as well have been the other side of the world. She wanted to be happy for him, she really did, but at such a cost. Him so far away. Long-distance relationships were difficult. She heard stories all the time of marriages going wrong because the men were away fighting. If they got leave the couple sometimes didn't know each other any more. They'd moved on without the other one or met someone new. People rarely got divorced, it was too expensive, but many effectively lived apart or sometimes lived together miserably for the rest of their lives.

She tried to push away these depressing thoughts. 'When would you leave?'

He squeezed her hand tighter. 'Not immediately, but I haven't got a start date yet. I came to tell you as soon as I knew for sure. I didn't want you to hear it from someone else.'

She struggled to make it seem real. Although they didn't see each other every day, in fact sometimes a whole week would go by without them managing to meet, she loved knowing he was nearby. He was her rock.

He crouched down in front of her, taking both hands in his. 'Sweetheart, I know it's a lot. It's not what either of us would have chosen. But it's not forever. It's just a step towards something better. For us, for our lives together if you want it to be. I know I do.'

'For us,' she echoed, her voice hollow. 'You talk as if everything will stay the same. Like being hundreds of miles from each other won't change things, but life's not like that, is it?'

He learned forward and tucked a stray hair behind her ear. 'It won't change how I feel about you. Maisie, you mean everything to me. And I should be able to get an occasional rail pass to come back to see you so that's something. I'll see if I can get one so you can come to see me too.' He was beginning to gabble in his haste to convince her. 'I'll write to you every day if you'd like me to.'

She wanted to believe him, be happy for him, proud of him. But all she could think about was how much she already had on her plate. He was her emotional support, even if they didn't see each other often. Letters couldn't replace that.

'What if something happens?' Her voice was hardly above a whisper. 'What if you meet someone else, or you love it up there and don't come back. I can't up sticks and move there. Not with the kids to look after and Mum still, well... you know...'

He kissed her hand. 'Maisie, listen to me. I'll never forget you or look at another girl. You mean too much to me. You're the reason I want to build a better future. And when this war's over, I'll come home and we'll have that life we've talked about. A house with a garden, maybe even some chickens like I said before.'

Maisie laughed. 'Chickens? Really? Is that the limit of your ambition?'

'Okay,' he conceded. 'Perhaps I want more than chickens, but you know what I mean.' He grinned again. 'But if we do get some, you can choose names for them!'

She leaned forward, resting her forehead against his. 'You'd better keep that promise, Frank. Chickens and all.'

'I will,' he promised. 'Chickens and all. Half a dozen at least.'

He stayed a little longer, but the atmosphere was bittersweet with so much unspoken. When it was time for him to go, Maisie walked him to the door, waiting while he put his coat and cap on.

'Maisie,' he said, pulling her close. 'We'll get through this. I know it's hard for both of us, but it's not forever.'

He kissed her tenderly before stepping outside. 'See you soon, love. I'm not gone just yet.'

When the door closed she leaned against it, feeling sadness weighing her down. *You'd better come back, Frank*, she thought. *How will I manage without you?*

38

The night was colder than usual, and Maisie shivered as she walked home through the market. Her shoes, worn thin from years of use, were already lined with cardboard, but they didn't stop the cold from seeping up, making her feet tingle with cold. Spring might be here, but winter seemed to fight back some days. She clutched her handbag tightly, her woollen gloves doing little to keep her fingers warm. At least she and her friends were making progress with Grace's wedding dress. Thinking about it always lifted her spirits.

Approaching her home, she felt the familiar weight of dread settle in her chest. Her mother swore she had given up alcohol but Maisie knew otherwise. She still found the occasional empty bottle in the rubbish bin and despite her mother's attempts to disguise the smell on her breath, she could often smell the strong whisky or cider she favoured.

The curtains were drawn and Maisie sent up a silent prayer that Rose and Ron would be happy. That their mother was sober and maybe cooking a meal for them all. She couldn't handle another scene tonight.

Turning her key in the old door, she stepped inside. The smell of boiled cabbage and damp wool greeted her, along with the muffled sound of the wireless playing in the kitchen. Rose appeared in the doorway. Her eyes were red, and she wiped her nose on her sleeve.

'She's gone again.' She didn't need to say more. Just as well as she could hardly speak for sobbing. Maisie knew exactly what she meant. She froze, her stomach churning. 'Oh, no.' She pulled Rose towards her in a hug. 'When did she go, love?'

Rose sniffed. 'I dunno, about an hour ago, I think. She said she was nipping next door to borrow some tea but she ain't there. I asked.'

'She'll be down the pub again,' Ron said. It seemed his voice grew harsher each time something like this happened. 'She's a drunk, that's what she is!'

Maisie sighed. 'That's enough, Ron, don't you think I know what's going on? She can't help herself, can she?'

He sneered. 'Helps herself to booze though, don't she, even if there's no money for food.'

Maisie tried to hug him, but he pulled away and went into the living room. She wanted to be cross with him, but like all of them, he'd had a lot to put up with and she'd heard he was being bullied at school because of their mother's drinking. She often felt angry with him, but she felt sorry for him too.

Shaking her head, she took off her coat and dropped her bag. She hated that Ron spoke about their mother like that, but what he said was true. She'd been to the library, reading about people addicted to alcohol. As she understood it, alcohol became the most important thing in their life, more important than their health or their family. It was like an evil spirit possessed them.

'Does Dad know?' Maisie asked, though she already knew the answer.

Rose's face darkened. 'He's in the kitchen, reading the paper. He said she'll come back when she's ready. He ain't bothered.'

Maisie clenched her fists, anger flaring in her chest. Their father's indifference infuriated her. He acted as though their mother's drinking was someone else's problem, as though it wasn't tearing the family apart. It left her feeling confused, not knowing who to feel more angry with – her mother for her drinking or her father for the way he ignored the family. But then she remembered what she'd read. Her dad had a choice, her mum didn't.

'I'll go and look for her,' Maisie said, grabbing her coat again. 'Make yourself some jam sandwiches while I'm gone. I'll try to bring a bag of chips back.'

Rose's eyes widened and tears sparkled in her eyes. She clung onto Maisie again as if she'd never let her go. 'Don't go, Maisie, we don't know where she's gone and you could be gone ages looking for her.'

The weight of the world on her shoulders, Maisie put her coat back on. 'Tell you what. I'll just go to the chippie and fetch us some chips. I might get lucky and find her while I'm out. How about that?'

Ron grunted. 'Have a look in the Rose and Crown while you're at it. She's probably there.'

Rose's lip quivered, and Maisie softened, pulling her younger sister into another quick hug. 'Stay here and get the plates and things out, Rosy. I'll be back soon. Keep the door locked.' It was only after she'd closed the door behind her that she realised she hadn't even consulted her dad about going. Still, there'd be little hope of him going out to look for his wife. Maisie often wondered why he hadn't upped and vanished like some men did that she knew about. In some ways, it would make their life easier.

Maisie decided to go to the pub before the chippie. She hated doing that. Everyone in their streets knew about her mother's drinking. Word about her collapsing in the street and an ambulance taking her to hospital had soon spread. Most people had no patience with her and either pretended not to know or made sarcastic comments if they saw Maisie. Only a couple of neighbours were sympathetic, offering what support they could. Considering how common being a heavy drinker was, people should have been more understanding, Maisie thought. The government had reduced pub opening times to try to deal with the problem, but most regular drinkers knew which pubs let people in the rear doors when officially closed.

The Rose and Crown was loud and rowdy, its patrons spilling onto the pavement despite the chill. Maisie hesitated outside, her stomach churning. She hated coming here, hated the way some men leered at her as she passed. One or two even made comments about following in her mother's footsteps. She pretended not to hear them and pushed her way in. Her mother might be inside, and Maisie couldn't afford to let her pride get in the way.

As she stepped through the door, the smell of stale beer and smoke hit her like a wall. The floor was sticky, and the ceiling was brown with decades of cigarette smoke. Above the bar was a picture of the King and an array of Toby jugs. The noise was deafening, laughter, shouting, the clink of glasses, the sound of darts being thrown at the dartboard. Maisie's heart raced as she scanned the room. But her mother wasn't there.

'Oy, Maisie!' a familiar voice called. She turned to see Alfie, a young man who worked part-time at the butcher's stall. He was standing at the bar, a pint in his hand.

'Don't usually see you 'ere,' Alfie said, his brow furrowing. 'Not your sort of place, is it?'

Maisie struggled to keep her voice steady. 'Looking for my mum. Have you seen her?'

Alfie frowned. 'She ain't been in 'ere for a while. Gone teetotal I heard.'

Maisie longed to search the other pubs she knew her mum used to visit, but remembered her promise to Rose. She'd be worried and Ron would be getting angrier and angrier.

There was a queue at the chippie as usual, and everyone was talking about the latest rationing restrictions. Thank goodness fish and chips weren't rationed. Maisie loved the smell in the chippie, even if it did cling to her clothes. The aroma of salt and vinegar made her mouth water and she moved from foot to foot with impatience, all the time looking around in case her mother went by. Finally served, she hugged the newspaper-wrapped chips and hurried home, trying to keep them warm. As she opened the door, Rose ran up to her, her eyes wide with fear. 'Where's Mummy? Did you find her?'

'I'm sorry, love. I couldn't find her, but let's have some chips and bread and marge. Then I'll tidy up and read you a story.' Her father had gone while she'd been out, but she shrugged her shoulders and dished out the chips.

When they'd finished eating, Maisie settled down with Rose to read her more *Winnie the Pooh*. It was Rose's favourite book and she'd read it so often the pages were a bit grubby. But as she began the familiar story, Maisie was delighted that Ron came and sat next to them. He pretended not to be interested, looking anywhere but at them, but she could tell he was. She knew better than to say anything though. It felt like a precious moment between the three of them to cherish. And it reminded her that even though the pair fought often, Ron did sometimes look out for his sister, even giving her a hug if she was upset.

By midnight, Maisie had given up all hope of her mother

returning. Rose and Ron were in bed, her father was who knew where, but she couldn't go to bed herself. She lay on the settee, pulling a knitted blanket over herself and eventually drifted off to an uneasy sleep full of nightmare scenarios of her mother being lost or run over or trapped in the underground. Twice she woke up with a start and looked around. Footsteps outside made her heart jump. Was it her mum, searching for her keys? But it wasn't. The next time it was the ARP warden shouting at a neighbour to 'close that bloody curtain'. Each time it took a while for her tortured feelings to settle down so she could get back to sleep.

Rose woke before her next morning and shook her awake. 'Where's Mummy? Has something happened to her? Is she dead?'

'Don't think like that, sweetheart,' Maisie said, struggling to hold back a sob. It was so awful that a little girl lived in constant fear of her mother being dead. 'She'll come back. She always does.' But reassuring Rose did nothing to calm her own fears. What if her mother had been hit by a car in the blackout or ended up drunk in some stranger's bed? What if she'd drunk so much her body had just given up and she was in the morgue somewhere? How on earth would Maisie be able to keep the family together when she worked full-time and part-time at the Petticoat? How could she stop Ron's behaviour getting worse?

She'd hardly had time to put the kettle on when there was a knock on the door, loud and urgent. The sound was too different from her mother's knock to be her, too forceful, too cold. Maisie froze, her breath catching in the throat as a chill travelled down her spine. She didn't need to answer the door to know something dreadful had happened.

39

Two policemen stood there, their expressions grim. They looked as if they'd rather be anywhere else. Maisie froze, her heart pounding so hard it seemed to echo in her ears. She immediately assumed the worst. Her mother must be dead.

The terror in her face must have been plain because the older policeman spoke first, his voice low and careful.

'I'm Officer Tiplady. It's about your mother, miss. Can we come in?'

Maisie's breath caught in her chest. Her knees felt unsteady, but she nodded, standing aside without a word. She longed to know what had happened but dreaded knowing too. Her breath came in small, sharp gasps as she tried to steady herself. Rose, who had been playing quietly with her doll a moment before, now clung to Maisie's skirt, her little face pale and anxious.

The older policeman stepped inside, taking off his helmet and tucking it under his arm. He glanced around the small room, his eyes softening slightly at the sight of Rose. Maisie led them to the table, where he carefully placed his helmet. 'We found your mum,' he said, his tone heavy, almost apologetic.

Maisie's stomach churned. She felt Rose's small, clammy hand slip into hers. The child looked up at her, wide-eyed, searching for reassurance Maisie wasn't sure she could give. 'Where is she?' Maisie whispered, her voice trembling. 'Is she...?'

'She's alive,' Officer Tiplady said quickly, raising one hand as if to calm her. 'But she's in a bad way. We found her near the docks, unconscious. It looks as if she'd fallen over and banged her head.'

Relief and dread warred inside Maisie. Her knees buckled slightly, and she gripped the back of a chair to steady herself. 'Where is she? Can she come home?' Her voice cracked on the last word as she clutched Rose tighter.

'She's in no condition to come home, I'm afraid,' the officer said, shaking his head. 'She's been taken to an institution for observation and treatment. The doctors think she'll need to be there for a good long while.'

Rose let out a wail, throwing her arms around Maisie's waist. Maisie held her tight, though she felt as if the ground were crumbling beneath her feet. Her mother. In one of *those* places. The words the officer had used, *institution, observation, treatment*, felt clinical, detached, but they couldn't disguise the truth. Maisie had heard the whispered stories about those places. The snake pits. The nut house. The loony bin. Once someone went in, they rarely came out the same. If they came out at all.

The younger officer, fresh-faced and stiff with discomfort, shifted awkwardly, his eyes scanning the modest room. His lip curled slightly, and he muttered something under his breath. Maisie caught the words 'some people...' and her chest burned with indignation. She wanted to scream at him, to shout, *Do you think we enjoy living like this? Do you think it's easy to stretch every penny, to keep a roof over our heads while the world is falling apart?*

Instead, she bit her tongue, feeling the taste of blood where her teeth had already cut into it.

Rose's tear-streaked face turned to Officer Tiplady. 'What's going to happen to Mummy?' she asked, her voice small and trembling.

The older man's expression softened even further. He crouched slightly to meet her gaze. 'The doctors will look after her,' he said gently. 'They'll do everything they can to help her get better.'

Maisie stood frozen, her mind racing. *Get better?* How? Her mother wasn't sick, at least, not in the way people usually meant. Yes, she'd been drinking more, disappearing for hours, sometimes days, but that was stress, wasn't it? The war? Struggling to make ends meet with a useless husband who was no help at all. Maisie had told herself it was temporary, that she just needed time even though she knew better. But now... now it felt as though time had run out.

She collapsed onto the settee, trembling so hard she could barely hold herself together. Her hands covered her face, but she couldn't stop the tears from spilling out between her fingers. 'Can I see her?' she asked finally, her voice muffled and broken.

'Not yet,' Officer Tiplady replied, his tone regretful. He reached into his pocket and handed her a small slip of paper. 'This is the number for the institution. Call them tomorrow, not today. They need time to get her settled, to figure out what's what.'

Maisie stared at the paper as though it were written in a foreign language. The institution's name, a cold, impersonal string of words, seemed to mock her. She folded it tightly in her hand, her knuckles white.

The officer straightened, his professionalism slipping back into place as he glanced at his colleague. 'Right,' he said. 'We need to be on our way. Sorry to love you and leave you, but we've got a lot on this morning.'

Maisie didn't respond. She didn't even look up as they moved towards the door. Rose reached out as if to stop them, her small voice trembling. 'Will Mummy be okay?'

The older officer hesitated, his hand on the doorknob. He looked back at Maisie, his face lined with sympathy and something else – uncertainty. 'She's in the right place,' he said finally. It was all he could offer.

When the door closed behind them, the silence was deafening. Maisie sat motionless, her hand still clutching the paper. Rose climbed onto the settee beside her, burying her face in Maisie's shoulder as her sobs grew louder. Maisie stroked her sister's hair absently, staring at the floor, her mind a jumble of panic, guilt and despair.

How had it come to this? She thought of her mother, that proud, sharp-tongued, fiercely independent woman now reduced to a patient in an institution. How could Maisie explain this to Rose, to Ron? How could she keep them together, keep things going, when she could barely hold herself together?

She leaned her head back against the settee, her tears slipping silently down her cheeks. 'We'll figure it out, Rose,' she whispered, though her voice wavered with uncertainty. 'We'll figure it out.'

But as she sat there, the weight of the paper in her hand and her sister's sobs filling the room, Maisie wasn't sure she believed her own words.

40

It was the day of the charity dance for victims and survivors of the Bethnal Green underground station tragedy. St John's church hall smelled of tea and polish as Amanda, Bethan and Maisie arrived early. They were loaded with decorations, tiny prizes and supplies. Four WI members were already there, bustling around, organising chairs and trestle tables, covering the latter with an old sheet. A few decorations were already up, homemade paper chains and some signs saying *Give generously to help the survivors and families of the underground tragedy.*

After getting agreement from the WI members, the friends also had two notices advertising their repair business. Amanda had made a great job of making the poster look attractive. As none of them had a phone, they were each wearing a homemade badge saying *Need a repair? Ask me for details.*

The three friends put down their things and began to applaud the women who had done the decorations. 'You've done a tidy job, I gotta say.' Bethan smiled and went to shake hands with each of the women. 'This old hall looks fit for royalty. You must've spent ages doing all this.'

The youngest woman, who must have nonetheless been in her mid-sixties, smiled. 'Mrs Brown here used to be a florist. She's the one with the skill to make garlands and things out of odds and ends. She's a miracle worker. I'm Mrs Goldstein.'

The door opened again and four men struggled in, carrying a variety of musical instruments. 'Hi, all,' the tallest said with a grin. 'I'm Bob. We're from Bryant and May, no spare matches though!'

'Come in, come in,' Mrs Goldstein said. 'We're very glad to see you. You'll be on the stage. I don't know if anyone has warned you but one way we'll be raising money is to let people pay for a request. Do you know plenty of songs?'

Bob laughed. 'That we do. We've been playing at weddings for years. Ain't many songs we don't know.'

Bethan liked the look of Bob. He was a bit old for her but he had good looks like Frank Sinatra with black hair oiled back. He walked with a confidence that spoke volumes, and he had a trombone under his arm.

Bethan fiddled with one of the curls in her hair.

'You must have strong lungs to play that all night.'

'That's not all he can blow!' one of the others said with a dirty laugh. 'But 'scuse us, we gotta get set up.'

Checking that Bob didn't have a wedding ring, Bethan turned back to the others with a smile and began loading cups and saucers on one of the trestle tables.

'Leave him alone, you!' The words hissed in her ear made Bethan jump and her heart race. She spun around to see a tall, stick-thin girl with auburn hair standing too close, her hands on her hips. 'He's mine, so keep your hands off, Welshie!'

'What? You talking to me?' Bethan was stunned. This girl must mean Bob, she hadn't spoken to anyone else.

'Yes, you, trying to get off with Bob. He's mine so back off if you know what's good for you.' With that she strode off and stomped up the three steps to the stage where she kissed Bob on the cheek, her eyes never leaving Bethan's.

'Good gracious,' Mrs Goldstein said. 'I heard that. What on earth did you do?'

Bethan was struggling to get her breathing back to normal. 'Nothing, only a little joke. I reckon that girl's a bit barmy if you asks me.'

Mrs Goldstein shook her head. 'You young people! But enough of that, there's a mountain of sandwiches to make. We don't get them out until after the raffle, dearest, or it'll all be gone within half an hour. But we need more sandwiches made. Go into the kitchen and one of the others will tell you what to do.'

Bethan grinned and walked into the kitchen. 'Right, what's occurring? What sandwiches are we making?'

Mrs Doherty ran the back of her hand over her forehead, brushing her hair away from her face. 'I'm glad to see you, that I am. Bethan, is it? Well, we're making a ton of sandwiches, Marmite, mock crab, fish paste, jam, and Spam and pickle. Mrs Jones here has cut the Spam very thin to make it go further, so don't be surprised if it falls apart when you pick it up. Now, get yourself an apron off the back of the door and get cracking. Make sure you cut the sandwiches into quarters. They'll last longer that way.'

While she was busy with sandwich making, the others were all finishing the decorations and getting the room ready. The vicar, Reverend Smithson, appeared with a couple of extra chairs, staggering under the weight. He put them down and stopped to look around. 'Ladies, you've excelled yourself, this tired old hall is transformed. I'm sorry I can't stay longer but I have an elderly parishioner in need of comfort.'

What felt like a few minutes later, it was time to open the

doors. Bethan was taking door money, sixpence each. She was ideal for the job, being lively and enjoying having a word with everyone. She complimented every girl on something about their appearance and each of them went into the hall feeling better about themselves. She eyed up all the good-looking lads as well but was disappointed when no GIs appeared.

The band was playing swing tunes as people began to filter in: 'In the Mood', 'Sing, Sing, Sing' and 'Tuxedo Junction'. Couples were soon dancing. Some men were in uniform, some in civvies. Many people knew each other and there was soon a great atmosphere in the hall. After all their planning, it was a relief to see everything going so well.

Maisie looked anxiously at the door every few minutes, hoping Frank would manage to get time off to come. She desperately needed to talk to him about what had happened to her mother and him being sent to Scotland. She was putting a brave face on for the evening, but inside her heart was breaking.

Then the door opened again and there he was. 'He's here!' With that she left her friends and, dodging around the dancers, rushed to the door. Frank saw her and picked her up off her feet, hugging her tight. 'Maisie. At last. It's been too long.'

She had to wipe a tear from her eyes. 'I thought you were working tonight.'

He winked. 'You know me! I managed to change shifts at the last minute. Couldn't let you go to the dance on your own. Some other bloke might have made off with someone as gorgeous as you!'

Maisie's heart sang. She wasn't used to compliments. Before Frank she'd never had more than one or two dates with any boy.

They went over to the drinks table, soft drinks only, but it didn't matter. It seemed far too long since they'd seen each other, and seeing Frank made Maisie's tension relax. Work, Mrs Duncan being awful, her mother in hospital and Ron and Rose playing up took their toll, without having to cook and clean every day. And she still had nightmares about helping the people that dreadful night of the underground tragedy. Frank provided exactly what she needed – some affection without any expectations of anything from her.

'How's your mum?' Frank asked. 'I'm so sorry I haven't been to see you or her. I've had to do double shifts. Old Mr Bentall is off sick with a bad back. He should have retired years ago, but he's still keen to do his bit.'

Maisie held his hand. 'You're here now, that's the important thing.' The band changed to a slower number, 'The Nearness of You'.

'Come on, sweetheart,' Frank said. 'Let's dance. We can cuddle up a bit to this number.'

They did indeed cuddle up, although Maisie struggled to keep just a little distance between them as they danced. But it was oh so tempting to forget her principles and close that space. She could feel Frank's breath on her cheek, and he once or twice whispered sweet nothings that sent her heart racing. Her raging emotions made her realise how some girls could get carried away and end up in the family way or being called a slag or other horrible names. Being so close chased away all her fears for a few minutes. She knew it wouldn't last, but closed her eyes, determined to enjoy the moment.

At the end of the number the music stopped and Mrs Goldstein went on stage. 'Time to draw the raffle, ladies and gentlemen. If you look around you there's sure to be someone who will sell you some last-minute tickets, while we get set up.'

Someone dragged a small side table from the wings and she put a big bag on it, full of the remaining half of raffle tickets sold. There was another small table with ten prizes on it. None were breath-taking. There was a bar of soap, another of chocolate, a pair of stockings, a tin of biscuits, a jar of homemade jam, a novel, a voucher for two iced buns from Griffiths Bakers, another for tea for two at Bert's Café, a knitted scarf and a mystery prize wrapped in brown paper.

'As you know,' Mrs Goldstein said, 'tonight's event is in aid of the victims and survivors of the dreadful Bethnal Green underground tragedy and I want to thank you all for so generously buying raffle tickets and making donations.' She paused to emphasise the seriousness of the event, then spoke more lightly. 'Every penny will be given to them and it will make a tremendous difference, I promise you.'

She picked up the bag of raffle tickets. 'So, who's going to pick out the first winner?' She looked around expectantly. Several hands were raised and the first person won the bar of chocolate. Each was then called upon to pick the next winner. Despite the modest prizes there was a lot of good humour. Amanda went on stage and handed Mrs Goldstein a slip of paper. 'Ladies and gentlemen,' she went on, holding up her hand for silence. 'I am thrilled to announce that this raffle has raised a wonderful fifteen pounds ten shillings for those people affected by the terrible tragedy. Thank you all for your generosity.'

She paused and called Amanda, Bethan and Maisie onto the stage. 'As well as our wonderful WI volunteers, let's have a round of applause for the three young women whose idea this evening was. They have done much of the work for making it happen.' When the applause died down, she continued. 'And I don't know if you're aware that these talented friends offer their services doing repairs and alterations to keep our war-tired clothes looking respectable.'

Amanda stepped forward. 'We're thrilled so many of you have come tonight to help people affected by this terrible tragedy. Mrs

Goldstein will let the local newspaper know how much has been raised in all so it will be wonderful to see that figure.'

The applause rippled through the hall as Mrs Goldstein stepped down from the stage. The band struck up again with 'Pennsylvania 6-555' and within seconds the room was buzzing with dancers again.

While the raffle was being called, the WI members had laid out the sandwiches and tiny finger cakes. The three friends made a beeline for them.

'That's tidy, that is,' Bethan said, standing behind the food table. 'It'll go a long way, that money. And some publicity for us!'

Maisie grinned. 'You know they'll be looking at the sandwiches, not you.'

'Then I'll have to get their attention, won't I, bach.'

By the end of the evening, they had several enquiries for their services and Maisie and Frank had made a date for the following week.

But Bethan still didn't find her dream man. Nor did Amanda have any inkling of what was soon to happen at the factory.

41

Earlier that day, Amanda had seen Turnbull loading crates into an unfamiliar van at the factory's rear entrance. He wasn't supposed to be there at that time, and the way he glanced around, checking no one was watching him, before he slammed the doors shut sent a chill down her spine.

Cursing herself for her cowardice, she hadn't dared to approach then but the sight had lain heavy on her mind all day. It had to be something to do with whatever he and Mrs Duncan were up to.

By late evening, she just had to act. The blackout shrouded everything in shadows, and she pulled her coat tightly around herself, hands buried deep in her pockets to stop them from trembling. She knew the small back gate would be unlocked. Although a security guard patrolled the area at night, she had slipped in once before when she'd had to go back, having forgotten something. No one noticed.

But that didn't stop the factory looking more threatening this time, a hulking silhouette against the dark sky. She stopped just outside the gate, her heart beating fast enough to make her feel a little unsteady. *Calm yourself*, she repeated over and over in her mind, slowing down her breathing.

The gate creaked as she pushed it open, the sound splitting the night air. Wincing, Amanda slipped through and into the yard, aware of the sound of her feet even though she was tiptoeing. The smell of oil and fabric waste hung heavy in the air, the faint hum of a bus passing by the only sound. She froze, listening, but the place seemed deserted.

Yet she couldn't help feeling watched. The warehouse loomed to her right, its dark windows unwelcoming. She crouched low, moving as quietly as she could, her shoes making little sound on the concrete floor.

For a long while nothing happened and she almost decided she was wasting her time. Then she heard voices. Her heart leapt. The voices were low, urgent and unmistakably familiar. She crept closer, pressing herself against the cool bricks.

'We've got to move it tonight,' Mrs Duncan was saying, her voice sharp and clipped. 'The longer it stays here, the more chance someone will stick their nose in, especially as it's not one of our vans.'

Amanda's stomach churned. She edged closer, peering through a gap where the door wasn't quite closed. There they were, Duncan and Turnbull, standing over several crates stacked near the loading dock.

'You're the one who delayed it yesterday,' Turnbull growled. 'Make up your bloody mind.'

'That was different,' Mrs Duncan snapped. 'We had inspectors sniffing around. But now, we need to act. We've got that bloody blonde girl suspicious, I'm sure of it, and that union woman.'

Amanda caught her breath. They were talking about her.

'She's been snooping around,' Mrs Duncan continued, her tone icy. 'If she doesn't stop, we'll have to deal with her.'

Amanda clamped a hand over her mouth, her pulse thundering in her ears. The shadows suddenly felt too thin to keep her hidden, too fragile.

'You're not asking me to...' Turnbull never finished his sentence before Duncan interrupted him.

'Don't be ridiculous. I'm not a bloody gangster. But we can't let her ruin this. I need the money for... well, never mind what. But if I have to, I'll get her fired.'

Turnbull muttered something Amanda couldn't catch, then turned towards the door, making Amanda duck back out of sight. 'Okay, okay, let's get this load in the van now then.'

Amanda's mind raced. They were definitely stealing fabric. But she needed proof, and there was no way to get it. Her eyes darted around, searching for a way out.

As she shifted her weight, her foot brushed against a loose stone on the floor. It clattered loudly, the sound ricocheting off the walls.

'What was that?' Mrs Duncan snapped. 'Is someone out there?'

Turnbull spun round, his eyes narrowing. 'Probably just a cat or something, but I'll check.'

Amanda's mind raced again. She crouched down, hoping the shadows would be enough. Would they? Turnbull's steps got closer and she was too terrified to breathe. Would he kill her if he found her?

He stopped just a few feet from her. 'Who's there? Show yourself!'

She had to move. Now. While his back was to her.

Seizing the moment, she darted towards the side door, staying low and moving as quickly as she could. Her heart pounded as she reached the door, her hand closing round the handle.

'There!' Mrs Duncan shouted. 'Someone's running!'

'Stop!' Turnbull bellowed, his voice echoing around the yard.

But Amanda wasn't about to stop. She yanked the door open and bolted into the night. Then she sprinted across the road, her breath coming in ragged gasps. Behind her, she could hear the thud of boots and the angry shouts of her pursuers.

Finally luck was on her side. A bus appeared down the road, its shielded headlights cutting through the gloom. Amanda waved her arms and it slowed enough for her to grab hold and pull herself on.

She collapsed into a seat, her chest heaving. The conductor gave her a curious look as she fumbled in her bag for her fare. 'You okay, miss?' he asked.

Too breathless to speak, she just nodded and handed over the fare, watching him deftly turn the handle of the ticket machine, the rhythmic *ka-ching* of the fare being rung up cutting through the hum of the engine. Taking her ticket from him, she rubbed it between her fingers as the bus gained speed and turned a corner.

She leaned against the glass, her body trembling with adrenaline. She didn't know if they'd worked out it was her, but they were certainly on to her.

Tomorrow, she'd go to Mrs Pain. She needed help. Fast.

42

Amanda swallowed as she approached Mrs Pain's home. The small terraced house was identical to its neighbours, its windows tightly curtained, the doorstep gleaming. She clutched her handbag with her notebook tightly, her heart hammering in her chest. She'd been terrified since going to the factory the previous night and now she saw threats everywhere.

But she had to do something. Knowledge of the stolen fabric weighed heavy on her mind, and the realisation that Duncan and Turnbull suspected she was on to them made her blood run cold. She'd barely slept all night, twisting and turning in her narrow bed, imagining all the ways they might try to silence her.

She approached the door, her hand trembling as she knocked. The sound echoed faintly down the street, but there was no answer. She waited, holding her breath, and then knocked again, louder this time. What if Mrs Pain wasn't home? What if she'd gone out for the day, or worse... Amanda shook her head, and struggled to get control of her fear.

She turned back towards the road, unsure what to do next. The morning air was warming, somewhere nearby a dog barked and a cart rattled over the old cobblestones. Amanda wrung her hands, glancing up and down the street. She couldn't leave without speaking to Mrs Pain. She needed help, and she needed it urgently.

About to sit on the doorstep, she heard hurried footsteps coming towards her. 'Oh, Amanda, I didn't know I'd see you today. Come on in.'

Amanda turned to see Mrs Pain bustling towards her, a string bag of groceries in one hand. Her face was as reassuring as Amanda remembered and it calmed her nerves.

'Come on in, love,' Mrs Pain repeated, opening the door with quick, experienced movements. 'It's good to see you, but I expect something's wrong for you to be here now.'

Amanda followed her inside, her shoulders sagging slightly with relief. The door clicked shut behind them, muffling the sounds of the outside world. Inside, the house was small, neat and organised. A ginger cat was asleep on one of the armchairs, ignoring them completely. They went into the living room, which was cosy and welcoming. A crocheted blanket was draped over a small settee, and a picture of a soldier stood on the mantelpiece next to a carriage clock. Along one wall was a bookcase with more books than Amanda had ever seen in anyone's house. She surprised herself with a pang of jealousy at the sight.

'Sit yourself down,' Mrs Pain said, gesturing to the settee. 'I'll just put this lot away and get the kettle on, then you can tell me what this is all about.'

Amanda looked at the books on the bookshelf, many were political works, along with Shakespeare and many books she'd never heard of. Her mind raced as she wondered how to tell her story. By the time Mrs Pain came back with two steaming cups of tea, Amanda's mouth was dry with fear at what she had to say.

'Now,' Mrs Pain said, gently pushing the cat aside to sit on the armchair. 'You look pale. Something must have happened. Come on, tell me, that's what I'm here for. Are you okay?'

'I'm fine, it's not me,' Amanda said. 'It's things going on at the factory.' She glanced towards the window as if someone might be listening. 'I think... I'm sure something illegal is going on. Something bad.'

Mrs Pain frowned. 'Go on, tell me all about it.'

'It's the fabric, you know, the uniform fabric. It must be expensive but...' Her voice had dropped almost to a whisper. 'It's my job to keep track of the inventory, not that anyone ever asks to see it. But it just doesn't add up. Bolts of cloth are missing and I've seen Duncan, the supervisor, and Turnbull, the warehouse supervisor... well, they're acting strange. The sums just don't add up and I've overheard things that make me think I'm not imagining it.' She took a sip of her tea. 'They are stealing fabric, I'm sure of it, and I don't know what to do. I hope you can help me. I'm scared and I think they're after me.'

Mrs Pain's expression darkened, and she set down her cup with a clink. 'You're sure about this?'

Amanda nodded. 'Yes, I'm sure. I've seen the figures, they're all here in my notebook. I've seen some dodgy things in the warehouse and the yard and I've heard them talking about me knowing too much. They're on to me.'

Narrowing her eyes, Mrs Pain leaned back in her chair, tapping her fingers against the armrest. The room was silent apart from the ticking of the carriage clock. 'You did the right thing coming to me. Now, tell me all the details, I'll write them down so I can plan action. You can leave everything to me. I'll see it's dealt with.'

Amanda told her everything she knew and handed over the notebook.

'But... what should I do in the meantime?' Amanda's voice was small and shaky.

'You go to work, just like normal,' Mrs Pain said. 'Don't let on anything's happening. Act as you always do. But make sure you're always somewhere where there are other people around. Don't be alone. If those two are on to you, it's best to play safe.'

Amanda's stomach clenched at the thought. 'But what if they...' She couldn't bring herself to finish the sentence.

'You'll be quite safe, my dear,' she said. 'Just go to work as usual. And don't breathe a word to anyone, not even your close friends.' Mrs Pain leaned over and took Amanda's hand. Her grip was firm and reassuring. 'Listen to me, love. I've dealt with people like them before. They think they can do what they like and no one will ever catch them, but they're not as clever as they think. You've proved that. I'll make sure the right people know about this. Today. We'll put a stop to it. You've done your part, now leave it to me.'

She wanted to believe Mrs Pain, to trust everything would be fine, but the image of Duncan's sneering face and Turnbull's aggressive eyes forced their way into her mind.

'Right, now finish your tea and get to that factory,' Mrs Pain said. 'The sooner we get dealing with this, the better. And leave your notebook here, I'll need it to show some people who will take action.'

Finishing her tea quickly, Amanda rose to leave. Mrs Pain walked her to the door, her hand resting lightly on Amanda's arm. 'Remember, act normal. Leave the rest to me.'

Although she didn't know what would happen next, Amanda felt less scared. Whatever came, she wasn't alone.

43

As ever, the factory floor was alive with the sound of sewing machines chugging their familiar rhythm. The radio was playing *Workers' Playtime* but could hardly be heard over the noise of the machines. Amanda usually ignored the chugging of them but now they felt oppressive, like a countdown to a bomb exploding. The fluorescent lights buzzed overhead, adding a faint, maddening whine to the cacophony. The factory floor felt like a trap, the walls closing around her. Her mind refused to concentrate on her work.

For her, the sound was suffocating. She had spoken to the union leader, and now she was following her instructions to carry on as normal, difficult though it was.

Remembering Mrs Pain's words made Amanda tremble, her head full of unanswered questions. *What's going to happen? Will I be in danger?* This had been her fear when she first realised something illegal was going on. Maisie and Bethan told her to be careful. She should have listened to them and done nothing else. Every instinct told her to stay quiet, to avoid trouble, but something stronger – the need to do what was right – had driven her forward. Now she wished she had said nothing.

Mrs Pain had put a hand on her arm. 'You'll be quite safe, my dear,' she'd said. 'Just go to work as usual. And don't breathe a word to anyone, not even your close friends.'

But acting normal was easier said than done. As she sat at her desk, her fingers shook slightly and she found it difficult to concentrate on her work. Her eyes kept flicking towards the far end of the room, where Mrs Duncan's office loomed like a fortress. This was one of the places she vanished to at regular intervals. But even then her presence was felt like a heavy cloud over the workroom.

Amanda struggled to stop herself looking around. Once already, on one of her regular walk arounds, Mrs Duncan had pulled her up sharp. 'What's wrong with you today, girl? Stop daydreaming and get on with your work.'

The outside door being flung open and the scrape of boots on the concrete floor made her jump. The air somehow shifted, heavy with tension. Machines stopped mid-seam, scissors stopped mid-snip, and heads turned in unison towards the intruders. Amanda's hands trembled as she gripped the edge of her desk, her pulse thundering in her ears.

Four men stood in the doorway. The tallest, an imposing man with a square chin and piercing blue eyes, scanned the room. He stopped in front of the nearest machinist and bent to ask her something. It was a new girl, Patsy. Her face drained of colour as she stammered, her finger pointing towards Mrs Duncan's office. The other machinists exchanged wide-eyed glances, their whispers growing louder.

Without a word, the men, who were in military police uniforms, marched towards Mrs Duncan's office. Amanda's throat tightened as they passed her, feeling their presence like a storm rolling through.

The lead man stood outside the office door and knocked firmly. 'Mrs Duncan,' he said, his voice calm but unyielding. There was a pause then the door swung open and Mrs Duncan appeared. She was as immaculate as ever, her hair swept into a tight bun, her glasses on a cord around her neck. Her expression was a mask of icy disdain, her evil eyes scanning the room for any sign of weakness. She moved like a predator, her heels clicking on the floor like gunshots.

'What is the meaning of this?' she barked, her voice clear across the whole room. Her chin lifted upwards, her eyes narrowing as she looked at the officers as if they were unruly machinists. 'What do you want? I'm a busy woman, I have a factory to run. If you have any questions, you can make an appointment like everyone else.'

'Mrs Duncan,' the officer said, ignoring her words. 'We have a warrant for your arrest.'

The workers gasped in unison, eyes widened and jaws dropped open. The room erupted in murmurs, a wave of disbelief and excitement spreading like a wave from person to person. Some craned their necks to get a better view, while others covered their mouths in shock. A few exchanged knowing looks, as if they'd long suspected something was wrong.

Amanda's stomach plummeted.

The supervisor wasn't going to give in that easily. 'Arrest?' she repeated as if she had misheard. 'What on earth are you talking about?'

The officer's jaw tightened. He nodded to two of his men who walked towards the warehouse. Meanwhile, he spoke again. 'You are under arrest for the theft of military supplies and violation of wartime regulations.'

Mrs Duncan took a step back, gripping the doorframe for support. 'This is ridiculous!' she spluttered. 'There must be some mistake. I have run this factory with the utmost...'

'Enough now, Mrs Duncan.' The officer's voice was firm. 'We have evidence. We know you've been selling on the black market. We've been watching you for a while.'

The room fell eerily quiet. Everyone looked at the hated supervisor whose face had turned ashen.

Seconds later, the other two officers returned, one either side of Mr Turnbull who was struggling to get away, cursing non-stop.

'Handcuff him,' the lead man ordered.

'Cor, it's better than a film,' someone said loud enough for everyone to hear.

'You, Mr Turnbull, are under arrest for the theft of military supplies and violation of wartime regulations.'

'What! It wasn't me,' the crook shouted. 'It's her, she made me do it! She threatened to ruin me if I didn't help her! She's the mastermind, not me!'

Mrs Duncan turned on him. 'You spineless coward,' she shrieked, almost spitting with rage. 'Don't try to blame me.'

Turnbull yanked his arm away from his captors and made a dash for the door.

'Grab him!' the boss shouted, still holding Mrs Duncan tight.

Turnbull's boots pounded against the concrete, each step echoing through the hushed room. Amanda's heart raced as Turnbull barrelled toward her. Her pulse screamed at her to run, but some instinct overpowered her fear. She thrust her foot into his path, her leg trembling as it met the weight of his rushing body.

His fall was brutal, his head cracked against the concrete with a sickening sound. Amanda recoiled, her stomach churning at the sight that reminded her far too sharply of the terrible scenes at the underground.

'Bitch!' he spat at her. 'You just wait...' But he didn't get to finish his threat. His arms were yanked behind his back and he was almost carried outside, still yelling protests.

Mrs Duncan looked over at Amanda as she was marched past. 'You did this!' she shouted, her voice sharp as a blade. 'You little rat! You think you're so clever, don't you? Meddling in things you don't understand. But you'll never be more than a silly East End girl!'

Amanda froze. Her fingers dug into her palms, leaving crescents of pain as she fought to steady herself. Her breathing was shallow, each inhale clawing at her throat. Why had she spoken to Mrs Pain? She could have just walked away, kept her head down, and avoided all this, all this fear and chaos. But it was too late now.

When Duncan and Turnbull were out of sight, the workers all turned to Amanda. 'Did you have something to do with it?' Patsy asked in awe.

Amanda's mouth was dry, but she swallowed hard and made herself speak. 'I just did what I thought was right.'

Bethan stood up. 'She's been keeping tabs on them for ages. She's a hero.'

Within seconds every woman left her machine and they all crowded round Amanda, congratulating her. She hesitated, her cheeks flushing under the weight of their words.

'You were bloody brave!' Bethan said, her voice full of pride. The room erupted into cheers and applause. Some of the women clapped her on the back, while others hugged her tightly. Amanda felt her eyes sting with tears as relief flooded through her body. Maisie grinned and nudged her. 'Don't let it go to your head, Amanda!'

Thrilled that the pair had been arrested, Amanda still felt a niggle of guilt. Everyone got something on the black market, and they were no better. She'd never asked Big Sal if what she sold was illegal, off the back of a lorry as they said, but only because she didn't want to know. Did that make her as bad as Duncan and Turnbull, complicit somehow? The parachute silk, the stockings she occasionally bought from a shady character at the Petticoat. Was she just another cog in the machine she had tried to stop? The thought grabbed at her, the cheers around her ringing hollow.

44

It was the day after Duncan and Turnbull were arrested and it was still uppermost in Amanda's mind, gnawing away like a rat at a bag of rubbish. Luckily, now she had something else to think about. Her sessions at the Petticoat and previous savings added up to enough for her to rent a room. Her heart sang when she discovered the room in Mrs Cohen's house was still available.

She knelt on the floor of her tiny bedroom, the room she'd slept in for as long as she could remember. She folded her few dresses into the battered cardboard suitcase. It was so old she knew she'd have to tie it shut with string. Her hands trembled as she folded the last item into her suitcase, an old pre-war cardigan. Was it fear? Or excitement? She wasn't sure any more. The weight of what she was doing pressed on her shoulders. This wasn't just a move, it was an escape.

The room was dim and she moved quietly, wincing every time the suitcase hinges creaked or the floorboards beneath her feet groaned. She knew she wasn't in danger. She was an adult and fully entitled to leave her parents' house any time she chose to, but she wanted no fuss. No mother standing looking helpless, silently pleading with her to stay. No father trying to get her to give him every penny she'd got so he could lose it on the horses. That would never happen again. But it wasn't just about getting away from the miserable atmosphere in the house. It was about finally claiming something for herself, something her father couldn't steal as he stole so much else. She was tired of living in a house where it felt as if she was some sort of prisoner whose dreams of escape and a better life would never come true.

Her precious post office book now showed an almost zero balance. It had taken most of her savings to pay for the rent in her new place. Nonetheless, she tucked the book firmly inside her handbag. If the repair business went well, she'd have more money to save soon.

The sound of a door closing downstairs made her freeze. She paused, trying to work out who had come in, but it was too early for her father, it must be her mother moving about in the kitchen. If her father walked through the door now, he'd notice the suit-case immediately. His face would soon turn red, his eyes bulging as they did every time he was angry, which was often. He'd demand to know where she was going. She'd refuse to tell him but that would just make him angrier. Inevitably he'd ask about money. He always did. But this time he wasn't getting a penny. He could rot in hell first. Bastard.

She exhaled slowly, willing her hands to stop shaking as she tied the string round the suitcase. She stuffed her sewing scissors and thread into the side pocket of her bag, then glanced around the room, doing a final check.

Satisfied she'd got everything, she lugged the case and two fabric bags down the stairs, being as quiet as possible, glad her mother had the wireless on listening to the news. She hated being so sneaky, but it was better this way. If she told her mother, she'd respond with that helpless look she had, helplessness combined with pleading. Amanda wasn't sure she was strong enough to resist her and leave. Better to just go.

She left a note on the bed saying she'd write to her mother soon. She'd arrange to meet her somewhere for a cup of tea, as long as she could be confident her mother wouldn't tell her father. She wasn't sure she could. She decided she would always meet her mother somewhere neutral, a café or after church some Sundays.

Amanda's chest tightened as she slowly opened the front door. She thought she'd got away with it but then her mother called from the kitchen, 'That you, Mand?'

'Just nipping out for a minute,' she called back. Her fingers slick with sweat, she pulled open the door and went outside. Outside the house and into freedom. The street was alive with people, men in flat caps heading home from work, or going to their next shift, women in scarves and coats hurrying to the shops, knowing there would be long queues to look forward to. Workmen from the repair gangs trying to repair a bombed house nearby, propping a half-collapsed wall with big wooden beams.

Her arms soon ached from the case and bags, but motivation kept her going despite the suitcase banging into her legs at every step. Keeping her head down, she focused on the rhythm of her footsteps. She didn't dare look up, afraid she might see her father striding towards her, fury in every step.

She paused for a moment outside Mrs Cohen's house. It was as she remembered when she looked at the room a while before, modest yet well maintained and welcoming. Halfway up the six steps to the front door she stumbled, the weight of the case and bags pulling her off balance. A passerby glanced at her with mild interest but walked on without any offer of help. Amanda took a deep breath, straightened herself and continued up the steps, blinking away the sudden sting of tears as she thought of her mother discovering she had left. She couldn't break down now.

Mrs Cohen's house was modest but welcoming with flower-pots in the tiny front garden and a brass knocker shaped like a lion's head. The cream paint on the front door was a bit chipped, but the steps were scrubbed clean, and the lace curtains in the window were sparkling white.

She knocked on the door. Mrs Cohen opened it almost immediately. 'Amanda, do come in, girl. Nice to see you again.'

The hallway was narrow, but tidy with pegs to hang coats and a small side table. It smelled slightly of lavender. Mrs Cohen led the way upstairs, chatting all the time. 'I'm sure everything's just as you saw it last time,' she said. 'Clean sheets on the bed and I've left a little milk and bread in the cupboard for you. I know how it is, moving to a new place. It takes a day or two to get settled, doesn't it.'

There was a lump in Amanda's throat as she followed Mrs Cohen up the narrow staircase. Although she'd liked her at her first visit, she hadn't expected this, this warmth, this kind welcome. After years of walking on eggshells at home, she wasn't used to people being kind without wanting something in return.

The small bed sat against one wall, covered with a faded patchwork quilt. A lace curtain hung over the single window, letting very little light in at this time of day. She'd have to close the blackout blind soon.

'It's perfect,' she assured her new landlady and handed her an envelope with the first week's rent.

'I'm glad you think so,' Mrs Cohen said. 'I like to think this is a good place to make a new start.'

'That's exactly what I need.' Amanda could have hugged her.

'Well, I hope you'll be very happy here. I'll let you unpack but

I'll just be downstairs if you need anything.' And with those final words Mrs Cohen went, closing the door gently behind her.

Amanda ran her fingers over the faded patchwork quilt on the bed, as though it were made of the finest silk. She arranged her belongings carefully, her dresses in the wardrobe, her sewing tools on the table and finally, her mother's photograph on the mantelpiece. The frame was scratched and worn, but the smile in the picture made the room feel warmer, more homely.

Her mother might drive her mad with her passivity, but Amanda knew she would miss her.

When she'd finished, she sat on the edge of her bed, and found her thoughts drifting to her friends. She felt deeply sad for Maisie, who had so much weight on her shoulders and an uncertain future for her mother. At least she had Frank, but with so much going on, their relationship was moving at a snail's pace. If he moved to Scotland it would be slower still. Long-distance relationships didn't always survive.

But thinking of Bethan, livewire Bethan, always brought a smile to her face. One day she'd find love, find the man of her dreams, but Amanda couldn't help but hope it would be someone local, someone who would be kind and faithful.

Her mind was made up, she would invite her friends round to tea in her new room. It might not be much, but it was hers and she no longer had to live in fear.

45

Bethan picked up a newspaper at the corner shop, waiting to pay, worried she'd be late for work. Her eyes drifted to the sunlight streaming through the shop window when a group of GIs strolled past. As always, their uniforms were immaculate, crisp and spotless, and their laughter carried through the street. Unconsciously, she straightened her posture slightly, smoothing her hair with a quick hand. She couldn't help herself.

The Americans were different. Confident, loud, and full of stories about places she'd only ever seen in films – New York, Chicago, California. As had happened so often before, she imagined herself walking arm in arm with one of the dashing GIs. He'd have a dazzling smile and be madly in love with her. He'd be rich too, of course. She'd be wearing a smart designer dress and heels, and other women would gaze at her enviously.

Yet somehow the image was growing thin, like a dress worn and washed too many times. Her mum would say she was growing up.

She sighed, her fingers clutching the coins she needed to pay for the newspaper. 'Bethan Harris?' she whispered to herself, trying out a name with an American twang. It sounded glamorous. She could be someone entirely new over there. A fresh start, far away from the grey skies and bombed streets of London.

'Daydreaming again, are we?' Mrs Evans, the shopkeeper, interrupted her daydream as she held out her hand for the money.

Bethan flushed. Was she that obvious? 'Only nice dreams,' she replied with a smile. She took her change and tucked the newspaper into her bag. Outside, she walked briskly. She knew where the GIs tended to hang out. She should do, she'd spent enough time trying to hook one. The church hall for a dance on Thursday nights, the Red Cross club near the station, she'd gone to both so many times she'd lost count.

'You're too obvious,' Maisie said after going with her once. 'You frighten the blokes away because you try so desperately to get their attention.'

Was it true? She'd certainly had no luck so far. 'Why don't you look for someone closer to home?' Maisie asked, echoing Bethan's mother's words. 'They can't be married then, not like that Buddy you went out with. Anyway, not all GIs are rich. What if you married one and he turned out to be dirt poor over there or have a family who didn't like you?'

But Bethan didn't want closer to home. She still wanted to be far away, leading a different life in a different country. Her mind full of dreams, she turned the corner near the post office and almost bumped into a man carrying a briefcase.

'Oh, sorry!' she said, stepping out of his way.

He smiled. 'No harm done. It's Bethan, isn't it? I've seen you before somewhere or other. I'm Graham.'

She nodded, vaguely recognising him but unable to think where from. He was an average-looking man, tall but a bit too thin. Not tall, dark and handsome though and nothing like a GI.

He wore a suit, but it was shiny with use, like the sort of man who would sit at the same desk all his working life, quietly dealing with paperwork and having some boring hobbies.

He looked at her bag, weighed down with some shopping she'd already done. 'That looks heavy,' he said. 'If you ever need help carrying something, I'd be happy to help. You'll know where to find me. The insurance office on King Street.' To her surprise, he reached into a pocket and handed her his business card. 'That's me,' he said with a warm smile. 'I'm glad we bumped into each other.'

Bethan simply gave him a half-smile that committed her to nothing. 'I must be getting on, or I'll be late for work.' She forgot about him within minutes, her mind on the other side of the Atlantic where a whole world was waiting for her. She just needed to find the right man to take her there.

* * *

The next morning, Bethan stopped at the paper shop again. The air was crisp, with the sun struggling to break through a thin layer of clouds promising a fine day. As she turned towards the post office, he was there. Graham, the man she'd bumped into the day before. He was standing looking in a shop window, still clutching his briefcase. When he spotted her, his cheeks reddened, giving away the fact he'd been waiting for her.

'Good morning, Bethan.' His voice was friendly and cheerful. 'I hoped I'd run into you again.'

She paused, caught off guard. 'Oh, hello. Graham, isn't it?'

He looked down at his feet. 'Um, well, I hoped I'd bump into you,' he said. 'Listen, I know a pretty girl like you probably has more beaus than you can count, but would you like to come to the pictures with me one evening? There's a new film at the Odeon that looks good.'

Bethan was taken aback. He didn't seem like the sort of man who would ask for a date when they hardly knew each other. But he seemed decent if a bit forward and he must have a good job if he worked in the insurance office, but he wasn't American. He didn't fit the bill.

'I don't think so.' She avoided his eyes as she spoke. 'I'm...'

'Oh, go on,' he said with a winning smile. 'I'm not a bad bloke and you'll get to see a good film. Who knows, we might even have a nice time.' She looked at him properly for the first time. She liked the way he held himself, confident but not cocky, and he had lovely blue eyes.

'I'm not sure I'd be good company,' she said after a pause.

'That's a risk I'm happy to take. Go on, take a chance on me. It's only a few hours.'

Bethan glanced at her watch. She needed to hurry or she'd be late for work. 'Oh, all right,' she said, then thought how ungracious she sounded. 'But only because I fancy that film.'

Graham's face lit up, and for a moment she felt a flicker of something, not excitement exactly, but interest, curiosity.

'Great,' he said. 'See you outside the Odeon tomorrow evening at six thirty. That okay?'

She nodded and checked her watch again. 'Okay, I've got to go now. I'll... see you tomorrow then.'

* * *

The next evening, she stood in front of the mirror in her bedroom, smoothing the fabric of her best dress. It wasn't new, nothing was since clothes rationing, but she'd remodelled a dress she found at a jumble sale. The previous owner must have been a big woman so there was plenty of spare fabric and it was hardly worn. As she looked in the mirror, she noticed how the blue pattern brought out the colour of her eyes and blew herself a kiss. 'It's just the pictures,' she reminded herself.

Graham was already waiting outside the Odeon, his suit freshly pressed and his shoes polished to a good shine. When he saw her, his face broke into that winning smile again. 'Bethan, you look just lovely.'

She gave a mock curtsey. 'And you're on time.'

'Always am. Mister reliable, that's me.' He insisted on paying for their tickets and bought her a small packet of sweets. She couldn't help but smile a little at his earnestness.

The Lamp Still Burns was a wartime drama about a nurse torn between duty and love. Bethan completely lost herself in the story, drawn by Vivian Leigh's glamour and charm, imagining herself in the heroine's shoes. But that didn't stop her being aware of Graham from time to time. Most men would have tried to put their arm around her shoulders by the first ten minutes of the film, but he behaved like a perfect gentleman. At one point their hands brushed as they reached for a sweet at the same time. She pulled her hand back quickly, feeling a strange flutter in her chest. *It's just a reaction to the film*, she told herself.

The streets were busy as they left the cinema, the sound of their footsteps echoing off the darkened shop fronts.

'What did you think of the film?' Graham asked.

'It was good,' Bethan replied. 'I really enjoyed it. She's such a great actress. She makes you really believe in her character.'

He nodded. 'But it was a bit sad too. It must be so hard to have to choose between duty and love.'

She'd been thinking the same thing. 'Do you always think so much about films?'

'Only if they're worth thinking about. Do you fancy a drink? We can fit one in before closing time.'

They passed a quiet pub, its warm light spilling into the street when someone left. Inside it was cosy, filled with the low murmur of conversation. While Graham got their drinks, Bethan looked around and smiled to herself. *I gotta say, this couldn't be more different from places I usually like*, she thought, and there wasn't a Yank in sight either. Usually that would bring her mood down, but she found she didn't mind. Perhaps it was because she still felt cheerful after seeing the film.

Soon they were sitting by the fire, glasses in front of them. 'I got you half of shandy,' Graham said, looking apologetic. 'If you'd rather have something else just say.'

As they talked, she learned more about him, his family, his job which bored him silly even though it was important. His poor eyesight had kept him from being called to the front, and for that Bethan was grateful. Then they got talking about hobbies. She was convinced he'd have boring ones like stamp collecting or reading. But no. 'I'm in an amateur dramatics society,' he said when she asked. 'I might seem a mild-mannered man but you should see me when I'm being a murderer or a philanderer. I love it.'

Her jaw dropped open. Perhaps there was more to this man than she'd expected. 'You sound like Clark Kent,' she said with a grin. 'You know, Superman.' She remembered not everyone had seen the American comics she'd seen. 'Mild-mannered man most of the time but when there's an emergency, he dashes into a phone box, twirls around and somehow emerges in a sexy tight outfit with a big S on his chest.'

He laughed. 'I think I've seen one of those comics. I'm no superhero though.'

She raised an eyebrow. 'Well, let me know if you change, I

could do with rescuing sometimes.' She thought about the episode with Buddy and her other unsuccessful attempts to find a GI husband.

'I don't think you need rescuing, Bethan, you're pretty smart. In fact, you're pretty and smart as far as I can see. Anyway, if I was Superman I'd probably fall over my own cape!'

He walked her home, and she found it easy to chat to him. Perhaps it was because he was an East Ender too and she didn't have to try to be someone she wasn't. She felt as if she'd known him for ages.

At her door, he turned and kissed her very lightly on the lips. 'I hope we can go out again, Bethan. I'd like that.'

She just nodded then watched him walk away, thinking she'd like that too. Later she couldn't help comparing Graham with the GIs she'd met. He certainly lacked their glamour and excitement, but he wasn't boring. Imagine, he was an actor and had played a murderer. She'd love to have seen that.

As often happened, she thought about her future. Should she hold out for the possibility of a life in America or accept Graham's offer of another date? All her friends would laugh at her if she went out with a local lad, and an insurance clerk at that!

46

It was difficult finding time to do everything while still working at the factory full-time, but at least Mrs Duncan was gone so the atmosphere there was much more relaxed. Then some time after Mrs Duncan and that bully Turnbull were arrested, Amanda was called into the office. She'd never been there before apart from the morning she was interviewed.

She immediately felt like a naughty schoolgirl called into the head teacher's office and racked her brain for anything she might have done wrong. Each step up the stairs to the management office felt like she was walking towards her doom.

She tapped timidly on the door and waited until she heard a harsh, 'Come in,' which did nothing for her nerves. She clasped her hands together to stop them shaking.

Mr Biggerstaff, the senior manager they rarely saw, stood up from behind his desk. 'Come in, girl. I don't bite.' He indicated a chair opposite. His office was pure luxury compared to the factory workshop. His desk was huge, there were three filing cabinets and a small side table with three chairs arranged around it. It even had a colourful rug on the floor.

Swallowing hard, Amanda sat down, smoothing her skirt over her knees.

'I'll come straight to the point,' the boss said. 'I've heard some good things about you, Amanda. May I call you that? And I believe you're good at keeping your eyes open.'

Amanda looked up for the first time. Whatever did he mean?

Mr Biggerstaff called his secretary over. 'Two cups of tea, please, Doris, and two of your homemade biscuits if you can spare them. We've a lot to talk about.'

He looked back at Amanda. 'I expect, like most people, you think management and unions are at each other's throats all the time. Sometimes we are, but we also try to work together when necessary. Mrs Pain told me how helpful you'd been in uncovering the criminal activities going on here. We're very grateful for that.'

Amanda was so surprised she sat with her mouth open. She'd never even met this man before and here he was praising her.

'Um, well, yes. I'd been suspicious for a while but wasn't sure what to do about it.'

Mr Biggerstaff shuffled some papers on his desk and took one from the pile, putting it on top. 'It's like this...' He adjusted his glasses, tapping the papers in front of him lightly as if organising his thoughts. They could hear the faint hum of the sewing machines downstairs and two of the warehouse men calling to each other.

But before he got any further, Doris came back in with a tea tray and the promised biscuits. She winked at Amanda as she set it down on the desk. 'There you are, ducks. Enjoy.'

When she'd gone, closing the door gently behind her, the boss handed Amanda a cup and saucer and encouraged her to take a biscuit. 'Go on, have both biscuits, you've earned them.' Amanda's mouth was so dry she wasn't sure she could swallow one mouthful, let alone two whole biscuits, and she didn't think it would be done to dunk it in her tea in front of her boss.

'Now,' he finally said when they were settled. 'As you'll be aware, Mrs Duncan has gone and she won't be coming back.'

Mention of Mrs Duncan caused a shiver to run down Amanda's spine as she remembered all the barely veiled threats the woman had hissed at her.

The boss was speaking again. 'That leaves us with a dilemma. We need someone reliable, someone we can trust, to take her place. Someone who gets on with people and can keep things running smoothly. Someone with an eye for detail.' He paused, looking into her eyes. 'Like you.'

Amanda nodded slowly, her mind racing. Who did he mean? Amanda wondered, who was good at detail?

'I won't beat about the bush.' His gazed fixed on her. 'Would you be interested in her job? We'd still expect you to check the figures like you've been doing, so it would be a challenge. It would mean more money for you, of course.'

Amanda's mind went blank. Was he really offering her a supervisor's job? Surely she had misunderstood.

'I... I don't know what to say,' she finally stammered.

'Say you'll think about it,' he replied with a smile. 'It isn't an easy role, Amanda. It'll sometimes mean longer hours, more responsibility and the occasional difficult decision if there is a problem with the staff. But it's a chance to prove yourself and make a real difference here. That's helping the war effort.'

Amanda swallowed hard, her thoughts whirling. She thought about the long days, the friendship of the other workers, and the pride she felt when a job was well done. Mostly she wondered how on earth she would fit everything in.

'I'll need some time to think it over,' she said at last, her voice barely above a whisper.

'That's all right, my dear, take a few days. Can you let me know by Monday next, do you think? We need someone sooner rather than later.'

He stood up, signalling the conversation was over, and reached to shake her hand. 'I do hope you'll accept our offer. We need someone like you.'

Amanda rose on unsteady legs. 'Thank you for thinking of me,' she said.

'Thank you, Amanda. Whatever you decide, know your work here hasn't gone unnoticed.'

She left the room in a daze and descended the stairs, her legs trembling with each step. Her thoughts swung wildly – pride that her work had been acknowledged, fear of how she would cope if she accepted the job and worry about finding time to fit everything in if she did. Her dream was still in fashion, not a uniform factory. Could she really step into Mrs Duncan's shoes and make a success of it or was this a mistake waiting to happen?

But then she remembered how far she'd come. She'd been doing a responsible job already, she'd spotted wrongdoing at the factory, she'd been the main driver getting the repair business going, and she'd dealt with the dreadful day of the underground disaster. Logically she knew that her friends would think she was mad to turn down the promotion.

She reminded herself that one day this war would be over. Some believed the end was in sight already. Then the uniform factory would presumably be less busy. Perhaps the end of the war would be the start of a new beginning for them all.

47

The bus pulled away with a groan of its engine, leaving Maisie and Frank standing on the grass verge. It seemed like they were miles from anywhere and she had lost count of how long it had been since they'd got on the bus in Spitalfields.

The road was quiet, stretching ahead in both directions, hemmed in by hedgerows and the occasional tree. They could smell faint traces of a bonfire somewhere and, distantly, the sound of a tractor. It was a mild afternoon but Maisie tugged her coat tighter around her, although she wasn't cold. The chill came from inside, a knot of fear and dread that no amount of warm clothing could counter.

The noticeboard on the big metal gates declared this was St Mary's. That's all, no indication of the purpose of the building. It could have been anything, a hospital, a monastery, even a workplace of some sort. But they knew differently.

Holding hands, they followed the winding gravel path, the crunch of their footsteps the only sound in the still air apart from some birds singing in the trees. The drive was meticulously maintained, with neat hedges and clusters of trees lining it to form a green avenue. It was pristine yet felt lonely.

Maisie glanced around and swallowed hard. 'Frank, it's visiting time, but it seems like we're the only ones here.' Her chest tightened at the thought of the patients inside. Surely many of them would be hoping, yearning for a visitor who might never come. She imagined their heads turning towards the door each time it opened, the hope in their hearts soon dashed. 'Poor souls.'

Frank squeezed her hand. 'Some of them may not have family. And some families I know soon disown someone who's not, well, not right in the head. Don't want to know.'

The hospital stood at the end of the drive, its grey stone walls rising starkly against the overcast sky. It was a Victorian building with tall, narrow windows that seemed more like prison bars to keep people in rather than being there to let in light. The roof sloped sharply, and several chimneys belched pale smoke into the air. Some of the paintwork on the windows and doors was peeling and the whole edifice felt forlorn.

Maisie stood and looked at it, the corners of her mouth turned down. 'It looks so... grim,' she murmured, her voice little more than a whisper.

'It's what's inside that's important. I've been reading about treatment people can have these days. I just hope the staff here are kind and up to date with all that.'

It was Maisie's first visit. Initially she'd been told there would be no visitors for a week or two while her mother settled in, and she'd honoured that.

'It was good of your aunt to come to visit her first,' Frank said. 'Is she staying with you now?'

She nodded. 'She can be a funny old stick, but she's been an absolute treasure. Says she'll stay until Mum comes home or things get sorted somehow. It's taken a load off my shoulders.'

The closer they got, the worse the place looked. Since the war started, many buildings had been neglected. It was hard to get paint and everything needed to maintain them properly. A lot of houses that had been partially demolished by bombs had been propped up by work teams. People kept their fingers crossed that the bodge job would last longer than Hitler.

A sign nearer the entrance read *St Mary's Hospital for Nervous Disorders*, the letters faded and chipped. Maisie stopped, unable to go any further for a minute. 'What's the point, Frank? Aunt Betty says Mum still doesn't really believe there's anything wrong with her, with all her drinking.'

Frank stepped in front of her and gently put his hands on her shoulders, his eyes meeting hers. 'The point is that you're here, you care. That's all that matters, Maisie, love. And she knows what's right, even if she can't admit it yet.'

Maisie bit her lip and nodded. Together, they walked up the last few yards to the heavy wooden doors. They were locked. Frank reached for the bell beside the door, a big brass button set into the crumbling stonework. A muffled chime echoed deep within the building. They waited, the silence broken only by the faint rustling of the wind through the trees and the occasional shout from inside. Maisie shifted nervously, glancing back towards the empty drive as if wondering whether to give up and go home again.

Finally, the door creaked open, revealing a matronly nurse in a starched uniform. Her lined face was brisk but also kind. 'Visiting?' she asked with a smile.

'Yes,' Maisie said, struggling to find her voice. 'I'm here to see my mum. Mrs Hawkins. I'm Maisie.'

'That's excellent. I'm sure she'll be pleased to see you. Right, follow me. She's in Nightingale ward.' She led them down a long shadowy corridor. 'Sorry about the locked doors, but some of them try to escape. It seems harsh but it's for their own protection.' Their footsteps echoed on the worn linoleum floor, adding to the feeling of desolation.

The ward was a large, rectangular room filled with rows of iron-framed beds. Some of the women sat in the beds, staring blankly ahead, others lay curled under blankets. A few wandered aimlessly, their slippered feet shuffling on the floor. A few more were reading books. The staff had tried to cheer the room up with pictures of flowers here and there on the walls, but in that huge space they had little effect.

Maisie spotted her mother near the far end of the room, seated in a hard-backed chair by a window. She was dressed in clothes that Maisie had never seen before and was staring out of the window at nothing in particular, her face pale and drawn. As she looked at her, Maisie struggled to remember her mother in days when she wasn't drinking, days when her eyes shone and her hair was neatly styled, when she was a good mother and fun to be with.

'She's had something to help with the shakes,' the nurse said. 'It keeps them calm but can make them a bit groggy. See if you can get her talking. It's lovely that you've come to see her. I must get back now. See you later perhaps.' Maisie and Frank hesitated. Although they were quite near, her mother hadn't turned to look at them. Unlike many of the other women, she hadn't even looked round when the door opened and they walked in.

Frank squeezed Maisie's hand again, pushing her gently towards her mother. 'Go on, say hello, love.'

Maisie felt a lump in her throat. She crouched beside her mother. 'Mum, it's me. It's Maisie. I've brought Frank with me.'

Her mother's eyes flickered briefly in recognition, but she said nothing. As Maisie leaned forward to kiss her on the cheek she noticed a faint, unpleasant chemical smell on her mother's breath, sharp and medicinal. She didn't doubt her mother needed the medication, but it made her sad that it had taken over her mind like that. But then so had the booze.

Frank found two hard-backed chairs for them to sit on. 'I brought you a few things,' Maisie said, the brightness in her voice sounding as false as it was.

'What you got?'

The voice made her jump. Another patient had come up behind her and was suddenly peering over her shoulder. 'Can I 'ave some?'

'Bugger off!' Maisie's mum said, but there was no strength in her words. It was enough to get the woman to go, although she still hovered nearby watching them.

'I've got you some pear drops, they're your favourites. It was hard to find any, and I used the last of my sweet ration for this month. Rose'll be cross with me.' She knew she was wittering on, but without any type of response from her mother, Maisie had no idea what to do to communicate with her.

She reached over and took one of her mother's hands, rubbing it gently. 'It's lovely to see you, Mum.'

'Pear drops? Can I 'ave one? Go on, give us one.' The woman was back again, standing so close they could smell her body odour.

Frank stood up and gently took the woman by the shoulders. 'They're not for you, sweetheart. Now, which bed is yours? Come and show me.'

Maisie could have kissed him as he took the woman away in the kindest way possible, leaving her to talk to her mum.

'I've brought you your favourite magazine too, Mum.' She'd got a copy of *Woman's Own*. 'It's got some nice recipes in it. We can make them together when you get home if you like. I'd like to do some cooking with you like we used to when I was a kid.'

Her mother's hands twitched slightly and slowly she turned her head towards Maisie. Her eyes, though dulled by whatever sedative she'd been given, landed on the bag of sweets. 'Pear drops,' she said, her voice hoarse and faint as if she hadn't used it for ages.

Maisie smiled. 'That's right, I know you like them.' She opened the bag and placed it gently on her mother's lap. Her mother's fingers hovered over it for a moment before clutching it protectively. 'They steal stuff in here.'

Maisie opened the magazine next, turning to a page that had a picture of Clark Gable. 'Look, Mum. He's so handsome, isn't he?'

Her mother's lips twitched, almost imperceptibly. 'He looks thinner.' Her voice was flat as she spoke. 'Must be on rations too.'

Eager to keep the conversation going, Maisie nodded. 'Yes, rationing's a pain in the neck, isn't it? Seems like they ration something new every week.'

They sat for a while in silence, each struggling as if they were strangers.

From across the room, a loud thumping noise drew their attention. A patient was rocking violently back and forth in her bed, singing a hymn the whole time.

'She's always doing that.' Maisie's mum said, her voice flat as a horizon on a misty day. 'Take no notice.'

Frank came back and sat beside them, looking at Maisie as if he was as lost as she was. 'Shall we go?' he whispered in her ear after a while.

She was so relieved he'd suggested that. Every minute here was torment. She bent and kissed her mother's cheek again. 'I've got to go now, Mum, but I'll come again.'

On the way out, they saw the nurse again. 'Will she ever get better?' Maisie asked.

'Mrs Hawkins? We can only hope so. She looks poorly now, but we have a lot of experience with people with issues like hers. If she's lucky, things will improve, but it will be very slow if at all. I wish I could be more positive, but we have to be realistic with what we can do. In a few weeks we may be able to transfer her to a convalescent place we use. It's much more comfortable there and they can get her off the medication. But we can't make any promises.'

Maisie was fiddling with the strap of her handbag. 'But will it stop her drinking?'

The nurse, who seemed too young for such a difficult job, gave a half-smile. 'There are no guarantees with this type of work, but it's the best chance she has. I know it's hard, but keep visiting when you can.'

Outside, they sucked in the fresh country air, a boon to their senses after the smells of the ward. 'She barely even knew I was there,' Maisie said quietly, struggling to hold back tears.

'She knew.' Frank's voice was steady. 'Maybe not as clearly as you'd like, but somehow she knew. And what that nurse said sounded a little bit hopeful.'

As they walked back to the bus stop, Maisie tried to imagine a future where her mother didn't drink, where they could sit together at the kitchen table and talk like they used to. But the thought was so fragile, it was like trying to keep a flame alight in a hurricane.

Would her mother ever recover?

48

Bethan's mum always offered a warm welcome to her friends. 'Come on in, girls. Welsh cakes you're after like last time, is it?' While they took off their coats and got settled round the table, she bustled about making refreshments.

On the settee, carefully folded inside a clean sheet, lay Grace's wedding dress. Bethan's eyes kept straying towards it, hardly believing they had managed to make something so beautiful.

'Here's your tea, girls,' Bethan's mum said, putting a tray full of cups, saucers and a big brown teapot in the middle of the table. 'Whatever you do, take this back to the kitchen before you look at that dress! I'm off to the shops now, taking the little ones with me. Give you a bit of peace and quiet, like.'

'I can't wait to see Grace this afternoon,' Maisie said. 'The dress is so beautiful. Your design is just lovely, Amanda. I've never seen the like.'

Amanda leaned forward and poured the tea. 'It's made me wonder, and tell me if you think I'm mad, but I wonder if we've been thinking too small with our repair business. If we can make a dress as lovely as this, we can make pretty much anything. Dresses, suits, whatever.'

Bethan's eyes lit up. 'You think we could?'

'Well, we're all experienced, and making this dress has taught us so much more. People are sick and tired of clothes rationing, wearing the same old stuff. We could remodel their clothes for a start, make them look different. And if we can get the material, we can make new things. Maybe even more wedding dresses.'

Maisie took a sip of her tea, thinking how much she'd loved being part of making the dress. After the worries about her family, every stitch was like a ray of sunshine knowing they would bring joy to Grace on her big day. 'It's a lot better than making uniforms, that's for sure,' she said, putting down her cup. 'Not that the uniforms aren't important though.'

Bethan laughed. 'Listen to us. Talking like we're business-women. But why not? The Petticoat might be the big break we need.'

They sipped their tea in companionable silence, the only sound the ticking of the clock and the sound of trams trundling by outside. Then Amanda leaned forward with a mischievous look in her eye.

'Enough about dresses for a moment,' she said. 'Tell us about this new bloke, Bethan. You've been very hush-hush about him. You'd think careless talk costs lives or something!'

Bethan blinked. 'New bloke?'

'Oh, come on. You let slip you'd got a date with a new man. How did it go?'

Bethan's cheeks went pink. She knew they'd pounce sooner or later. There were few secrets between them. She fiddled with her teaspoon. 'It was nice. Very nice actually. I enjoyed myself.'

'Nice? Is that all? We need details. Where did he take you?

Did he try to get fresh? Did you have to fight him off like some of them Yanks?'

Bethan laughed, flustered. 'We went to the pictures and then for a drink. He told me about his family and his work. He's, well, he's easy to talk to. Makes me laugh.'

Maisie's eyes softened. 'That sounds lovely. He must be kind.'

'He is. He walked me home even though it was out of his way. And...' She hesitated, knowing the response her next few words would get. 'He's a local lad, not a GI.'

Amanda let out a low whistle. 'Not a GI? That's a first! Wonders'll never cease. What does he do?'

Bethan hesitated. 'He... he works in insurance.'

That was all it took. Her friends looked at each other then let out peals of laughter. 'You're kidding. An insurance man! That's precious. You couldn't have picked a more boring job if you'd tried. Out of all the possibilities, a pilot sweeping you off your feet, a GI whisking you away somewhere exotic, and you pick a man who spends his days with policies and paperwork!'

Maisie hadn't had so much fun for ages. 'You'll have to be careful. Next thing you know, he'll have you signing forms in triplicate if you want sugar in your tea!'

Bethan bristled. 'He never mentions insurance. The job bores him to death.'

Amanda wagged her finger. 'Course not, he's saving that for the next date! I can see it now. If you get as far as walking down the aisle, instead of saying "I do" he'll ask you if you have insurance cover for your wedding dress!'

Bethan groaned, burying her face in her hands, though she was smiling. 'You two are impossible.'

'And when the air-raid sirens go off, does he whip out his notebook and ask if you're insured against falling masonry?'

Even Bethan laughed at that, swiping Amanda's arm. 'You're

terrible. He's not like that. He listens. And he makes me laugh properly. And he acts! He's in amateur dramatics. He's even played a murderer.'

'Listen to her,' Maisie said. 'She sounds quite smitten. If I was writing a comedy I couldn't have picked a better job for a new man for you.'

Bethan stood and began collecting the tea things, not looking at her friends. 'He's a decent man and I can be myself with him. With the Yanks, well, I always felt I had to be someone I'm not. I had to impress them.' She turned her back to them and took the tray to the kitchen, returning with a tea towel to make sure there were no spills on the table.

'Did he kiss you?' Amanda said, unwilling to let her off the hook yet.

Bethan rubbed the table hard even though she could see it was dry. 'Yes, he did, and he's a good kisser too.' She didn't really mind her friends teasing her but she didn't tell them that just being with Graham made her insides feel funny in a way that had never happened before. She wasn't sure what that meant but she was willing to find out.

'Right, you horrible pair. Let's get the dress out for a final check before Grace comes round, shall we?'

49

'Bride or groom?' the usher asked the three girls.

'Um,' Maisie replied. 'I suppose we're bride, but...'

'Yes, bride,' Amanda said, giving her a nudge. The usher looked at them askance, and they were relieved when another couple arrived, and they could slip in unnoticed. It was Grace's wedding and although they hadn't been invited, they couldn't resist a chance to see the dress on Grace on her big day. She'd been thrilled at the final fitting when the dress hung from her elegant frame like a dream, giving her skin a magic glow. She'd looked at herself in the mirror as if she couldn't believe her eyes, turning this way and that, the silk gently swishing around her legs.

Bethan had borrowed her dad's camera to take a photo of Grace in the church. Although she'd taken one in her living room, the church background was so much more romantic. 'Gotta get a what-do-you-call it? Portfolio. Yes, a portfolio of our creations to show prospective customers, if we're going to build a business, like.'

Maisie laughed. 'Get you.'

The small stone church, St Brigid's, was nestled in the corner of a quiet street near Weaver's Fields. It was an ancient church, with arched windows, perfect for a romantic wedding. The friends had stopped at the edge of the park, the church spire just visible through the canopy of leaves. The sound of the city faded, replaced by the rustle of the leaves and the faint laughter of children playing nearby. All the way there they'd worried about gate-crashing the ceremony. What if someone spotted them and they got thrown out?

But they'd got in and sat quietly at the back of the church on the bride's side. Like all weddings, the guests were dressed in their best. Wartime fashions were about utility, practical and hard-wearing. Looking around, the girls could see many of the women had gone to town with their outfits nonetheless. Some wore old-fashioned but elegant dresses and jackets, others had adapted a utility style, changing buttons or adding a frill to the neckline. Hats tended to be small and neat, often with a feather or a piece of net to make them more individual. Many men wore utility suits, cut narrower to save fabric. A couple of older men wore their old army uniforms with the insignia removed and the addition of a tie.

As newcomers came into the church, some sat near them. 'How do you know Grace?' one woman asked, leaning towards them.

Bethan was nearest but her mind went blank. 'Um, we...'

Maisie rescued her. 'We knew her from way back. Our secret is we made her dress. Don't tell anyone.'

The woman, middle-aged and rather well dressed, raised an eyebrow. 'Oh, so it's you. Grace has told me all about her dress. She wouldn't let me see it before the wedding though.'

'See,' Bethan whispered to the other two. 'She's been talking about us. She must be pleased with the dress.' She was tightly clutching the camera. 'I'm glad we took extra time to get the fit just right.'

Amanda nodded. 'It's not just about the fit though, is it? It's about making her feel a million dollars.'

Maisie grinned. 'You should be writing for one of them women's magazines, you should.'

The low hum of the organ filled the small church, its solemn notes weaving through the hushed conversations of waiting guests. The melody shifted to the gentle strains of 'Amazing Grace' and for a moment the chattering stopped. The music seemed to hold the air still, as if the building itself was waiting for the bride to join her groom who was in place in his wheelchair at the front of the church.

'It's starting,' Bethan whispered.

The congregation turned their heads towards the back of the church where the rustle of fabric and light footsteps filled the brief silence.

And then, there she was.

Holding her father's arm.

The dress they had spent so many hours on shimmered softly in the light that stretched through the church door. The fabric flowed gracefully, the simple lines emphasising her slender frame. The tiny hand-sewn pearl beads at the neck and cuffs twinkled in the pale sunlight from behind her. The veil, which Grace's mother had worn on her wedding day, looked superb, completing the magical look.

Maisie let out a quiet breath. 'She looks...'

'Beautiful,' Amanda finished, her voice so quiet it was barely above a whisper.

The girls seemed to hold their breath as Grace moved closer to the altar, their creation moving around her like a dream. She looked radiant, as though the weight of the war, of her husband-to-be's injuries, had momentarily lifted.

As Grace reached her groom, his face lit up with a smile that seemed to negate the weight of his injuries. Grace responded with a small laugh, her hand reaching for his as if they were the only two people in the world. Then the organ music faded, replaced by the soft murmur of the vicar's voice.

The girls sat back, their earlier worries about being caught when they hadn't been invited forgotten in the glow of their accomplishment.

Even from the back of the church, they could see the groom looked at his bride with a face full of love. 'Look at him,' Maisie whispered. 'He can't take his eyes off her.'

The ceremony began, the words of the service carrying through the church in a steady, calm rhythm. Each of the girls was lost in their own thoughts. Bethan was imagining her wedding, although since she'd met Graham dreams of an American wedding had faded fast. Maisie imagined herself with Frank, walking down the aisle of St Mark's Church, her sister as her bridesmaid and her mother so proud she could burst. But Amanda wasn't thinking of a wedding for herself. That was far off in the future, if it happened at all. While she had loved making the wedding dress, she had hopes to achieve a career, a profitable business. Perhaps even travel when this rotten war was over.

As the vows drew to a close and the bride and groom exchanged rings, each girl felt a lump in her throat. Despite wartime austerity and the ever-present threat of an air-raid alarm, there was something profoundly moving about the ceremony. It promised love and caring in a time when so much in life was uncertain.

Grace had been sitting for much of the ceremony to be at the same level as her husband. Now she stood up and they both turned round to face the congregation as husband and wife. Applause filled the small church. Leaning into the aisle, Bethan took another three photos of the couple. Glowing with pride, she whispered to her friends, 'We did good.'

But as Grace passed them, holding the hand of her wheel-chair-bound husband, she glanced their way. Her smile widened and she mouthed, 'Thank you!' Her eyes shone with happiness and gratitude.

The three friends held back as the congregation filed out behind the bride and groom, not wanting to be asked awkward questions.

'It makes all our hours of work seem worthwhile to see her so happy,' Amanda said. 'And so much nicer than sewing army uniforms.'

But someone else had dawdled to let others leave the church ahead of her. It was the lady who spoke to them about making the dress. 'Her dress is just beautiful, so elegant and simple. It makes a real impact,' she said, looking at them with interest. 'My daughter has just got engaged and I know she would like a unique dress for her wedding. Can you tell me where I can get hold of you? She might want to ask you to make her dress.'

As the lady left her details and followed the other guests, the girls exchanged wide smiles. They looked at each other, full of hope. They might be realistic in their business dreams after all. 'We're really onto something lush,' Bethan said, clutching the slip of paper. Amanda nodded. 'This is just the beginning. We're on our way.' It was so exciting that the three girls linked hands and did a little jig, hoping no one could see them.

When the wedding party gathered outside the church for the photographer to take photos of the happy occasion, the three friends stepped back. They weren't invited, after all, but were reluctant to leave such a joyous sight. Grace and Robert had been chatting to their guests, but then Grace spotted the girls and smiled, waving. 'Maisie! Bethan! Amanda!' Her voice was warm and delighted. Pushing her new husband along the path, she made her way to them, the silk of her dress shimmering with each movement. 'I saw you inside the church. I hoped you'd come.' She turned to Robert. 'These are the three girls who made my dress!' She twirled round as if letting him see it properly for the first time. The sight of it filled their hearts with pride.

Grace took each of their hands in hers in turn. 'I don't have the words to tell you how much this dress means to me. It's perfect, better than I could ever have imagined.'

Robert reached for her hand. 'She's right. You've made an already beautiful girl look even more lovely. I'm the luckiest man in the world.'

Bethan held up the camera with a grin. 'I've already taken a couple of photos. Do you mind if we take a couple more? We might want to make wedding dresses in future and it would be good to show what we can do.'

Grace laughed. 'Oh, yes, you should have a portfolio. You girls are going places, I know it.' She turned to Amanda with a smile. 'You've given me something I'll treasure forever. I'll make sure everyone knows who made this dress. You deserve it.'

Amanda, usually so composed, felt her throat tighten. 'It was our pleasure,' she said gently.

Grace's mother came and stood by her side, smiling. 'Oh, it's you three, the dressmakers. You've done a wonderful job, everyone says so, but Grace, the photographer is ready and people are waiting. We should move on.'

Giving each friend a brief kiss on the cheek, they moved away. Maisie let out a breath she hadn't realised she'd been holding. 'We did good, and wasn't it lovely to make, even if it got difficult at times?'

Bethan nodded, clutching her camera. 'Better than good.'

Amanda nodded, her mind already whirling with plans for the future. For now, she let herself bask in the moment, the joy of their success, the knowledge they'd made a difference on Grace's special day.

'You two are the best things in my life,' she said, hugging each of them in turn.

50

It was the day Maisie had been dreading. The day Frank was leaving her for his new job in Scotland. A new life, although she tried to brush that thought aside.

He'd begged her not to see him off. 'It'll be too upsetting, love, for both of us, and the train'll probably be hours late.' She wasn't listening, unwilling to miss a minute of his company.

The station was alive as it always was, full of the sound of feet on the platform floor, of steam escaping from a waiting train, and the cacophony of voices, some cheerful, others sad. There were plenty of soldiers there, many with people who'd come to see them off, like she was. The air smelled faintly of coal smoke and oil. Maisie stood at the edge of the platform, gritting her teeth, determined not to cry.

Frank stood beside her, holding her hand, his brown suitcase at his feet, the corners scuffed from years of service. His hair was slicked back, although a few stubborn strands fell around his forehead. Maisie longed to brush them away but didn't trust herself to move.

She wouldn't cry. Not here, not in front of other passengers.

But her heart ached with the weight of unspoken words, and her throat felt raw from holding back her emotions.

'I know it's hard,' Frank reminded her, squeezing her hand. 'But it's a good opportunity. They don't come up very often and remember, it's for our future.' He let go of her hand and put his arms around her. 'We'll be apart but I'll still love you and I'll write so often you'll be bored of my letters.' He hesitated. 'But remember to write back if you get time, what with your new business and everything.'

Maisie let herself sink into his arms, afraid that if she spoke, her voice would simply give way. But the thought of him leaving seemed to cut her heart in two. So much in her life was uncertain; the bombings, her mother's health, trying to make ends meet were all everyday stories. And she wouldn't have his support, no matter how often he wrote. It wouldn't, couldn't be the same.

He kissed her soundly, and several people whistled or called encouragement, making Maisie blush.

'You'll be brilliant, Frank. They're lucky to have you.'

He let her go, but kept hold of her hand. 'I'll miss you, you know.' His grip was warm and firm. She wanted to remember the feel of it for ever. 'Before we know it, a year will be gone.' He did his best to reassure her. 'I'll let you know when I get some leave and a train pass to come to see you.' He trailed off and Maisie knew what he wasn't saying. Maybe she could join him in Scotland, build a life up there even. But she knew that was hopeless. Her mother still needed her and so did Rose and Ron. She was the one who held the family together and that wasn't likely to change any time soon.

The train whistle blew, a long mournful sound that cut through the hum and hubbub of the station. For once it was on time, when Maisie wanted nothing more than for it to be late so she could spend more time with her love.

Around them, other passengers began picking up their belongings, and the doors were flung open as existing passengers got off the train. Maisie felt a surge of panic rise in her chest. She wasn't ready to lose him. She longed to tell him to stay, to forget about the promotion, but she knew that would be a selfish thing to do. She hated herself for even thinking of it.

She forced a smile, although Frank wasn't convinced by it. 'You'll make a great senior engineer,' she said, her voice thick with emotion. 'Just don't let them work you too hard. And stop for plenty of cups of tea. All right?'

Frank chuckled. 'I'll try but you know how it is. There's a war on and a lot of engineers have been called up. But we've still got to keep the trains running.'

The whistle blew again, and this time Frank bent to pick up his suitcase. 'Maisie,' he said, his voice low and serious. 'I'll come back to you, I promise.'

She swallowed hard to stop a tear.

'And don't you go worrying about me meeting some bonny wee lassie up there either. There's only one girl for me, and she's right in front of me now.'

She wanted to believe him, but the fear still gripped her like a vice. 'You'd better get going or the train'll go without you,' she whispered, reaching up to kiss his cheek.

'I love you, Maisie,' he said simply.

'I love you too,' she managed to struggle out the words without breaking down.

He turned and climbed on the train, finding a seat near the window where he could still see her. Maisie closed the gap between them, holding her hand against the glass. He did the same, as if the warmth of their hands could be felt through the barrier.

When the engine started, she stepped back and watched as

the train gradually moved away, waving even when she could no longer see him. For a long moment, she didn't move. The platform emptied around her, the other passengers going on with their lives. Her shoulders slumped and she struggled to suppress a sob.

Finally, she turned and began walking back towards the station building, her slow steps an echo of her emotions. Outside the sun was shining, the early-summer warmth wrapping around her, but it did little to ease the chill in her heart.

She would be brave. Frank deserved that of her. She would write to him regularly, making her letters bright and cheery even if she felt low.

But as she made her way home, dodging people going about their everyday lives, she couldn't stop the tears from falling. Life was so unpredictable, who knew what could happen in a year?

51

The British Restaurant was as busy as ever as Amanda sat down with her cup of tea to wait for her mother. She smiled as she'd handed over the one penny it cost. The place was bustling as it always was. Many people went there for their midday meal from their jobs and others went there because their homes had been bombed and they could get a full three-course meal for a shilling.

She sat at a corner table, running her finger round the rim of the teacup, keeping an eye on the door for a familiar face. It had been a while since she'd left home without warning. She hated doing it, but knew her mother would beg her to stay and couldn't face the heartache. Fear of her father tracking her down meant she didn't tell her mother where she was going either. But she'd left her a note on her bed, promising to get in touch. She worried that if she told her mother where she was, her father would worm it out of her. She hadn't been bothered by her father, so her plan had worked. But it broke her heart to treat her mother that way.

Although she was often frustrated at the passive way her mother put up with her father's behaviour, she still loved her. Loved sitting round the little kitchen table talking about this and that, just sharing time together. She hoped they could do that again over a meal today. But what if her mother didn't come? What if her father had found out and stopped her or, worse still, turned up with her?

She kept looking at the clock, worrying something had happened when the door opened again and there she was. Her mother. Amanda stood and waved to get her attention and was rewarded with the widest smile she'd seen from her mother since... well, as long as she could remember.

'Mum!' Amanda said, embracing her tightly as soon as her mother came over to her.

'Oh, Mandy, it's so good to see you, love.' Her mother's voice almost cracked with emotion. 'Shall we go and get something to eat before we talk? I've been up since the crack of dawn and I'm famished.'

They walked to the serving counter, the smell of stew getting stronger with every step. They each got a tray and joined the queue to be served. It gave them time to consider what they wanted to eat. 'I'm going to have fish pie,' her mum said. 'It's only 9d, and I think I'll have some pease pudding with it. What about you?' Amanda decided on stew and dumplings for the same price.

It was only when they took their meals to the table that Amanda had a chance to look at her mother properly. 'Mum,' she said, a small frown on her smooth forehead. 'You look different somehow. Happier. Has something happened?' A wicked part of her mind wondered if perhaps her father had died. It would solve a lot of problems.

'Well,' her mum said, speaking slowly as if she was hugging a delicious secret to herself. 'You're going to be real pleased with me, Mand. I've gone and done it, what you kept saying.'

They had to move aside as a burly man pushed past them to

get to another table. His elbow caught Amanda's shoulder and she let out a little yelp. He either didn't hear or didn't care.

Regaining her composure, Amanda had a mouthful of stew and swallowed it before speaking. 'What? You've done what?' Her mind roamed over all the conversations they'd had around that kitchen table, anything from her father's behaviour to the latest recipes issued by the government to help people cope with rationing.

As if to tease her, her mother took a bite of her fish pie before answering. 'I've done it.' She swallowed her food and smiled the widest smile Amanda had ever seen. 'I've left him. Your dad. I've only gone and left the bugger.'

Amanda was so surprised her mouth dropped open.

'You've... what?'

This was something she'd been telling her mum to do for as long as she could remember, but she didn't think she'd ever do it. She'd always been too passive, too willing to put up with her lot.

'I'm not joking, Mand. I've left him. Really. And not before time. I've been thinking about it for a long, long time but didn't want to get your hopes up in case I chickened out.'

Amanda's heart leapt with happiness. 'Blimey, that's a surprise, Mum,' she said, leaning over and clasping her mother's hand. 'No wonder you look like the cat that got the cream!' But then she remembered how her mother never had two halfpennies to rub together, her father had always gambled it away. How had she managed to leave? Amanda remembered her struggle to save enough for a week's rent for her new room. She couldn't see how her mother could possibly have done that.

So many thoughts went through her mind, she was letting her stew get cold. 'But how? When? Why?' She stopped herself and shook her head. 'No, I know why, but how did you manage it?'

Her mother ate her last mouthful of pie and put her knife and fork together neatly. 'It's been a long time coming, hasn't it? I know you kept telling me to go, but it wasn't that easy. The vicar always says we should honour our husbands – daft sod – and I fell for it for years. Be a good wife, never complain.'

'And you never had the money either,' Amanda said, remembering all the times her mother was in tears because her father had gambled away all the housekeeping. 'How did you manage it?'

Her mother reached for her tea. 'You remember I've talked about one of the ladies I do cleaning for, Mrs Tomkinson? Nice woman, busy, a widow, works all the hours God sends to keep herself afloat. Well, her mum's been getting forgetful, getting into all sorts of muddles, she has.'

Amanda frowned. 'She surely hasn't asked you to work for nothing for her mum?'

'No, much better. She asked me to move in with her mum, keep an eye on her, cook her something every day, that sort of thing. I'd met her a few times, nice old thing she is, she won't be any trouble. So I've already done it. I've moved in with her a few days ago, got my own bedroom and everything. No rent to pay and Mrs T gives me a little bit extra on top of my cleaning money. I still have time to do work for one of my other ladies too.'

Amanda couldn't have been more surprised if her mother had flown to the moon. 'That's... that's great, Mum. I'm so pleased for you, and you look ten years younger already.'

Her mum was eyeing up the menu board. 'I think I'll have treacle pudding in a minute, but no rush. I'll tell you what made me agree to the job. You did. You having the courage to move away. I cried and cried when you went. Even though you left me a note explaining why you did it like you did, it cut me to the core. It took me ages to understand, but now I do and it gave me courage.' She smiled again. 'It doesn't matter what the vicar says, I'm doing the right thing.'

Tears pricked in Amanda's eyes, but she blinked them away. 'Where are you living now then?'

Her mum pulled a piece of paper out of her pocket. 'Here's the address. But don't tell your dad, will you? We'll keep our secrets tight.'

The couple at the next table left, struggling to manoeuvre their tray between people.

'Still, I keep wondering how he's getting on. At six o'clock every night I imagine him coming in, expecting his dinner on the table, knife and fork at the ready, wireless off.' She gave a happy sigh. 'I expect he's having his dinner at Joe's Café every night now, good job too. Bet he doesn't throw it at the wall if he thinks it's no good neither!'

Amanda began to laugh. 'Can you imagine? Him looking after himself, doing his own washing, cleaning the house. I bet he hardly knows how to cook himself some toast.'

Her mum shook her head. 'You're not wrong there, but I've heard through the grapevine that he's got a woman doing housekeeping for him. Has to pay her, mind, not free like a wife. And I bet a penny to a pound he finds some poor sod to move in with him. Nice as pie until he gets her there, then he'll be back to his old tricks.'

They had a wonderful few minutes imagining him trying to look after himself with no wife and daughter to boss about. The scenarios caused them to laugh out loud.

'Mum, I'm so proud of you,' Amanda said, reaching for her hand again. 'You did good. We're both free now and we've got each other.'

They went to get their treacle tarts and custard, then returned to their table. 'So tell me what's been happening to you,' her mum said. 'And those mates of yours.'

There was so much to tell Amanda hardly knew where to start. 'Well, as you know, the military police came round the factory and arrested that horrible Mrs Duncan. On the fiddle she was.' She didn't bother telling her mother her part in the woman's downfall. Her mother would worry even though it was all over. 'And you'll never guess what? I've got her job! Me, your daughter, is a supervisor.'

'Good gracious.' It was her mother's turn to let her jaw sag. 'That's wonderful. How are your friends coping with you being their boss?'

'Good as gold, they are, but there's one or two others who I might have to deal with before long. Still, I'll worry about that when the time comes. And the three of us have started earning a bit on the side with our sewing. That's going okay too. And look at this.' She took a photo of Grace at the wedding out of her bag and showed it to her mother. 'We made that!'

Her mother looked at the photo then looked at Amanda, pride in her eyes. 'That's just beautiful, Mandy. The bride looks so happy. You've always had so much get up and go and you're really going places.'

When it was time to leave, they walked to the door together, arm in arm. Outside the sky was pale blue and you could forget there was a war on for a few minutes.

'Will I see you again soon?' her mother asked, looking at her anxiously.

'Of course, Mum. I'd rather not give you my address but I'll put a note through your door soon. Maybe I could come to see you there and meet the old lady you're looking after.'

Her mum nodded. 'That'd be good. She gets in a muddle, but she's a sweet old thing. You'll like her.'

They hugged tightly, and Amanda watched as her mother walked away, her step light and confident for the first time in years. Amanda felt like her future was something to look forward to instead of something to fear.

As she turned and began walking to her own little rented room, she smiled to herself. Her mother had found a way out, and so had she. They were both free and that was worth everything.

52

Like every Sunday, the market was heaving, the usual muddle of stalls and voices, the air thick with the smell of food from different countries. Just as they liked it. Housewives haggled for everything, children darted underfoot, and a spiv with a suitcase full of stockings tried to entice them. 'These'll make you look sexy, girls!' His eyes darted around the whole time in case the police appeared and he had to make a quick getaway.

They came to Big Sal's stall, a riot of fabrics, ribbons and baubles all piled high. Sal herself was impossible to miss.

"Ello, girls,' she boomed. 'Got the wrong day, ain't ya!' She laughed as if she'd said something hilarious, but it was impossible not to laugh with her. 'I got some new stock 'ere, you'll love it.' Her outfit was even more outrageous than usual. A flowing caftan made of some exotic African print and a matching turban round her head made her look like something from a travel book.

'Look at you, Sal,' Bethan said with a grin. 'You're brighter than the rest of the market put together.'

'Gotta keep up appearances, ain't I? How'd people come to my stall otherwise?' Bethan hid a grin. Sal's loud voice could be heard halfway down the market.

Amanda stroked the new fabric longingly. They'd been thrilled when the woman they'd met at Grace's wedding had been in touch. Her daughter wanted to speak to them about making her wedding dress. 'We're on our way!' she told the others and they went to the pub to celebrate with a shandy or two.

'Got any more you-know-what tucked away in your shop?' Amanda asked conspiratorially. 'We've got another wedding dress to make.'

Sal's face dropped. 'Sorry, sweetheart, you 'ad the last. But come to the shop later and see if anything else takes yer fancy.' She stopped to serve a customer. 'See you later, girls.' They didn't leave immediately but instead studied the fabrics, feeling the weight of them, imagining what they could make if money was no object.

It was a warm early-summer day so the friends decided to forego Bert's Café and instead went to a tea stall nearby. They found three empty stools and sat down, but the ground was uneven and they tipped this way and that. Maisie almost spilled all her tea down herself. The sun found its way through the clouds, and they basked in the warmth.

'I was just thinking,' Maisie said. 'A lot's happened since we first thought of starting our little business. Old Duncan getting arrested. We never did find out what happened to her, did we? Did you ever hear anything, Amanda?'

'Not a dickybird. I may be a supervisor now but I'm still in the dark apart from quotas.'

'I'm just relieved you haven't turned into a monster like Duncan. Not that we'd let you, mind.' Bethan chuckled at the idea.

'I'll drink to that,' Maisie said, raising her mug. She leaned forward, brushing a strand of hair out of her face. 'And I've had another letter from Frank. He's kept his promise and he writes twice a week like clockwork.' She smiled, remembering his words of love, and talk of their future together.

'You still worried he'll go off with some Scottish lassie?' Amanda asked.

Maisie shook her head. 'Nah. I don't think he has time from what he says, and there's some good news. He thinks he can get me a travel pass to go to see him. I can't wait!'

'More tea, girls?' The stallholder could see people waiting to take their stools.

'Go on then,' Amanda said, keen to hear Maisie's news. 'My treat this time.' They waited until their mugs were filled again to carry on. The scent of freshly brewed tea mingled with the tang of fried onions from a nearby food stall. Bethan cupped her hands around the mug, enjoying the warmth from it despite the mild day. Around them the market buzzed with life, a chaotic symphony of voices, shouts and laughter.

'You haven't mentioned your mam lately,' Bethan said. 'How's she doing? Any sign of her coming home?' She immediately kicked herself. It was a sensitive subject for Maisie and she should have waited until they were alone to ask it.

Her question made Maisie remember the last time she'd visited her mother. There was no doubt she was improving. They'd reduced the drugs they were giving her so she was more alert, and was finally admitting that she had a problem with drink. But she wasn't yet ready to fully accept responsibility. 'It's me mum and dad's fault,' she'd said. 'They brought me up to think drinking was normal. Lots of people around us did too, so you can't blame me.' Her words made Maisie feel less confident about her recovery. While what she said was true, her parents were long dead, and her mum had to take responsibility for herself now.

She sighed, realising she hadn't answered Bethan's question. 'She's a lot better, thanks, but there's a way to go. I just take every day as it comes.'

'Hello, ladies!' Graham's words came as a surprise. He had a bag full of vegetables in one hand.

'I didn't know you would be here today, cariad,' Bethan said, eyes glowing at the sight of him. 'Oh, you haven't met these two before, have you? This is Amanda and that one almost spilling her tea is Maisie.'

He stepped forward to shake both their hands. 'Beth has told me a lot about you two, all good stuff. I've been looking forward to meeting you.'

'Why don't you grab a cuppa and join us?' Amanda asked, impressed by his striking eyes and friendly smile.

'I wish I could but I've got to get a few things then I'm off to an audition for the latest play. I'm hoping to be the dastardly villain! I'll see you again soon, Beth. Nice to see you two as well.'

'He looks nice,' Amanda said. 'I can see what you see in him. Looks like your romance is going well. Has he asked you to sign any policies yet?'

Bethan nudged her. 'Give over, you. Why can't you forget his job? He's a nice bloke and it's nearly... well, nearly made me forget about moving to America.'

'Only nearly?' Maisie's voice was high. 'Surely you don't still have that dream, do you? You haven't been two-timing him with any GIs, have you?'

Bethan looked uncomfortable. 'No, but one or two I bumped into have asked me out. Gorgeous one of them was, but I said no.' The others didn't miss the regret in her voice. Would she ever learn?

There was a moment's silence between them and Bethan knew they thought she was crazy. Graham was lovely, after all. But America...

Amanda shifted on her stool, brushing crumbs off her lap. 'Let's talk about something else.' She glanced around at the market stalls. 'Now we've got our second wedding dress order, we need to get back to Sal's and estimate how much the fabric will cost.' She tapped her mug with her nail, already thinking ahead. 'They're not broke like most of the people round here.'

Bethan's eyes went dreamy as usual. 'It's so lovely working on something beautiful like a wedding dress, especially after uniforms all day. You got some designs in mind, Amanda?'

Amanda grinned. 'Of course, but you know me. I don't like to spend too much time on it until after I've met the bride. But I know what I'd design for you.'

'You do? Show me!' She looked dreamy again. The others had sometimes said she spent so much time daydreaming about romantic scenes, she should write a book. She hadn't told them, but she'd been giving the idea some serious thought.

'The ideas are in my head. I'm not showing them to you or you'll be proposing to Graham just to wear one!'

'Meany!' Bethan said, but she was smiling. One day...

'Anyway,' Maisie said. 'I reckon we've got a lot to look forward to. We're earning a bit here at the Petticoat and we can build up our business making dresses.'

'What, wedding dresses? When would we sleep?' Much as she loved the romance of making Grace's dress, she knew how long it took.

'Not just wedding dresses. Ordinary dresses, only with Amanda's special touch...'

'What's that then?' Amanda asked, surprised at the idea.

'No idea, but you'll think of something. You're clever. Who

knows, one day we might be able to work full-time making clothes. Our own fashion brand. Look out, Norman Hartnell, we're on our way!'

They fell silent for a moment, each of them lost in their thoughts. Around them the market carried on in its usual busy way. The war might have been going on for years, but life had to go on too, people still had to eat, people still fell in love, or out of love. All life was around them.

'I think we're going to be okay,' Amanda said finally, her voice steady and confident. 'The three of us. We've been through so much, and look at us now. We're on our way, I'm sure of it.'

They finished their tea and stood up to leave, feeling optimistic for the future. It wasn't certain, nothing was in wartime, but they believed they could support each other with their plans to face whatever came their way.

Walking arm in arm towards Big Sal's, their laughter wove its way around the bustling stalls, a joyous sound telling of friendship and resilience. Petticoat Lane market with its chaos and colour was the perfect backdrop for their new beginning. A place where dreams could come true.

* * *

MORE FROM PATRICIA McBRIDE

The next instalment in Patricia McBride's uplifting and heartwarming Petticoat Lane series is available to order now here:
https://mybook.to/PetticoatLane2BackAd

AUTHOR'S NOTE

I hope you have enjoyed reading this book as much as I enjoyed writing it. I am sometimes asked why I write books about World War II and the answer is simple. I am one of the oldest baby boomers so grew up with stories about 'the war' every day. Some of the stories were tragic – for example, my grandmother, who was somewhat psychic, knew which lads wouldn't be coming home when they set off to war. Also she was suddenly widowed in the middle of the war when her husband, my grandfather, died of a brain haemorrhage. She had four children to care for.

On a more light-hearted note, the little aside in this book about a girl arranging dates every half an hour in case any lad didn't turn up is true. It was one of the stories my mother told. She was a teenager in Swansea, a port town, during the war and had plenty of men keen to date her. If you've read any of my other books, you may have noticed I often have a Welsh character. My mother was half-Welsh and I have a huge Welsh family so find it easy to 'hear' their voices when I want to write dialogue for characters like Bethan.

I love research and spend a lot of time researching my books, hoping to make them as authentic as possible, indeed I have bookshelves full of books about life during wartime, especially life in the East End. My mother was a Cockney and her parents, after much moving around looking for work in the depression of the 1930s, ended up living in a tiny flat near Petticoat Lane market. A very exciting place for a child to visit.

The dreadful story of the tragedy in Bethnal Green underground station is based on truth. The council had indeed asked the government for funds to make the stairs safer on three occasions but had been turned down. Soon after the tragedy, this was remedied. One hundred and seventy-three people died in this horrific event which was the biggest civilian disaster of the war period. There are many sources to read about this and I particularly recommend https://stairwaytoheavenmemorial.org/background-to-the-bethnal-green-tube-disaster as this includes information about a memorial built to commemorate the lost.

This is the first book in a series about Amanda, Bethan and Maisie, so if you'd like to be notified when the other books come out (if they aren't already when you're reading this) do follow me on Amazon.

As an aside, my husband, born at the end of 1949, was convinced as a child he had been alive during the war as it was talked about so much. He was very embarrassed when he said something to that effect during a lesson at school and was heavily mocked!

ABOUT THE AUTHOR

Patricia McBride is the author of several fiction and non-fiction books as well as numerous articles. She loves undertaking the research for her books, helped by stories told to her by her Cockney mother and grandparents who lived in the East End. Patricia lives in Cambridge with her husband.

Download your exclusive bonus content from Patricia McBride here:

Visit Patricia's website: www.patriciamcbrideauthor.com

Follow Patricia on social media here:

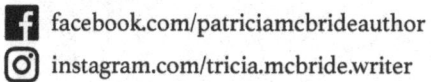

facebook.com/patriciamcbrideauthor
instagram.com/tricia.mcbride.writer

ALSO BY PATRICIA MCBRIDE

The Lily Baker Series

The Button Girls

The Picture House Girls

The Telephone Girls

The Air Raid Girls

The Blackout Girls

The Bletchley Park Girls

Christmas Wishes for the Bletchley Park Girls

The Library Girls of the East End Series

The Library Girls of the East End

Hard Times for the East End Library Girls

A Christmas Gift for the East End Library Girls

A Better Tomorrow for the East End Library Girls

Wedding Bells for the East End Library Girls

The Petticoat Lane Series

The Market Girls of Petticoat Lane

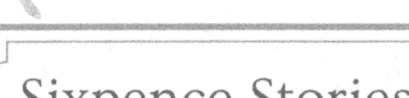

Sixpence Stories

Introducing Sixpence Stories!

Discover page-turning historical novels from your favourite authors, meet new friends and be transported back in time.

Join our book club Facebook group

https://bit.ly/SixpenceGroup

Sign up to our newsletter

https://bit.ly/SixpenceNews

Boldwood

Boldwood Books is an award-winning fiction publishing company seeking out the best stories from around the world.

Find out more at www.boldwoodbooks.com

Join our reader community for brilliant books, competitions and offers!

Follow us
@BoldwoodBooks
@TheBoldBookClub

Sign up to our weekly
deals newsletter

https://bit.ly/BoldwoodBNewsletter